C000143250

The Sp
Sank the Armada

David West

ACKNOWLEDGMENTS

I would like to thank my wife Claire, our friend Marius Grose and my editor, Debz Hobbs-Wyatt for their valuable input to this book, and Jacqueline Abromeit for a brilliant cover design.

CHAPTER ONE

1567, Paris

Don Francés opened his study door and called for Captain Rodriguez. In less than a minute, he heard the familiar steps of Rodriguez rushing up the stairs. In contrast to his normal practice, Don Francés held the door open for his captain.

'Your Excellency.'

'It is intolerable! They have gone too far this time.'

'You have interrogated your secretary I take it, Your Excellency?'

'Yes, this Venetian spy has offered him money. He was using Ramón to get at our correspondence. Ramón told me everything as soon as I confronted him. I have some pity for Ramón. His son is unwell and he cannot afford a doctor, thanks to the tightness of His Majesty's purse strings. But we must show the doge that he has overstepped the mark. I cannot let him get away with this.'

'What shall I do, Your Excellency?'

'The Venetian spy. You must make an example of him. See how many of his bones you can break without actually killing him. Then leave him on the Venetian ambassador's doorstep. That should be clear enough.'

'It will be a pleasure, Your Excellency. My men have had no entertainment for quite a while. Would you like me to dispose of Ramón as well?'

'Ramón? No, I have had my physician attend to his son. I think I can be quite certain of his loyalty now. And it takes so very much time to train a new secretary.'

The flames were biting into Anthony's flesh as he struggled against the ropes that bound his limbs firmly to the stake. He could smell the roasting flesh and hear his screams, like the screams he had heard in Smithfield. He glanced across to see flames licking upwards around Marie's thighs, reaching, feeling higher and higher, her soft, pale skin burning, crisping, crackling. His eyes followed the flames upwards as the fabric of her dress burnt away. His agony danced with ecstasy for a moment, then he lifted his gaze to her face, which smiled before dissolving into a jawbone, teeth and skull, then transforming into another smiling face, that of the lovely Donna, wife of Fabris, his fencing master from Hampton Court.

A bright light swept everything from his sight and a deep voice called. He must have crossed. It hadn't been as bad as he had feared.

'Who is your master?'

'You are, lord, you are my only master.'

'I am not your master. We have never met. Who is your master?' A test, of course. He had felt the flames of hell, and now he saw the light. He would not deny his god.

'You are my only master, lord.' He hoped Marie would make it through too, and Donna. He tried to reach out to hold her hand, but could not move his wrists. 'You are the one true master, lord.'

Who am I? Who is Marie? Why was I at Smithfield, and who was being burnt? Hampton Court, I see a man. He scolds me, but with love in his eyes. He wants me to read law, but it's not for me. Father, is that you? His father's mouth opens. He can see him mouth 'yes'. Who am I, Father? His father's mouth opens and closes, but no sound emerges. Where am I? Why can't I move? The mist is thick on the water, the lookout at the bow peering ahead. The oarsmen pull steadily. We glide through still water. A shadowy shape rises to our right. A bell tolls, twice. There is a bump. The oarsmen ship their oars and one of them leaps onto the quay with a warp. As they tie the boat up alongside, the mist clears. I'm in Paris, that's where I am. What am I doing here?

Anthony paid the boatman and climbed onto the jetty. He slung the strap of the small sack holding his spare shirt and hosen over his head. Then he pulled the hand-drawn map from the purse tied to his belt and studied it. The towering spire of Notre Dame on the island in the river gave him his first landmark. Turning around, he saw the turrets of an enormous palace, the Louvre, just as shown on the map. Orientated, he set off towards it. His right hand went to his neck, and he clasped the Saint Christopher medallion that his mother had given him on his seventeenth birthday, just before he set off for Scotland two years ago. She said it would keep him safe on his travels. As he made his way through a market, he listened to the cacophony of conversations. There were accents very different to the French he had learnt from the diplomats' children he had played with in his youth. He mouthed the familiar words with strange accents and guessed at the meanings of the probably vulgar words in common use. He passed a man and boy. The man was chastising the boy for neglecting his school work. Anthony felt for his St. Christopher again, winced, and moved on, turning right when he identified the Rue des Deus. He marvelled at the elaborately decorated stone buildings, then paused as a herd of sheep passed. Then he crossed the street and turned left into Rue St. Honore. Here he found the English Embassy, at number 26. He knocked on the massive oak door, which was soon answered by a manservant who spoke reasonable French, although his accent betrayed him as English. Anthony presented the manservant with the document that Sir Nicholas had given him, addressed to Sir Henry Norris. The manservant led him into a reception room.

'Please take a seat,' the manservant said, and departed. It was an impressive room; the painted plaster walls were hung with several portraits. Dominating the wall opposite was a portrait of Queen Elizabeth. To the right of the queen, stretched a series of smaller portraits. Since the last but one in the row was of Sir Nicholas Throckmorton, he assumed that the very last one must be of Sir Henry Norris, the current incumbent as England's ambassador to France. The manservant reappeared and beckoned him towards a door which led into a smaller room, where his assumption was confirmed. Glancing up from reading the letter, Sir Henry motioned him to sit. He sat facing the ambassador across a large desk. After some minutes, Sir Henry placed the letter on the desk and looked up.

'So you are Sir Anthony Standen. Welcome to our embassy in Paris.' Sir Henry stood so Anthony stood too and they shook hands.

'Thank you, Sir Henry,' said Anthony as they both sat down again.

'First, may I enquire how you met Sir Nicholas, my predecessor here?'

'I met him in Edinburgh, sir. I was engaged as master of horse by Lord Darnley and travelled there with him when he was to marry Mary Queen of Scots. Sir Nicholas, as I'm sure you know, sir, was Queen Elizabeth's envoy to Scotland, sent with the aim of trying to prevent the marriage to Lord Darnley. I met him a second time, quite by chance. He had with him a protégé, Francis Walsingham.'

'From what I know of Francis Walsingham, very little is left to chance. Where did you meet him?'

'It was just after Lord Darnley was killed. I was left without a position, making a small living by doing some language teaching. I was having lunch in the Sheep Heid Tavern when they came in and Sir Nicholas recognised me. He had travelled to Scotland to secure the release of Queen Mary following her arrest by the Scottish lords. It seemed to be a very fortunate chance encounter to me, sir. I was down on my luck, scraping a living and unwelcome in my homeland. Now, here I am in Paris with, I hope, sir, a chance to redeem myself.'

'How did you secure the position with Lord Darnley?'

'My father is a lawyer and works in Hampton Court Palace. We lived in East Molesey nearby. My mother knew Lady Margaret Lennox, Lord Darnley's mother, and suggested me for the role.'

'So your father is a lawyer. Where did he train?'

'At Gray's Inn, sir.'

'Gray's Inn. I have a lot of friends at Gray's. Did you ever go there with your father?'

'Only once, Sir Henry, when I was ten. While my father was in meetings, I went for a walk to see the market at Smithfield. There was a huge and noisy crowd, and I wanted to see what was going on. When I worked my way to the front, I found they were just starting to burn men and women. I discovered later they were the Islington Martyrs. The screams and the smell still haunt me. I never went back, sir.'

'That was an unfortunate experience for a boy of ten, very unfortunate,' Sir Henry repeated, deep in thought. 'Why didn't you follow your father into a career in law?'

'My father wanted me to. He tried to teach me about law, but I'm afraid very little of it made any sense to me. I preferred languages, art and fencing, I seemed to have a natural talent for them. My younger brother, who is also Anthony, although we call him Freddy to avoid confusion, and my youngest brother Edmund, are both following father into law. I'm afraid I was rather a disappointment to him.'

'What ambitions do you have now, what is it that drives you?'

'I want to serve my queen and country, Sir Henry.'

'Yes, yes, we all do. That's what you think you should say. What is it you want to achieve?'

'Just the usual things, Sir Henry, to see the world,

seeking fame and fortune. I suppose I want to show my father that I can make a success of things, my way.'

'I can understand that. If you can help us, then I think you may well see quite a lot of the world. Your fortune, however, is likely to be quite modest. Her Majesty is very careful with her purse strings. Fame is certainly not appropriate for the work we have in mind. Sir Nicholas thinks you may be of use to us since you know many of the officials, messengers and visitors to the Scottish court. You also speak many languages fluently, I understand.'

'Yes, sir, as a child I played with the children of the diplomats who came to Hampton Court. I found I have a gift for languages, I'm a mimic for accents. Having some natural ability for languages, I found I enjoyed them at school. My language teachers praised me, and I worked harder and harder. I found that learning the grammar of Latin and Greek helped me learn other languages, and as I felt I was achieving something, I redoubled my efforts. But other masters, my history master, for example, said I was sinfully self indulgent to only work at the subjects I enjoyed. He was a friend of my father, and I think my father agreed with him.'

'Yes I see. Your languages will be of much more use to us now than ancient history, but modern history you will need to learn.'

'Very well, but I'm still uncertain what you have in mind for me.'

'The Scottish lords are still holding Queen Mary prisoner. They also hold the child, Prince James. Queen Elizabeth is trying to secure their release and the re-instatement of Mary. Scotland is in absolute turmoil.

After Mary married Earl Bothwell, the leading suspect in the murder of your former employer Darnley, the lords divided. Bothwell fled to Norway, and then to Denmark, where he is now imprisoned. The French want to get hold of the young prince so that they can further French influence in Scotland. The Spanish are desperate to stop them. It's an absolute powder keg.' Sir Henry paused.

'I understand that Queen Mary, and, in turn, Prince James, are the Catholic favourites to succeed Queen Elizabeth in England. So why should France and Spain, both Catholic countries, be at odds over it?'

'France is only partly Catholic. Most of the south is under Huguenot control, the north is Catholic and the centre is hotly disputed. Spain could rightly fear that France might fall to the protestant Huguenots. If that were to happen, then Spain would be cut off from its dominion in the Low Countries by both land and sea.' As Sir Henry paused, Anthony nodded.

'So how can I help?' Anthony asked.

'By keeping your eyes and ears open. When you spot anyone you know from the Scottish court, you will follow them. I want to know who they visit, and if possible, what they have to say. When they visit a tavern, see if you can keep in earshot. Report back to me as soon as you have something.'

'What if they recognise me?' asked Anthony.

'We must make sure they don't. My man Robert will help you with dyeing your hair and beard. That will be a start. Then we shall establish an alternative identity for you, a merchant of some sort. Wine, cloth, whatever interests you the most. Then I suggest making you an

Italian with passable French but poor English. We'll find you lodgings somewhere nearby. Both the Scottish and Spanish embassies are just around the corner from here. How does that sound?'

'It sounds rather exciting, but there's just one thing,' said Anthony.

'What is it?'

'What shall I use for money?' Sir Henry smiled.

'That will be taken care of. A salary of ten crowns a month, plus approved expenses.'

'And what are approved expenses?'

'When you have exceptional expenditure to loosen a tongue, either through wine or monetary inducement, that will be reimbursed depending on the value of the information obtained.'

'I see,' said Anthony.

'Good,' Sir Henry said as he stood up. 'Now come along and Robert will get you started. There is one other thing. When did you receive your knighthood? I try to keep tabs on who's who. One has to, you know. And I don't remember you.'

'I saved Queen Mary's life when Lord Darnley, his uncle and the others assassinated her secretary, David Rizzio. Queen Mary knighted me for that.'

'Ah, I see. Not an English knight then, Standen.'

Sir Henry's servant Robert Clark dyed Anthony's hair and beard black, then trimmed both. Anthony inspected his reflection in the mirror he was offered, and was surprised at the difference it made. The change from his natural brown hair made him look every bit the Italian wine merchant they had decided he was to become. Robert had also got a change of clothes, knitted woollen hose, fine linen shirts, coloured waistcoats and doublets in the Venetian style. Robert had quite an expert eye, and they fitted perfectly. Robert then took him to a house on Rue Des Augustines, where Madam Dufour had a room for him. Robert explained that Madam Dufour had been on the embassy's payroll for many years and was trustworthy.

Next, they went to a wine merchant just off Rue St. Honore, and Robert introduced him to Monsieur Lavigne as Antonio Foscari. Once again, Robert explained that Monsieur Lavigne had been a supplier to the embassy for many years. Anthony was to spend a month or two working with Lavigne full time, developing his cover as an Italian wine merchant working on a trading relationship with Paris in fine wines and spirits. After that, he would spend most of his time looking for Scottish messengers and spending half a day a week maintaining the cover story.

He rather enjoyed learning about wine. He found that corrupting his French with a Venetian accent was a challenge, but it became easier after the wine tastings. Monsieur Lavigne introduced him to the local grape varieties, particularly the exceptional Ay wines of Marne and the Beaune wines of Burgundy.

'Now try this wine, Antonio, and tell me what you think.' He took the goblet and swirled the wine, breathing in the aroma as Monsieur Lavigne had taught him. He took a sip and ran it around his mouth.

'It is, how do you say, tasting of strawberries,' said

Anthony.

'Excellent, you learn quickly. What else?'

'Slightly spicy?'

'Very good. This is the Sangiovese grape, otherwise known as the blood of Jupiter. It is one of the finest Italian grapes and one that is the foundation of the best Italian wines. You will need to know this grape well if you are to be an Italian wine merchant.'

Throughout the rest of the summer, Anthony worked on his new persona and visited all the taverns near the Louvre. This was the palace where Charles IX held court with his mother, Catherine de Medici, when in Paris, and around which all the significant embassies were located. He even sold some wine, which rather surprised Monsieur Lavigne. Using his fake Italianesque French, he tried engaging tavern customers in conversation. Usually they were polite, but restrained. There had been very little diplomatic activity, but Sir Henry had explained that King Charles and his court were in the country for the summer, near Meaux, a day's ride east of Paris. Anthony gradually discovered that people opened up to him far more readily when he volunteered some revelation about himself. His first success was when he invented a girlfriend back in Venice and wrote himself a letter breaking off their relationship in favour of a fencing instructor. He found many people ready to console his sorrow and recount their own tales of treacherous wives and paramours. When he moaned about his parsimonious boss, who was always late paying his wages, he found himself in good company.

At the end of September the king and his mother

returned to the city, and the rumour spread that Louis, Prince de Condé, leader of the Huguenots, had tried to seize Charles, Catherine and the rest of the royal family, using as his excuse a supposed Italian plot to capture the king. Days later, news arrived of a massacre of Catholic priests in Nîmes. Anthony found his cover as an Italian a little difficult for a while and lay low.

After a few weeks he ventured out again, and it was on a sunny morning, as he approached the English embassy, that he passed a figure he recognised as John Beaton, the brother of James Beaton, Mary's ambassador in Paris. Beaton didn't give him a second glance. When Anthony got to the next junction, he turned left and stopped, then peered back around the corner to see Beaton still walking down the street. Anthony followed him. He watched Beaton enter a grand, three-storey house on Rue St. Thomas, then he strolled past, looking through the ground-floor window, where he saw Beaton being offered a seat by a tall, smartly dressed man in his mid-thirties. Anthony continued down the street for fifty yards, then crossed the street and stood by a tree from where he had an unobstructed view of the house.

From his third-floor office on Rue St. Thomas, Don Francés de Alava, the Spanish ambassador to France, gazed out of the window at the busy street below. There was a knock on his door.

'Come in.'

'Your Excellency, there is a Mr John Beaton here to see you, a messenger of the Queen of Scots.'

'Thank you, Rodriguez. I saw him from the window.

He has been followed. Here, see for yourself.' Captain Rodriguez joined his master at the window. 'There, see the athletic-looking young man across the street? Black hair and beard.'

'Yes, I see him, Your Excellency. Shall I arrest him?' asked Rodriguez.

'No, but follow him. Find out who he is and who he's working for. And show Mr Beaton up.'

'Yes, Your Excellency,' Rodrigues bowed and closed the ambassador's door behind him.

What do I do now? Anthony thought. I suppose when Beaton leaves, I should follow him and see where he goes next. But if someone else leaves before that, do I follow them instead? This is clearly where Beaton was sent, so it must be the key link. I need to find out what is being said in there. Sir Henry needs something of value, if I am to make much from it. He had made that clear. The front door opening again and John Beaton leaving interrupted his thoughts. Anthony let him get almost to the corner of the street before setting off after him. He quickened his pace as Beaton reached the corner opposite the city wall. Anthony didn't notice Captain Rodriguez and two other men slip out of de Alava's house and spread out before following him. Beaton returned to his brother's house, the Scottish ambassador's residence, and Anthony took a seat outside the Champs des Oiseaux tavern and watched the Beaton house. He bought a pitcher of ale from the innkeeper and considered what his next move should be. The innkeeper moved on to take the order of another new arrival, who had taken a table behind him. As the shadows grew longer and his pitcher grew emptier, Anthony decided that nothing else was likely to happen at the Beaton house that night. What he needed to do was find out what had sent Beaton to the house on Rue St. Thomas, and what message he had delivered. Best to sleep on it, he thought as he got up and left the tavern, oblivious of the man from the table behind him rising a few seconds later.

For the next few days, Anthony went about his work for Monsieur Lavigne, concentrating on selling wines and making deliveries to taverns and large houses in the Louvre area. He regularly passed the house on Rue St. Thomas that Beaton had visited. Anthony hoped to see him again, but didn't. He did, however, occasionally notice people entering or leaving the building and studied them carefully, committing them to memory. He had to find out more about the household. But of course, how could he be so stupid? It was a large household, very much larger, in fact than many of the houses he had called on to sell wine to. He would make a call and see what he could find out.

'What have you learnt, Captain Rodriguez?' asked Don Francés de Alava.

'He is a Venetian wine merchant, working for a local firm, Lavigne's, just off Rue St. Honore. He has lodgings near there, on Rue Des Augustines. He has made it his business to sell wine mainly in this area and around the Beaton house.'

'Venetian, you say, one of the Doge's spies, then. They are everywhere. If we had a hundredth of their espionage budget, there is nothing we would not know.' The floorboards creaked as Don Francés de Alava paced the length of his study under the gaze of King Philip's portrait above the fireplace. 'Has he visited the Venetian embassy?'

'No, Your Excellency. He has kept his cover. We have not observed him pass any messages to anyone. I have men keeping a discrete watch on him, Monsieur Lavigne and his landlady. None of them have given us any cause for suspicion.'

'Have you questioned any of them? Do you have a name for our mysterious Venetian?'

'No, Your Excellency, I thought it best we should not show our hand yet. I am certain that he does not know he is being followed.'

'Good, good. Let us keep up the surveillance for now.'

'Perhaps if I could have a few more men, Your Excellency. At present we cannot follow both him and his associates.'

'If His Majesty were a little less careful with his purse, then you would have your men, captain. As it is you must do the best you can. You may go. Oh, and send Ramón up would you.' Captain Rodriguez bowed and left the study.

The captain's footsteps receded down the corridor and Don Francés crossed the room to his large walnut desk and sat down. He unlocked a desk drawer and withdrew some papers. As he leafed through them, there was a knock on the door. Don Francés grunted, and the door opened. A short, plainly dressed man of about forty entered. Without glancing up, Don Francés waved his hand towards the seat in front of the desk. The man crossed the room towards it but remained standing.

'Your Excellency, I wonder if I could trouble you. My son is very sick.' Don Francés looked up from his papers and noticed the fear etched in his secretary's face.

'I am very sorry to hear that, Ramón. Has he seen a doctor?'

'We cannot afford a doctor, Your Excellency. I don't like to mention it, but it is three months now since I last received my salary, and, well…'

'Ramón, you know as well as I do how many urgent requests for funds we have dispatched to the king, with nothing yet to show for them. I am doing the best I can with my own resources, but they are limited. I am sure the king will send funding soon, and then you shall have the money we owe you. In the meantime, you have work to do. There are some letters from the Queen of Scots that I would like you to decipher.'

'Thank you, Your Excellency, of course.'

Anthony put down his basket of wine flagons and knocked on the heavy oak door of the house on Rue St. Thomas. After about a minute, he heard footsteps and the door opened. A young man in a smart but cheap looking tunic over woollen hose looked him up and down.

'What do you want?' asked the young man in accented French. Anthony thought it sounded like a Spanish accent.

'I am a wine merchant with some samples that I'm sure your master would like. Is he in?'

'His excellency is not to be disturbed.'

'Well, is there anyone in authority who could sample these fine wines? They are of resounding quality at exceptionally low prices.' The young man looked dubious and began to close the door. 'Hey, I shouldn't want to be in your shoes when his excellency discovers you have turned away the finest wines in Christendom. I shall be back, and the prices will not be as low as they are today.'

'I don't know. His excellency's secretary is in, but he is working.'

'I'm sure he will welcome a sample of fine wine, then. Would you ask him please?' Somewhat reluctantly, the young man opened the door, and Anthony stepped into the hallway. He looked around as the young man closed the door behind him. The ceiling was high and elaborately decorated. A wide staircase lay to the left, half-way down the hall, and there were three closed doors on the right-hand side. Beyond the staircase, there was an open door at the end of the hallway. From the sounds and smells escaping, he guessed it led to the kitchen. The young man opened the first door on the right.

'If you wait in here, I will see if the secretary can speak to you.' The young man left and closed the door behind him. Anthony looked around. It was a fine panelled room with a window overlooking the street. There was a rectangular table with six chairs in the middle of the room, with an oriental-looking carpet under them, and extending about half-way across the wooden floor towards the walls. Paintings hung on the walls, an eclectic mix of religious art, landscapes and seascapes. It was the room that they had shown John Beaton into. At the opposite end of the room to the window, there was a large portrait he recognised as King Philip of Spain, the late Queen Mary's husband. The man who he had seen with John Beaton in this room had been older and far better dressed than the young man who had just shown him in. He had exhibited a military bearing, he thought. He put his basket of wines on the table and was just wondering whether or not he should sit when the door opened again and a short man came in.

'I'm told you are here to sell wine. I have to tell you we have our own supplier.'

'I'm sure, but you must get through a lot of wine at an embassy. This is the Spanish embassy, isn't it?'

'Well, yes, but it isn't convenient now. Please come back another time.' Anthony thought there was something dejected about the man.

'Yes, of course. I'll come back another day.' He picked up his wines, and the secretary showed him to the door. Anthony left, and the secretary closed the door behind him.

Anthony was having a drink at a table outside the Champs des Oiseaux tavern on Rue St. Honore when he saw the Spanish secretary walk past, staring at the ground a few feet in front of him. Again, Anthony thought he looked dejected and deeply troubled. Perhaps this was an opportunity to find out what was happening in the Spanish embassy. He called out to him. The secretary turned and looked at Anthony blankly.

'Hello again. I didn't have a chance to introduce myself the other day. My name is Foscari, Antonio Foscari.'

'I'm Ramón Aguilar,' sighed the secretary. 'I am sorry, I was rather curt the other day.'

'Why don't you join me for a drink, and we can start again?' Anthony said, indicating the vacant chair opposite.

'I don't know, I should get on, but thank you for the offer.'

'You look exhausted. Where's the harm in taking a rest for five minutes? I haven't spoken to anyone all morning, nor sold a single bottle of wine,' Anthony lied. Ramón shrugged and sat down at the table. Anthony lifted his goblet and signalled to the waiter for another. The waiter brought the goblet. Anthony filled it from the flagon of wine and handed it to Ramón.

'How long have you worked at the embassy?' Anthony asked.

'It's coming up to six years now.'

'That's quite a while. I never seem able to settle anywhere for very long. You must be well regarded.'

'I hope so. I'm certainly never short of work. The pile of papers is never ending.'

'Well, that's something, it's good to have steady work, don't you think? I carry my case of wine from door to door, and if I get an order from one in ten, I consider myself lucky. Yours must be interesting work, I should imagine. Is it a well-paid position?' Anthony enquired.

'It has its moments, and it should be well paid.' Ramón sighed, swilling the wine around and around in his goblet.

'You should take a sip, it's actually quite a decent wine. It's not as good as my wines, obviously, but quite palatable,' Anthony said, studying Ramón's face.

'I'm sorry, I'm not very good company, perhaps I should go.'

'No, finish your wine first, it'll do you good. Do you live in, at the embassy, or do you have rent to pay?'

'No, I live with my wife and youngest son in a house near the Les Halles market.'

'How many children do you have?' Anthony asked.

'Two girls and three boys.'

'What are their names?'

'My eldest son is Juan. He's a teacher back home in Madrid. He recently married a nice girl and they are expecting our first grandchild.'

'That's wonderful. You must be very proud.'

'Our second son, Bernardo, is training for the priesthood in Santiago de Compostella. Our daughters, Sophia and Maria, are soon to be married as well. They are staying with their aunt in Madrid. We hope to get back for the weddings, but it doesn't look as if that is going to be possible.'

'Why not?' Anthony asked.

'We don't have the money, and there is a something else.'

'That's a pity. But your children must be a great blessing to you. I hope to find a wife one day and have a family. You're a lucky man, Ramón.'

'You are right. In many ways I am.'

'You said you had three sons. You told me about Juan

and Bernardo. What's your other son's name?'

'Our youngest son, Miguel, is only five. It was quite a surprise when we found my wife, Donna, was pregnant again. He lives here with us, but poor Miguel is very ill and we can't afford a doctor. We can't even think about the weddings of our daughters while he is so ill. Donna and I are almost at desperation point.'

'I'm very sorry to hear about Miguel. Not having a family of my own, I can only imagine what you're going through. But I'm quite familiar with being short of money. There isn't a fortune to be made from selling wine door to door, unless you're the boss. Mr Lavigne does all right. My commission is miserly and often late.'

'I haven't been paid for three months now. It's very worrying. We're desperate to get Miguel to a doctor.'

'Can't you borrow the money? Wouldn't the ambassador give you an advance on your salary?' Anthony asked.

'I've asked him, but he cannot at the moment. And little Miguel just gets worse every day. I don't know how long we can wait.'

'Oh, that's awful. I think I may be able to help you. When do you finish work?' Anthony said, and Ramón looked up.

'You can help my son?' Ramón asked, and for the first time since they had met, Anthony saw a glimmer of hope in the man's eyes.

'Yes, I'm sure of it. What time can you get away from the office?'

'Around sunset. My eyes are too poor for the candles and oil lamps these days.'

'Meet me back here at sunset tomorrow, then. I'm sure I can fix something. I may be able to arrange a sort of loan, to tide you over.'

Don Francés was adjusting the wick of his oil lamp when there was a knock on his study door.

'Come in!' The door opened and Captain Rodriguez entered and bowed.

'Your Excellency, there has been a development. I had the Venetian spy under observation and he met someone in the tavern on Rue St. Honore this evening.'

'Anyone of interest?' asked Don Francés.

'Your secretary, Aguilar, Your Excellency. They spoke for around half an hour.'

'Dios! Ramón! Are you sure? Of course you are, I'm sorry. I will question Ramón in the morning. Have a man keep the Venetian's lodgings under observation. Thank you, Rodriguez, you have done well.'

It was early morning and Marie Dufour was sweeping the kitchen floor, but her mind was elsewhere. She was thinking about the handsome young Venetian who had come to stay. They had exchanged glances, but there had been little conversation as yet, although his French was excellent. Marie's mother had always found some chore for her whenever he came down in the morning. This morning Madam Dufour had gone to fetch the bread herself and Marie was alone in the kitchen when Anthony came downstairs.

'Good morning Monsieur,' said Marie, 'Mother has

just gone to fetch some bread. Will you wait? There is a little wine and water on the table.'

'Thank you, Marie, but I have much to do today. I have had some success, at work, and expect some extra money soon. I wonder, would you like to come to the theatre with me? The Hôtel de Bourgogne on Rue Mauconseil, I've heard that the troupe there perform some very amusing farces.'

'Oh, Monsieur Foscari, that sounds wonderful. I have heard of them, of course, and always wanted to go.'

'Perfect, we shall go this evening. And you must call me Antonio.' Anthony smiled and Marie blushed as he put on his hat and cape and left by the front door.

Anthony waited all day at the Champs des Oiseaux tavern on Rue St. Honore. He had brought some money that he had saved from his monthly allowance. The plan was that he would exchange this for some small letters, something that the Spanish ambassador would not miss, yet he could use to convince Sir Henry to invest a much larger sum for more. There was no sign of Ramón. What could have happened? Some crisis with his son, perhaps? The ambassador may have had work for him which kept him from the rendezvous. Either way, he must be patient. He was close to something big, a genuine breakthrough, he could feel it. He would come and wait again tomorrow. The sun was setting and the citizens of Paris were scurrying back to their homes. The merchants were packing away their goods and wheeling their stalls away. Despite his disappointment at an unproductive day, he smiled at the thought of Marie. He drained his wine goblet and called the waiter over, paid his bill and left. Behind him Captain Rodriguez and three of his soldiers also paid their bill and followed.

Anthony kept to the centre of the road, side-stepping the horses and carts. He was intent on avoiding any excrement flung from a window, that might take the edge off his amorous intentions with Marie. As he passed the English ambassador's house he thought of popping in to alert Sir Henry about his impending success, but he didn't want to keep Marie waiting. He hurried on, oblivious of the shadows closing in on him from both sides of the street. As he turned into Rue Des Augustines two burly men seized his arms, and someone behind him jerked his neck back with a hand firmly placed over his mouth. Anthony writhed as they dragged him into a dark alley off the street to the right. He tried to shout, but the hand was too firmly fixed over his mouth. Anthony tried to bite it, but couldn't get any purchase on the palm. His left arm became almost free as the assailant on his left changed his grip and he tried to pull his arm up to his mouth just as a fist landed hard in his stomach and every breath of wind left him. He fell limp and then a bright light was replaced by blackness as he slipped from consciousness.

CHAPTER TWO

'Ah, you are awake.'

'Where am I, and who are you?'

'I am Father Michael, and you are in the hospital of Abbey Saint Germain des Prés. You were brought to us by men of the Venetian ambassador. You were found severely beaten on his doorstep, but the ambassador has no idea who you are or why you were on his doorstep. He has visited you, but we have been trying to calm you with something from the east, a tincture of opium. You could not answer his questions. So who are you, my son?'

'I'm, er, I don't know.' Anthony tried to sit up, screamed and sagged back on the bed. He thought. *I'm in France. I'm speaking French, but I'm not French. Who am I?*

'You have needed more opium than we have tried before, and you have been in and out of consciousness for almost a month. But you are alive and your bones will heal in time. I think if you rest some more, your memory may return. Now drink this broth then sleep.'

When Anthony next woke, moonlight shimmered across the stone floor of the hospital. There was snoring coming from a bed nearby. Anthony crawled his right hand over his chest, walking his fingers across his ribs. He felt for his St. Christopher, but couldn't find it. Next, he lifted his head a little and swivelled his eyes down, and saw that it had gone. Then he tried to move his legs, but winced and stopped. *I'm Anthony Standen. I live in East Molesey, but I work for Lord Darnley in Scotland. No, that's not right. He murdered David and then… I'm a spy, spying for Sir Henry Norris.* Memories flooded back. *I'm obviously not a very good spy.* Relieved that he could remember who he was, but terrified the Spaniards may come after him again, he decided that he'd better play dumb until he could contact Sir Henry.

It was late November 1567, and Anthony was making painful circuits of the abbey gardens on crutches. He was, by this time, able to manage almost an hour of this a day. Father Michael approached.

'Antonio, you are getting much faster. I'm glad because…' he faltered.

'Why, Father?'

'It's the civil war. More and more wounded flood into the city every day, and I'm afraid…'

'Afraid?'

'I'm afraid we need all the beds we have for the sick and wounded. We have done all we can for you, Antonio. You will have to go now. I'm sorry.'

'Yes, I see. Thank you, Father, I would be dead were it not for you. I will leave now. What about these?' he asked, lifting one crutch.

'Keep them for now and return them as soon as you can walk without them. But come inside before you leave. We can spare you a blanket and some bread and cheese to see you on your way.' Father Michael walked with Anthony back to the hospital wing of the abbey. He kept glancing at Anthony.

'What's the matter, Father?'

'I don't like to worry you, but your hair seems to be turning brown at the roots. It's not unusual for a man's hair to turn white after the sort of beating you've had, but brown is a first on me. It may be an effect of the dosage of opium we have tried on you. I will make a note of it in the hospital record.'

Sir Henry Norris was sitting at his desk reading a decrypted letter from William Cecil, the Secretary of State.

Whilst your reports of the Huguenot success in September and the ongoing civil war are well detailed, I find your reports lacking on both the French ambitions in relation to Prince James and how Spain's embassy are positioning themselves. We remain vulnerable in the north. Walsingham assures me you have talented resources at your disposal, so I shall hope for better intelligence before long.

'Robert!' barked Sir Henry to his secretary. His study door opened and Robert walked in.

'Yes, sir,'

'Has there been any news about young Standen?'

'Nothing at all, sir. Neither Madame Dufour nor Monsieur Lavigne have seen him for six weeks now.'

'Have you been round the taverns?'

'Yes, sir, no sign of him at all.'

'This is a terrible business, Robert. I fear we may have played him too soon. He should have been better prepared. Keep looking, Robert, I want him found.'

'Yes, sir.'

The abbey gates closed behind Anthony. A small sack with a loaf of bread and some cheese in it hung by a loop of string around his neck. He limped along on his crutches towards the riverbank to gather his thoughts. By the river, he found a low wall to sit on with a view up and down the riverbank. He manoeuvred himself into position and lowered himself onto the wall.

Anthony needed to see Sir Henry. But if the

Spaniards were watching his house, what chance would he have? Should he go to Monsieur Lavigne, or should he return to his lodgings with Madam Dufour? The Spaniards may be watching both the wine merchants and his lodgings. It seemed more likely that they would watch the wine merchants. Since he left the Spanish embassy, he hadn't been to the English embassy. If they had dumped him on the Venetian ambassador's doorstep, perhaps they thought he really was a Venetian.

A group of sailors walked along the riverbank and Anthony watched them from the corner of his eye, aware that he was defenceless if they proved to be Spaniards looking for him. They passed by without giving him a second glance. Why would they think he was English? Since the Venetian ambassador didn't know him, would he have complained to the Spaniards? Why would he? He wouldn't know who had beaten him up. It might have been the English, for all he knew. Anthony opened the sack and took out the bread and cheese. He broke off a lump of each and chewed on them. He decided he must return to Sir Henry's, but not before dusk. He would find somewhere where he could watch the embassy unobserved, then make his move.

CHAPTER THREE

Anthony sat on the ground in a small alleyway off Rue St. Honore from where he could observe the English embassy. His crutches leant against the wall and a few small coins lay in his lap, where they had been tossed by the occasional Good Samaritan. The sun had set an hour ago. Lanterns and candles had been lit in the houses. He saw the embassy door open, and Robert leave, closing the door behind him. Anthony pulled himself upright, using the crutches, and limped after him as quickly as he could. He heard the coins fall to the ground, hesitated, then continued as fast as he could. Robert had just turned the corner into Rue des Deus when Anthony caught him. Robert turned when he heard the tapping of crutches on cobbles.

'Who's there?'

'Robert, it's me, Stan… Foscari. Antonio Foscari.'

'My god! We've been looking for you everywhere. What happened to you?'

'Not here. Can we go somewhere safe?'

'Down here, we'll go to the backdoor of the embassy.' Robert led the way down a dark alley, fumbled in his pocket for a key, felt for the keyhole, and then opened the door and helped Anthony inside. Oil lamps illuminated the embassy kitchen and a middle-aged woman, who Anthony assumed was the cook, looked with evident disapproval at this dishevelled man in her kitchen. 'Through here.' Robert led Anthony through another door and he found himself in the hallway. He recognised the door to Sir Henry's study and Robert knocked on it, then they both entered. 'Sir, I found him.

It's Standen.'

'My god, so it is.' Sir Henry stood up. 'Sit down, Standen. Pull up that chair for him, would you, Robert? Erm, I think the fewer of us that hear Standen's story, the better for now. That will be all, Robert, thank you.' Robert closed the door behind him as Sir Henry paced his study, regarding Standen from various angles. 'So what on earth happened to you, and where have you been?'

He recounted his story and Sir Henry listened until he reached the point where he had learnt from Father Michael that they had dumped him on the doorstep of the Venetian ambassador.

'Your cover wasn't blown then. They think you are a Venetian spy. That makes sense, the Venetian's have the most extensive and the best spy network in the world. That could be very useful to us.'

'But since the Venetian ambassador doesn't know me, he will know that I'm not a Venetian spy. So might the Spaniards learn from him that they got it wrong?'

'Possibly, but probably not. Why would the Spaniards brag to the Venetians that they have exposed their spy and beaten you up? Why would the Venetians protest that one of their spies has been assaulted? Also, the Venetian ambassador might think you are a Venetian spy.'

'Wouldn't he know, if I were?'

'The Doge is the elected leader of the Venetians. But councils made up from the wealthiest families in Venice elect him. There are councils of up to a hundred men, all vying for greater power and influence. Not every Venetian spy is run by the Doge.' Sir Henry paused and rubbed his temples with the tips of his fingers. 'In your capacity as a renegade Venetian spy, it is possible that the Spaniards, or indeed the French, may try to turn you to spy for them. We could feed you some plausible but worthless information to give to them, and by getting inside their web, you might find something useful to us.'

'It sounds dangerous.'

'It would be. What experience of spying did you have before you came to Paris, Standen?'

'Just the normal things, sir. I spied on girls bathing in the lake, when I was a boy. But other than that, well, nothing really. Oh, I hid under Lord Darnley's desk once and listened at his keyhole.'

'You mean you hadn't been spying for Sir Nicholas before he sent you to me?'

'No, sir. As I said, we only met a couple of times and I impressed him with my language skills. He thought I would be useful to you.'

'He didn't make that clear in his letter, the oaf! I'm sorry, Standen, I thought you had more experience with this sort of thing. I think you can be very useful, but we need to prepare you for a very dangerous task. I know some people who can teach you a few tricks. Some people I can trust, and some who fear me enough for me to rely on their silence. Now, from what you've told me, you maintained your cover story well. You also cleverly gained the confidence of this fellow Ramón. What you failed to do was check whether you were observed or being followed. We have a fellow, a reformed thief, who can teach you a few things. I also know an old soldier, the best dirty fighter in the army. He can teach you how to defend yourself if you are jumped on again. But given the state of you, I think we'd better start with something less strenuous. What do you know about codes and ciphers?'

'Sir Henry has asked me to teach you what I know of the arts of secrecy, Sir Anthony.'

'So I understand Robert. Thank you for using my

title, but we will progress faster if you do not. Anthony will suffice. I understand you handle all the embassy's secret correspondence.'

'That's right. So let's begin with some history.'

'Must we?'

'I think it will help. There are two principal ways of sending and receiving secret messages. One is to hide the message. For example, the ancient Chinese wrote messages on fine silk, scrunched it into a small ball, encased it in wax and then the messenger swallowed it.'

'That's disgusting.'

'Quite, and the Persians, or was it the Greeks? Someone, anyway, shaved the head of a servant and wrote on his scalp. When his hair had grown back, the servant was dispatched. If the enemy stopped him and searched him, there would be no message to discover. When he reached the intended recipient, he would shave his head and show it to the recipient.'

'I hope the message wasn't urgent,' Anthony laughed.

'Quite,' agreed Robert. 'Then there is invisible ink. The ancient Greeks used the milk of the Thithymallus plant as invisible ink. Once dry, it is invisible, but if you heat it gently, the ink turns brown. Urine will work too. So there are many ways of hiding a message. But if your enemy searches you and warms a blank page, or shaves your head, the message is revealed. Then there is encryption. Julius Caesar used ciphers. He employed a substitution cipher in which each letter of the alphabet was moved a set number of places.' Robert sketched out the cipher on a piece of paper.

a b c d e f g h i j k l m n o p q r s t u v w x y z
D E F G H I J K L M N O P Q R S T U V W X Y Z A B C

The lower case letters on the top are the alphabet and the capital letters below are the cipher alphabet. As you can see, the cipher alphabet has been shunted to the right by three letters. The writer and the receiver agree three, which is the key. But it could be any number between one and twenty-five as long as they agree on it. So now decode this message.'

"JRGVDYHWKHTXHHQ"

Anthony began writing,

"GODSAVETHEQUEEN" 'It is simple, but effective. And you just have to agree on the number.' Anthony smiled. 'This isn't as hard as I thought.'

'Right, I'll attend to some of Sir Henry's letters for half an hour, and you write me a simple message. Don't tell me by how many spaces you have shunted the letters. How long do you think it will take me to decipher it?'

'With twenty-five possible keys, let's say ten minutes per key, that's just over four hours. But you might strike it lucky. I'd guess two hours.'

'Anthony, you get started and I'll be back in half an hour. Don't let me see your key.' Robert smiled and left the room. Anthony thought a while and started writing out his key. He started his substitution with Q so that A became Q, B became R, etc. Whichever end of the alphabet he starts from, it will take him quite a bit of time to get to that, he thought. Then he began writing out his message.

HERUHJWIWDTUUTQWHUQJJUQSXUH

Anthony looked up at the clock on the wall of Robert's office. It had taken him twenty minutes to encipher his message. He took the paper his key was written on, and tucked it up the sleeve of his doublet. Shortly after that, Robert re-entered the room.

'There you are, Robert,' said Anthony, handing him

the paper with his message. 'Shall I go for my walk now, while you try to decipher my message?' He reached for his crutches.

'No, just give me a few minutes.' Robert's pen flew furiously back and forth over the message.

'But I could get my exercise while you do that. It's a fine morning, why waste it?'

'Oh, Anthony. That is kind. I think I shall frame it and hang it over my desk.' Robert smiled and Anthony looked stunned. ROBERTISINDEEDAGREATTEACHER

'How on God's earth did you do that so quickly? Is there a secret spy hole you were watching me from?' Anthony examined the wall and the ceiling above the desk.

'No, I just did some counting. There are six Us in your coded message. The next most frequent letter is H, which occurs four times. The most frequently occurring letter in the alphabet is E. So I assumed E was U, which meant that A was Q and the rest was easy.'

'That's incredible!'

'No, that's cryptanalysis! But I think that's enough for this morning. You take your walk and we will continue this afternoon.'

Robert's lesson had so amazed Anthony that he couldn't wait to learn more. Over the next few weeks, he learnt more about frequency analysis and the patterns that letters occur in. He learnt that E can appear before and after almost any letter, but that T is rarely seen before or after B,D,G,J,K,M,Q or V. He learnt that once you have accurately identified a few letters, the cipher begins to unravel quite quickly.

'So how can you keep messages secret? It isn't easy, but you've demonstrated that any code can be broken.'

'Firstly, we have been learning about ciphers. A code

is when a code word is used to replace a plain word, rather than a cipher letter substituted for a real letter. So, in a code, we might substitute the word ALE for QUEEN, say. Frequency analysis can not break a code. However, the sender and receiver both need a codebook, and if the codebook falls into enemy hands, then all previously intercepted messages are immediately decoded. Also, be as clever as you can be in both disguising the medium of the message and its content.'

'The invisible ink sort of thing.'

'Yes, and if your message to me had been ROBART IS A MOST GRAIT TUTOR, do you see how difficult that would have been for me to decipher?'

'No Es, yes I see. Yet the meaning is still clear.'

'You are learning, Anthony, you are learning.'

Anthony's next tutor was the thief Sir Henry had mentioned, a middle-aged man by the name of John Pollard. In fact, Pollard had been handed onto Sir Henry by Sir Nicholas Throckmorton. Sir Nicholas had been Under Treasurer of the Tower Mint when one evening, by pure chance, he discovered Pollard stuffing a sack with gold coin in the vaults. Pollard had evaded all the guards and picked his way through the most secure locks England had. Sitting in the drawing room around a table covered in locks of various types, both complete and dismantled, Pollard explained.

'I thought I was dead meat, honest I did. But Sir Nicholas thought I might be more use alive than dead.' Pulling open his shirt, he showed Anthony the Throckmorton coat of arms which had been branded on his chest. 'He did this, so that if I went back to my old ways, I'd be found, eventually. But he was good to me, too. He paid me well and I've been advising on security.

I've also stolen a few things for him when required, and occasionally returned them unnoticed when he'd finished with them.'

'So how did you learn about locks?' Anthony asked.

'My father was a locksmith. He died when I was a boy, but not before I'd learnt a lot about locks. I was too young to take over the business. We were starving, my mother, sisters and me, so I started stealing. I got very good at it, and at not getting caught.'

'Until Sir Nicholas caught you relieving the Tower Mint of its gold.'

'Your luck has to run out, eventually. You can stack all the odds in your favour and consider every eventuality. He was lucky and my luck had just run out. Anyway, let's get on with the lesson.' Pollard picked up a dismantled lock and its key. 'This is a five-lever lock. See, these are the levers. I'll put the key in and turn it slowly. Now see how the notches on the key fit between the levers and how the projections on the key lift each lever a slightly different amount until these slots, or gates in the levers, all line up.'

'Yes, I see.'

'Well, as we continue turning the key, this other projection on the end of the key engages with the bolt, and this projection on the bolt now slides through the gates on the levers which are now all lined up, and the bolt retracts. The door is open.'

'Yes, but you have the key!'

'Please be patient, sir. You have to know how a lock works before you can pick it.'

'Sorry.'

'Now do you see these other gates on these two levers, here and here?'

'Yes I see them.'

'Well, those are false gates. Locksmiths put those on to try to fool pickers. Now these are the tools of the trade. This is the pick.' He showed Standen a thin piece of metal about the same length as the key, with its end bent at right angles. 'And this is a tensioner. They look similar, but they do different jobs. You insert them both into the key hole, like this. The tensioner you use to do the task that the end of the key was doing. It engages with the bolt and is what retracts the bolt. You keep up a gentle pressure on the tensioner. Then you feel for the first lever. Obviously, we can see it, but when the lock is assembled, you have to feel for it. Now see how as I turn the pick, it lifts the lever. Did you hear that slight click?'

'Yes.'

'That was the projection just lining up with the gate in the lever because I had that little bit of pressure on the tensioner. Now I'll move onto the second lever, see that's one with a false gate in it. It's not as deep as the true gate. If it were, it would be a gate. I can feel that's a false gate, but I've had a lot of practice. So I'm going to keep turning the lever with the pick, and there, I've got the true gate. Now for the third lever. There's the click. Now four. See, there's the false gate on four. Feel on and there's the true gate. Just the fifth to go, and there you are, lock open. Now you have a go with the lock dismantled so you can see what you're doing, till you get the feel, then we'll put the lock back together and you can try it for real.'

Anthony found it simple enough with the lock dismantled, but once it was reassembled, he struggled. 'This is impossible. I simply can't get the hang of it.'

'Well, you've only been trying an hour, sir. If it was easy, there'd be no point having locks at all now, would there, sir?'

It was several days before Anthony picked the first

lock.

'Well done, sir! Now we need to get faster. Keep at this lock, sir, then when you can open it in a minute, we'll move onto some different locks.'

At the end of four weeks, Anthony was opening a variety of locks, from castle gate locks to padlocks and cabinet locks. Although it had been intensely frustrating at first, he felt quite a thrill when he felt the pick as an extension of his fingertip. He was also now able to walk without crutches, so the time spent on ciphers and locks had been a useful distraction while his limbs healed.

'You're doing well, sir, but you need to keep practising, every day if you can. You keep these locks and this pick set, sir to practise on. But shall I now teach you what I've learnt about avoiding being followed?'

'Yes please, Pollard. Some fresh air would be very welcome.'

'Very good, sir. But let's talk about the art a little here first, where we can't be overheard, before we go out onto the streets.'

'If I'm going to break into somewhere, it's best to do it at night. The first thing I do is make a reconnaissance. I want to know the layout, and especially the escape routes. The reconnaissance is best done in daylight, but I don't want anyone to be suspicious. I think about having a good reason to be there. I've had quite a collection of priests' habits, and beggar's rags in my time, to use as a disguise. Once I've decided on the best disguise, I don't go straight to the target. I plan a route to the target. I'll go to at least three other places first. I'll carefully plan the route so that there will be pinch points where anyone following me will have to show themselves.'

'What do you mean by a pinch point?' Anthony

asked.

'It might be a dark alleyway, for example. If I walk down the alleyway, a few yards and stop. I can wait and see or hear, if anyone has followed me into the alleyway. Or it might be a bridge. I can stop on the bridge and see if anyone behind me stops too. Although I'm trying not to be observed, I'm also discretely observing everyone around me. I look at their faces, their shoes, their clothes. I visit at least three places before the target and if I've seen the same person at more than one of the places, I assume I'm being followed.'

'But that might just be coincidence.'

'Indeed it might, sir, but it's safest to assume it isn't. Patience is a great virtue of the good criminal, sir. The other thing, sir, like you've learnt with lock picking, is to hone your senses. That feeling that the pick is an extension of your fingertip, that enhanced sense of feel. You need to use all your senses. When you're in that dark alleyway, can you hear footsteps, breathing? Can you smell anyone?'

'Smell anyone?'

'Yes sir, try it. I'm not suggesting you go around sniffing people. Just close your eyes occasionally and find out what you can sense with your ears and nose. Chef, for instance, has a distinctive smell. I don't need to go in the kitchen to find out what's for lunch, if she passes me in the hallway. Robert has a distinctive aroma of ink and blotting powder. As I said at the beginning, most of the time I work at night, so I use all my senses. Now then, sir, are you up to trying a bit of cat and mouse on the streets?'

They took it in turns to be the cat and the mouse, around the streets of Paris by both day and night. Anthony was getting better.

'Right, sir, I think it's time to introduce a few more actors. Sir Henry has agreed a few trusted members of staff that I can use to try to track you. Some you already know, and some you don't. We'll start that tomorrow, and see how you get on.'

'Excellent. Do you think we deserve a goblet of wine after that?'

'Indeed I do, sir, if you're buying.'

The following day, Anthony woke in his attic room in the embassy. He found a note pinned to the inside of his door.

Go to the graveyard of St. Eustache Church. Look for a gravestone with a chalk circle marked on it. You will find a secret note under a rock beneath the circle. I will not follow you, but others will try. The note will have your next set of instructions.

He read the note several times. Then he quickly washed and dressed and set off towards St. Eustache Church. He paused at several stalls in a street market. He picked up some vegetables, turning them over slowly in his hands whilst discretely looking around. A monk had stopped at the neighbouring stall. His hood concealed his face, but his shoes bore the same scuff marks that Robert's shoes did. Anthony put the vegetables down and ambled very slowly down the road. When he came to a junction, he timed his crossing the road to be just in front of a cart and ran a few yards beside the cart until he could dive off down a side street unseen. He took further turnings then paused, waiting to see if Robert would reappear. He didn't. Anthony took a wide loop around the district, avoiding the direct route to the church. When he reached the church, he kept his distance and waited patiently, observing the graveyard. There was a beggar by the church doorway who was the same size and build as

Stephan, who helped in the embassy kitchens. Anthony waited. Eventually, the beggar moved on. Anthony checked all around and entered the graveyard. It didn't take long to find the chalk circle and a piece of paper under the rock. He stuffed the paper inside his purse and hurried out of the graveyard. He alternated zig zagging through side streets with pausing to see if he was being followed. When he was sure he wasn't being followed, he slipped into a small tavern, ordered some wine and sat at a corner table. He then examined the paper. It was a shopping list.

6 onions
6 carrots
3 shallots
1 beetroot
1 lemon
5 apples
4 fish
3 gooseberries
4 prunes
2 pomegranates
3 parsnips
2 peas

He was bemused for a while, but Robert had been an excellent teacher. He used his lock pick to make a mark under the 6th letter of onions, then the 6th letter of carrots, the 3rd letter of shallots and so on. They spelt STABLE HONORE. He finished his wine and made his way through the gathering darkness towards the Stables on Rue St. Honore, carefully checking that he was not being followed.

It was dark when he reached the stables. He made his way around to the side door which was padlocked. It was a simpler padlock than the ones he had practised on, and he had it open in seconds. He pushed the door open, quietly at first. Then the hinge creaked, and he felt a heavy hand land on his right shoulder. He spun around and then looked down at a grey-haired, short, squat man.

'Who are you?' Anthony asked.

'I'm Harrison, sir, your next instructor.'

'Instructor in what?'

'Combat, sir.'

'Combat? I must be at least a foot taller than you, and thirty years younger. What can you teach me about combat?'

'Oh, I think you'll be surprised, sir. Shall we meet here tomorrow morning, as the clock strikes nine?'

The central area of the stable was covered in a six-inch layer of straw, and bales of it had been stacked up around three sides. To one side, there were bales on which an array of swords, muskets, and pistols were laid out. The stalls were all empty. The horses must have been moved out.

'Good morning, sir. I hear you have been recovering from a bit of a beating. How are you now?'

'I am much recovered thank you, Harrison. A few aches and pains, but I'm feeling much better every day.'

'Very good, sir. I think Sir Henry told you a little about me. I've spent my life fighting for king and queen and others who paid me. Not being a large man, I've had to learn to fight clever and dirty. Sir Henry wants me to pass some of that on to you, so that hopefully you don't take such a beating again. What are you like with a sword?'

'I can hold my own.'

'Well, let's see.' Harrison picked up two swords from the straw bales and offered Anthony his choice. They both had blunt edges, and the tips had been flattened. Anthony made his choice, and they circled around each other. Harrison made the first lunge and Anthony parried. 'Very good, sir.' Harrison then launched a furious assault, forcing Anthony to retreat towards the edge of the square. Blades crashed and as Anthony saw Harrison launch his next lunge, he sidestepped and landed his own lunge with the blunt tip of his sword, catching Harrison in the ribs. Slightly winded, Harrison panted, 'Fair play, sir. You can more than hold your own with a sword. How are you with firearms?'

'I had some experience of them in Scotland.'

'Very good. So can you tell me what we have here, sir?' Harrison asked, leading Anthony to the bale with the weapons laid out.

'These are matchlock muskets, or arquebuses. This is a matchlock pistol and I don't know what this is,' Anthony said, picking up one of the pistols.

'Very good, sir. But they are not both muskets. Look down the barrel of this one, sir.'

'The barrel is not smooth, there is a sort of spiral pattern running down it.'

'It's quite new, sir, and it's called rifling. Very expensive and rare, sir. The rifling puts a spin on the ball and makes it much more accurate. Don't ask me why, that's beyond me. But we shall see for ourselves a little later. Now this pistol that you don't recognise. This is also very new, and very expensive. It's a wheellock. The significant thing about this is that when you pull the trigger, a spring mechanism spins this wheel and brings this arm with a piece of pyrite in it into contact with the spinning wheel. The mechanism also moves the cover of the pan forward, exposing the powder and as the pyrite contacts the spinning wheel, sparks fly into the pan and bang!'

'My god! No match to keep blowing on?'

'That's right, sir. It's like magic, isn't it? You can carry this gun loaded, then pull it from your belt, cock the lever, aim and fire it with one hand, in seconds rather than minutes. But we'll play with that later, sir. First, let me see if you can load the matchlocks and hit the targets pinned on those bales over there.'

Anthony was pleased to note that there were leather buckets of water and sand ready in case a flash of powder ignited the hay. He picked up the unrifled musket, took a paper cartridge of gunpowder, and bit the end off. Next he filled the pan with gunpowder then swivelled the pan cover over the pan and blew the grains of powder that had not fallen in the pan away, all the time holding the glowing match cord well clear. Resting the butt of the musket on the ground, he emptied the rest of the gunpowder down the barrel. He picked up a musket ball and put that into the barrel. Then he scrunched up the paper cartridge and poked that down the barrel. After withdrawing the scouring stick from the slot under the barrel, he used it to ram the paper and ball down the barrel. He replaced the scouring stick in its slot and blew on the glowing match before fixing it into the jaws of the lever and adjusting it to the right length to contact the pan. Finally, he turned to face the target, slid back the cover of the pan, took aim and squeezed the trigger. The lever swivelled towards the pan and, with a flash and a bang, the musket fired.

'You handle the musket perfectly, sir. Let's look at the target.' They walked over to the target. The hole was six inches left of centre. 'That's pretty good from twenty yards, sir. I'm impressed. Now try it with the rifled one.' Anthony carefully repeated the process with the rifled weapon. The result was a hole a half inch from the centre. 'See how much more accurate the rifling is, sir?'

He was even more impressed when Harrison showed him how to use the wheellock. He could load it, fire and load it again very quickly. In fact, he could fire three shots in the time it took Harrison to count to sixty.

'This wheellock is incredible. Without a match to worry about, I imagine you could use it in heavy rain.'

'If you keep your powder dry, sir, yes.'

'So why haven't these replaced matchlocks?'

'As you can see, sir, the mechanism is very complex. So it takes a very good gunsmith to make one. If it breaks, you need a gunsmith to fix it, whereas any blacksmith can fix a matchlock. This all makes them very expensive. Also, the Holy Roman Emperor Maximilian banned them. Anyway, you're more than handy with swords and guns, sir. But they were no use to you when you were set upon unexpected. So let's clear these things away and set to fighting without weapons.'

Anthony helped Harrison clear the guns and swords away. They spread some more loose straw over the ground. Then Harrison led him to the centre.

'Okay then, sir. Hit me.'

'Where, and how hard?'

'Anywhere you like, sir. And as hard as you can.'

'Well, if you're sure.'

They began circling around slowly. Anthony crouched a little and had his fists raised, but Harrison stood upright, his arms hung at his sides. Anthony threw a punch to Harrison's jaw but found himself gazing at the roof joists, flat on his back and winded.

'… what. How did you do that?'

'Wrestling, sir. It's all a question of balance and mechanics.' He helped Anthony to his feet. 'You see, sir, you adopted a bit of a crouching stance and had your feet a little wider apart. That slows you down. I keep upright and my feet are shoulder width apart. Like this. If your feet are too close together, you lose stability. Too wide apart and you lose mobility. Now look at my feet. If you imagine a line drawn between my toes, then I am very stable along that line, but quite unstable at right angles to that line. It doesn't matter whether one foot is slightly forward or back. Look at the line between the toes. The weakness is at right angles to that line. When you threw your punch, your upper body was twisting and powering forward behind the punch. All I had to do was step aside, grab your arm, and sweep your rear foot away with my right leg. Your weight was moving forward and off your rear foot. You were already twisting. You did it all for me, really. All I had to do was react quickly and attack you below your point of balance. Your momentum did the rest.'

Over the next few weeks, they fought six hours a day, every day. Anthony learnt a wide variety of throws, armlocks, holds, and strangleholds.

'Now wrestling, sir, is what you do with friends, with people you like and don't want to kill or cripple. If you aren't too bothered with crippling or killing, then there are faster ways of stopping your assailant. It isn't easy to fight several people at the same time, as you know, sir. So, for each move you make, one of your assailants has to go down and not get up again. Eyes, throat, knees. The knee is a weak point. Land a kick hard enough on a man's knee and he won't get up again. Spread your fingers like this, and land a jab with your fingertips, hitting both eyes, and he won't see to hit you again. Chop with the edge of your hand like this into his throat, and he's out of the game. Obviously we can't practise this on each other. I've got a dummy made of sacking over here that I've stuffed with straw. I've painted the eyes and knee targets. I'll string it up to the joist and we can work on those killer moves.'

CHAPTER FOUR

'Enter!' barked Sir Henry, looking up from his correspondence as Anthony opened his study door. 'Standen, do sit down. How are you feeling now?'

'Fighting fit, sir.'

'Hah, technically as well as physically, I hear. I've had excellent reports of your progress. Are you ready to start work again?'

'Yes, sir.'

'Well, I've done a lot of thinking. Much has happened in the last year. The civil war in France appears to have ended, for now, with a peace treaty, in which the Huguenots have secured considerable concessions. Mary Queen of Scots has fled to England and is under Queen Elizabeth's protection. Mary's son, James, has been made King of Scotland at two years of age. Mary has become a figurehead for English Catholics, and we are weak in the north. With the rise of the Huguenots in France, Cecil thinks that the biggest threat now comes from Spain.'

'I see, sir. So how can I help?'

'You remember we spoke about how the Spaniards think you are a Venetian spy, and how they may try to turn you to spy for them?'

'I do, sir. Do you want me to get close to them again? Perhaps I could make another approach to Ramón?'

'No, I've had another idea, and I think it's a rather good one. You take up your cover as Antonio Foscari, the wine merchant with Monsieur Lavigne again. It's quite normal to have occasional social events with other embassies, so we will hold a drinks reception here. You and Lavigne will serve the wine. I will invite the Spanish ambassador, his senior staff and some French diplomats too.'

'Do you think the Spanish ambassador will recognise me, take me to one side and try to recruit me here?'

'Well, I base my plan on either him or one of his senior men recognising you, but you didn't exactly cover yourself in glory as a spy on your first mission. We need to make you a bit more attractive to them. I will keep my eyes on the ambassador and his staff to gauge their reaction when you appear. If it looks like they recognise you, I'll give you a signal. Then when the wine is flowing you slip out and go to my study. You pick the door lock, then pick the lock to my desk drawer and go through my correspondence. With luck, one of the Spaniards will have followed you and will catch you red-handed. They will be sure you're a Venetian, spying on us now. They may want to know what it is the Venetians are after.'

'What if they just take your correspondence from me and leave?'

'We will carefully craft false information. But my guess is that they won't be able to resist getting an inside man in the Venetian spy network. What do you think?'

'When do we start?'

'Tomorrow. You will need Robert to dye your hair and beard again. I'll get messages to Madam Dufour and Lavigne, then you slip away from here tomorrow night.'

'What if the Spaniards are watching Lavigne and Dufour, sir?'

'I doubt they will be after this length of time. But it's a good point. You will need to stay away from here until we spring the trap. If you need to get a message to me, or if I need to get one to you, we will need to have a signal. Perhaps something like a hidden note in the graveyard again. I heard about that, you did well. I'll ask Robert to come up with something, and you can talk it over tomorrow.'

A quartet comprising three lutes and a virginal were playing in the corner of the second-floor ballroom. Sir Henry was talking with a group of French courtiers.

'It is a very good turnout, Sir Henry. Are you expecting many more?'

'Just a few more, Your Excellency. I was hoping the Spanish ambassador, Don Francés, would join us. Ah, there he is now. Please excuse me, Your Excellency.' Count Charles of Anjou nodded and Sir Henry crossed to greet Don Francés, who had just been ushered in by Robert, followed by Captain Rodriguez.

'Don Francés, I'm so glad you came. We have several people here that you may know. Have you met Count Charles of Anjou?'

'No, I don't think I've had the pleasure. Can I introduce Captain Rodriguez, my military attaché.'

'I'm delighted to meet you, captain.' Sir Henry said as they shook hands. 'I'll just get some wine for you, then I'll make some introductions. Lavigne, some more wine over here please!' Monsieur Lavigne acknowledged with a wave, and Sir Henry steered Don Francés and Captain Rodriguez towards the group of French courtiers. 'Your Excellency, may I introduce Don Francés, the Spanish ambassador and Captain Rodriguez.' Sir Henry saw Anthony approaching with a tray of goblets and a flagon of wine. Sir Henry stood back to make room for Anthony to serve. Don Francés took the goblet offered by Anthony without breaking eye contact with Count Charles, but Sir Henry noticed Captain Rodriguez's eyes widen and his nostrils flare as Anthony offered him a goblet. Anthony had seen the reaction himself, so he hardly needed Sir Henry's signal, but Sir Henry rubbed his right earlobe, anyway. 'Do excuse me again please, I see we have more new arrivals.' Sir Henry left the group and greeted a group of Italian diplomats who had just arrived. Anthony returned to the table where Lavigne was uncorking some more wine. He whispered in his ear, then left the room carrying a box of empty flagons.

Anthony went down the stairs and turned towards the kitchen. As he put down the box to open the kitchen door, he heard the brief babble of voices as the ballroom door opened and then closed again. He carried the box into the kitchen and left it on the floor. Then he went back into the hallway and approached the door to Sir Henry's study. Anthony looked around and up the stairs. The door to the ballroom was closed and there seemed to be nobody about. He took out his lock picks and started working on the study door lock. He noticed a reflection in the brass door knob as a shadow moved across the second-floor hall window. Anthony opened the lock in less than a minute and entered Sir Henry's study. He left the door ajar and crossed to the desk. He knelt down behind the desk and picked the lock on the desk drawer. He opened that in seconds and took out the letter he knew would be in there. He pulled out a piece of paper from his purse, spread it on the desk beside the letter and sat in Sir Henry's chair. He used Sir Henry's pen and ink to copy the letter. He had just finished, replaced the original and locked the drawer when the door opened.

'I'll take that.' Anthony looked up to see Captain Rodriguez enter and close the door behind him. He also saw the pistol levelled straight at him. 'That was impressive. I didn't know locks were that easy to open. Now bring that copy of the letter and come with me.' Rodriguez waved the muzzle of the pistol towards the door. Rodriguez opened the door and glanced into the hall. He pulled his cape around him to conceal the pistol, but keeping it pointed at him, he motioned Anthony to walk in front of him. 'Now lock the door again.' Anthony used his picks to lock the study door and then they both left through the front door. He felt the muzzle of the pistol pressing into his back. 'The last carriage on the right, get in!'

The carriage took him and Rodriguez to the Spanish embassy on Rue St. Thomas. He thought about all the ways he could use Harrison's techniques to overpower Rodriguez, but escaping wasn't the plan. He allowed himself to be taken to the third-floor ambassador's office. There he and Rodriguez sat facing each other in silence for an hour, the pistol pointing at him the entire time. At last, the door opened and Don Francés entered. He and Rodriguez spoke in Spanish.

'What happened?'

'He opened the lock of Sir Henry's study with some kind of needles, then opened the desk drawer a similar way and made this copy of a document.' Rodriguez handed the paper to Don Francés. 'I caught him red-handed. I made him replace the original, re-lock the desk, and the study, and brought him here.'

'You did well, Rodriguez. I think you can put the gun away now. I assume you have checked him for weapons?'

'Yes, sir, he's clean. These are the needles I was talking about.'

'Interesting. You can wait outside now while I talk with Signor Foscari.' Rodriguez left the room. Don Francés addressed Anthony in French.

'So you can open locked doors without a key with these things. You Venetian spies are good.' Don Francés looked at the paper. 'We will get our code breakers to look at it.'

'We can talk in Spanish. It's all the same to me.'

'Ah, a master linguist too. Now the question is, what are we going to do with you? Perhaps I could tell Sir Henry what we caught you at and let the English deal with you. I could just have Rodriguez kill you and dump you in the Seine. On the other hand, I could show the Venetian ambassador how we outwitted his spy, maybe he would buy you back.'

'I doubt it, we have many more.'

'I'm sure you do. Does it pay well?'

'It's a living.'

'What if you made twice as much? What if both the doge and King Philip paid you for the same secrets?' Anthony remained silent. 'Come on, Signor Foscari, what's the matter with you? It's a better offer than another beating or death.'

'So it was you.'

'Yes, but you were trying to spy on us, and that we cannot allow. Now I see how useful you may be to us.'

'Can you pay? Your secretary hadn't been paid in months.'

'Yes, that was a hard time, but our king has been more generous recently. For good information, we will pay well. Do we have an understanding?'

'I don't see why not. What do I get for the paper I copied today?'

Don Francés stood up and paced back and forth for a few minutes.

'Yes, we will pay. We will pay two gold ducats for this.' He opened his desk drawer and took out two gold coins and handed them to Anthony. He inspected them, turned them over in his hands and bit one, as he had seen his father do once.

'We have a deal. Just one thing.'

'What?'

'I need my needles and that document back and another piece of paper. I'll need to copy it again for the Doge.' Don Francés looked surprised. 'If I am to serve two masters, and be paid twice, then I need two copies.'

'Yes, I suppose you do, and the Doge must not suspect our arrangement.'

Anthony found that the new arrangement suited him very well. The Spaniards seemed very pleased with the carefully crafted misinformation that he passed to them from Sir Henry. Sir Henry was being pressed for information that might influence the marriage proposal Queen Elizabeth had received from Duke Henri of Anjou, as well as plans the Spaniards might have to free Mary Queen of Scots. So he began picking his way into several targeted French residences, that Sir Henry suggested, under cover of night. Each time, he copied the correspondence he found for Sir Henry and made an extra copy to sell to Don Francés. He was very wary of Rodriguez, but the volume of information that Don Francés was now receiving made him careless. Anthony memorised some snippets of correspondence that Don Francés had been reading or writing on the occasions when they met. There were also the pieces of conversation he overheard. Marie Dufour had been impressed with his new wealth, the jewellery and perfumes he bought her, and the evenings at the theatre. When Anthony wasn't spying by night, he enjoyed her embrace very much indeed.

In August 1570, things changed. Francis Walsingham

arrived in Paris as special ambassador dealing with the marriage proposal. Soon afterwards, a dispatch arrived from Queen Elizabeth. Sir Henry invited Walsingham into his study.

'Francis, it appears my work here is complete. The queen has recalled me to London and appoints you ambassador in my place. I believe you have met Anthony Standen. Sir Nicholas sent him to me.'

'Yes, an exceptional linguist. I recall meeting him in Edinburgh shortly after I started working on the Scottish problem with Sir Nicholas. If I remember correctly, Sir Nicholas thought his knowledge of the Scottish court might make him useful in intelligence gathering.'

'And so he has been, but the affair began badly. We set him up as a Venetian wine merchant. He identified some Scottish agents in league with the Spaniards and tried to recruit an agent in the Spanish embassy. Unfortunately, he was observed and was thoroughly beaten up then dumped on the Venetian ambassador's doorstep.'

'So they thought he was Venetian then?'

'Yes. He was taken to the hospital of Abbey Saint Germain des Prés, where the monks treated him for several months. I then discovered that he had received no training at all for the role Sir Nicholas recommended him for. I employed several specialists to train him in some skills that I thought would be useful to a spy. Since the Spaniards thought he was a Venetian, we have exploited that misconception and contrived to have them recruit him to work for them as well as the Venetians. I am feeding them some plausible but false information.'

'Sir Henry, I am impressed. This may be just the opportunity I have been looking for. Since the rebellion in the north, supported, we are convinced, by Spanish gold, it is increasingly clear that Spain is the greatest threat to the realm. Now that the civil war in France has ended, and they reinstated the Huguenots at court, we are on much better terms with France.'

'The Northern Rebellion, where are the Earls of Northumberland and Westmorland now?'

'Hiding in Scotland, but we will get them. Sussex and Essex made a quick job of suppressing the rebels. We have executed eight hundred of them so far.'

'So where does Standen fit in?'

'I have been trying to persuade Cecil that we should work with France and the Protestant German princes to support William of Orange against the Spanish rule in Flanders and the Netherlands. If we could get more intelligence on the balance of power there, it would help us.'

'I see. Well, it's no longer my affair. I'll get my secretary Robert to contact Standen and arrange a meeting for you. In the meantime, I'll pack my things. Good luck Francis.'

'Good luck to you Sir Henry.'

In Ferniehirst Castle, set in the gently rolling Scottish Borders, just south of Jedburgh, an anxious group was gathered in the music room. Anne Percy, Countess of Northumberland, cradled her nine-month-old daughter Mary in her arms. Her eldest daughter, Elizabeth, was playing the harpsichord, and the middle daughters, Lucy and Joan, were reading. With them were their hosts, Sir Thomas Kerr and his wife Janet. Also, with them was the twenty-eight-year-old Charles Neville, 6th Earl of Westmorland. Sir Thomas gazed out of the window. He turned to Charles.

'Charles, a rider approaches, you had better go to the

priest hole again, I'm afraid.' Charles got up, walked over to the bookshelves, and removed a book. He pulled a lever, and the bookshelves swivelled, revealing a six-foot square hiding place behind, with a stool. He entered and sat on the stool. Sir Thomas pushed the bookshelves back into place. A catch clicked, and he replaced the book. A few minutes later, Sir Thomas's butler, Cranston, knocked on the door and entered.

'There is a message, sir.' The butler handed a letter to Sir Thomas. Sir Thomas opened and read the letter.

'No reply, thank you, Cranston, you can send the messenger on his way.'

'Certainly, sir,' Cranston said and left the room.

'I'm sorry, Anne, your husband has been captured. He's being held by Morton. The heretic blackguard is haggling for a reward from Elizabeth. He is asking for two thousand pounds.' Anne started rocking back and forth, clutching her baby. Sir Thomas walked over to the bookcase and released Charles from the priest hole. Elizabeth crashed out a D minor chord with a discordant 8th then got up and rushed out of the room. Lucy and Joan threw down their books and followed her. 'Did you hear the news, Charles?'

'Yes. Poor Thomas, this can't end well. I hoped he might get away to Flanders.'

'I'm afraid there is more news, Charles. Your cousin, Robert Constable, has, according to my sources, been paid to track you down and betray you. Is there anything that may lead him here?' Thomas asked.

'It's possible. He knows we are friends. I will have to go now.'

'Where will you go, to Flanders?'

'Yes. I'll join the Duke of Alva's army fighting the damn Protestants there. Can you get a message to Jane and my children? I can't bear not seeing them, but it would be too dangerous, not only for me, but for them too.'

'Of course I will, my friend. Write your letter and leave it with me. I'll get the stable boy to saddle my fastest horse. How are you for money?'

'I haven't got a penny.'

'I'll let you have enough to get passage on a ship, and set you up until you find Alva. Do you speak Spanish?'

'No, but my Latin is excellent and my Italian is quite good. I'm sure I'll get by.'

'Good man.'

Walsingham was unpacking his things and filing his papers in the study. There was a knock on the door.

'Come in!' Robert entered, followed by Anthony.

'Sir Henry asked me to fetch Sir Anthony for you, sir.'

'Ah yes, Sir Anthony, please come in and sit down. Thank you, Robert. Leave us would you for now.' Robert nodded and left.

'Sir Henry has told me of your remarkable exploits.'

'Thank you, er, how should I address you? Ambassador perhaps?' Walsingham smiled at his difficulty. Although he was landed, had considerable influence with the queen, and had been a Member of Parliament for ten years, he had not yet been knighted.'

'Francis will suffice. May I call you Anthony?'

'Yes, Francis.'

'Your work so far, impressive as it is, has not yet produced results to impress the queen and overcome her poor impression of your association with Darnley. But I think there is something you can do that would help to improve your standing with her.'

'What can I do, Francis?'

'Since the pope excommunicated the queen in February, there have been Catholic plots to remove her and free Mary, putting her on the throne. We have outwitted them so far, and have come down hard on the heretics. The major threat to the realm now seems to be Spain.'

'I'm sorry to interrupt, but I thought the Spanish were our allies. Sir Henry doesn't tell me all the news.'

'You're quite right. And trade with the Low Countries and Flanders has been very important to us. But did you hear about the affair of the ships held in 68?'

'No.'

'In November, some Spanish ships took shelter during foul weather in Plymouth and Southampton. Whilst waiting for the weather to improve, our harbour masters discovered they were carrying a great deal of gold and silver to the Spanish in Flanders and the Low Countries. The queen discovered that it was in fact owned by Italian bankers, so she seized it and negotiated with the Italian bankers, such that it became a loan to England rather than to Spain. The Italians were quite happy with that arrangement, so she kept it. The Spanish didn't take it so well.'

'They wouldn't.' Anthony laughed.

'Our merchants in Flanders have found things very difficult since then. This excommunication business has made things considerably worse, particularly with Spain. My chief reasons for coming to France were to help broker a peace between the Catholics and Huguenots, and to advance the marriage prospects of our Queen with the Duke of Anjou. Well, the war was thankfully over, almost as I arrived. Now I have to try to advance this marriage. An alliance between our countries would deter Spain a little.'

'So where do I fit in, Francis?'

'You have engineered a situation, your employment with the Spaniards here, that may be of great use to us. The Low Countries are now the tinderbox of Europe. The Spanish governor there, Fernando Alvarez, Duke of Alva, the Iron Duke they call him, is a ruthless suppressor of good Protestants. The Venetians must be as interested in having intelligence there as we are. Do you think you could tell your Spanish masters you are being sent to Flanders, and see if they could secure you an introduction? If so, any intelligence you can get on the balance of power there would help us consider our options.' Anthony tried to gather his thoughts.

'It may be possible. I'll see what I can do. Will Robert be staying here for a few days?'

'Yes, he'll be staying. Why?'

'I've had an idea. I think I might just need him.'

That evening, Anthony returned to his lodgings to find Marie preparing food in the kitchen.

'Antonio, Mother is out visiting a friend. We have a few hours. Would you like your supper, or something else perhaps?'

'Something else, and then supper I think.' Marie left the casserole simmering over the fire and led Anthony upstairs. They made love, Anthony like it might be his last opportunity for quite a long time, and Marie like it was the best opportunity she would have in a very long time.

'Have you brought me any new jewels, Antonio?'

'Not today, Marie. I'm going to have to go away for a while. Will you wait for me? I may be away for a few months or even a year. Will you wait and marry me when

I get back?'

'Of course, Antonio. Will it be a profitable trip? Will you buy us a big house when we are married?'

'That's the plan, a big house in the country where we can raise a family. How many children do you want, four, five?'

'Will we have lots of servants to look after the children? If we do, then perhaps four. But the country? What's wrong with Paris? They don't have theatres in the country, or shops or jewellers.'

'The country is so good for children. You can climb trees, lay in the grass, swim in lakes. I had a wonderful childhood in the country.'

'I don't enjoy climbing trees or swimming in lakes. In fact, I can't swim. Don't you care what I want?' Marie said, turning away from him.

'Of course I do, my love. It's just that I thought you would like the country. I'll make an enormous fortune and we can have a big house in Paris and a house in the country. How does that sound?'

'Well, let's wait and see how big a fortune you return with. How about some dinner now?'

'Don Francés, I have some news. The Doge wishes me to go to Flanders and gather intelligence on the protestant rebels led by William of Orange. I'm afraid I must leave immediately, so I thought I should let you know.'

'I am sorry to hear that, Signor Foscari. Since the misunderstanding, you have been very useful to us. And it has been profitable to you too, I trust.'

'Yes, I will miss the extra income,' Standen said slowly. Don Francés stroked his beard.

'What if you didn't have to lose the extra income?'

'That would suit me very much. But how would that

work?'

'I'm sure our governor there, the Duke of Alva, would welcome the assistance of a Venetian spy. Come back in two hours and I will have a letter of introduction for you to the duke.'

'Thank you, Don Francés. I will.'

Anthony went back to his lodgings. He bade a fond farewell to Marie, paid Madam Dufour his outstanding rent, and packed his things into a canvas bag. Then he walked down to the quay at La Grieve, near the Les Halles market. He watched the river boats being unloaded, their cargos lifted onto carts and taken to the nearby market. He approached a sailor who seemed to be directing the unloading of the sturdiest looking boat.

'Excuse me, how can I get from here to Antwerp?'

'Antwerp, eh? These boats all ply back and forth to Rouen. From Rouen you'll get a vessel that'll call at Antwerp, maybe once or twice a week.'

'How long will it take to get to Rouen?'

'Depends on the wind. If we have to row all the way, two, maybe three days.'

'And from Rouen to Antwerp?'

'You have the tide to help you from Rouen. Two tides should see you down to Honfleur, so a day. Then, so long as you don't get an easterly wind, three fair tides should do it. A day and a half or two days.'

'Heavens, four, maybe six days. I didn't realise it would take that long.'

'On French roads it'll take you a lot longer, if you get there at all.'

'You do take passengers, don't you?'

'Yes, for a small fee.'

'When does your boat leave?'

'Six o'clock this evening, or thereabouts.' Anthony

thanked him then returned to the Spanish embassy.

'Here is a letter of introduction to Fernando Alvarez of Toledo, third Duke of Alva. Good luck!' Don Francés passed him a letter folded and sealed with a wax seal with his crest imprinted. 'How do you intend to travel to Brussels?'

'There is a ship leaving at six this evening for Rouen, from where I'll get a ship for Antwerp. I'll make my way overland from there, that's just a day's ride.'

'Adios Foscari' Standen bowed and left. Don Francés waited until he heard Standen reach the bottom of the stairs, then called to Captain Rodriguez. 'Follow him, Rodriguez, discretely. See that he gets on the ship.'

Anthony made his way from the Spanish embassy back towards the port. He stopped several times and discovered that Rodriguez was following him. There was one of his men with him, too. He made his way towards the quay, but when he encountered a large group of people in the bustling market, he gave them the slip. He checked that he was no longer being followed and made his way via side streets to the backdoor of the English Embassy.

'Robert. Can you open this, decipher it and then forge a new letter with this seal?' Anthony asked.

'Well, first I'll have to take a cast of this seal imprint. Then I may be able to decipher it, as long as it's in English or French.'

'Damn, it'll be in Spanish but I speak Spanish.'

'How long have we got?'

'Four hours.'

'That's extremely tight. We'd better get on with it then.' Robert took down some jars from a shelf and started mixing some plaster of paris. Robert applied it over the wax seal. After a few minutes of waiting, Anthony got up and began pacing up and down the room.

'How long is this going to take, Robert?'

'I'm afraid it takes as long as it takes. I'm doing it as quickly as I can. There aren't really any shortcuts. I have to wait for the cast to set before removing the cast from the letter. The ring pressed into the wax makes the wax a mould of the ring. It looks dry now,' Robert said, pressing his index finger against the plaster. 'We have now made the plaster of Paris into a copy of the ring. Now follow me to the kitchen.' Robert took a container from a shelf and took out what looked like clay. Anthony followed him to the kitchen. 'First, I'm going to melt the wax, which is stuck to the plaster cast by holding it near the fire. Now that it's clean, I'm taking some butter and smearing it thinly inside the cast. Now I'm pressing the clay into the plaster cast. The cast was a copy of the ring remember, so the clay becomes a mould of the ring. Now we have to wait for the clay to dry and hope the butter will ensure that we get a clean break when I chip the plaster away. We only get one shot at this.'

They went back to Robert's study and broke the seal and opened the letter. Robert wrote on a scrap of paper and frequently asked Standen to tell him Spanish words that would include particular letters. 'This isn't a simple Caesarean cipher. The alphabet isn't just shunted a set number of spaces. It seems to be a random substitution that receiver and sender must have agreed.'

'But can you solve it?'

'With a bit more of your help. We're getting there.'

'I need to be down at the quay to catch a boat in two hours. Is an hour and a half enough time?'

'To crack it maybe, but to forge a new letter and seal it definitely not.'

'Keep going then.' In just under half an hour, Robert whistled.

'I've got it.' He wrote it out, and Anthony laughed.

'Give me the pen. I'll draft the forgery in Spanish. Then you encipher it in the same hand and seal it to look the same as the original.' Anthony looked up at the clock. 'Damn, I don't have much time. What if I just delete one small word and change one word?'

'Only one word to encipher. Ten minutes to write it out, half an hour to fake the seal.'

'Great.' Anthony took Robert's deciphered Spanish text, crossed out one word, and changed another. Robert then started work on the forgery.

'What have you changed?'

'Well, there are the usual salutations and good wishes. Then he tells the Duke of Alva that I am a Venetian spy, fluent in many languages, who is being sent to spy on the Protestants. Here he says he is "not sure that I can be completely trusted" I've deleted the "not".'

'Very clever. And this new word?'

'That's where he says he has paid me around eight pieces of gold a month for my information, so that would make a reasonable pension to retain me. I changed the eight to twenty.'

'No wonder you're a spy! Right, let's see if the clay is dry enough.' Robert took something else from his shelf and they went back to the kitchen. 'Right, keep your fingers crossed,' Robert said as he chipped away at the plaster with a knife. 'Yes, that will be good enough. Grab that spoon, would you? Thanks, now I'm hacking off a piece of this lead and placing it in the spoon. I'll take one of cook's oven gloves and hold the spoon in the fire until the lead melts, then we pour it into the clay mould, wait for it to cool and we have a lead imitation of the ring used to seal the document.'

Anthony slipped the forged letter inside his doublet, picked up his sack and thanked Robert. Then he slipped out of the back door, checked he wasn't being followed, and made his way back to the quay. From a side entrance of the market, he saw Captain Rodriguez and his man standing on a street corner observing the quay. Anthony doubled back and entered a tavern from the back door. From there, he could leave the tavern from the front entrance and be certain that Rodriguez would see him getting on the boat.

'Hello again,' Anthony said to the sailor. 'Can I come aboard?'

'You made it then. We were just about to cast off. Two francs to get you to Rouen.' Anthony gave him the money. 'You can sit over there, against that wool sack.'

He sat down against the wool sack and glanced towards Rodriguez. As the warps were untied and thrown onboard, sailors used their oars to push the boat off the quay. When they had sufficient room to row, they sat and started pulling at the oars in unison. Anthony saw Rodriguez and his man turn and walk back towards their embassy.

The sun went down and a gentle wind picked up from the south. The oars were shipped, and the sail was unfurled. The boat pressed forwards silently, apart from the gentle, relaxing sound of water rushing down the boat's side. Anthony pulled his cape from his bag and wrapped it around himself. He leant back against the wool sack and closed his eyes.

Oh Marie, Oh Antonio, yes, yes, yes, soft, smooth flesh, perfumed flesh. The smell. Burning flesh, clinging stench, stomach churning, burning flesh. God forgive them. You can be a Protestant with my blessing, son, but I'm not sure about your mother. You won't make a living out of languages, it's law that puts bread on the table. You disappoint me son, why can't you be like Freddy and Edmund? They'll make their mother proud. Catholic heretics, priests cut down alive, stomachs slit open. Intestines plucked out and dangled in front of staring, wide eyes. Beautiful firm thighs, opening, inviting, writhing. Screams, stomach turning screams, burning flesh, acrid stench clinging. Screams. Are you English or are you a Catholic? I'm just a man. I'm just a fucking man.

Anthony's eyes opened wide, and he wiped sweat from his face with his cape. The helmsman stood peering forward through the moonlight, sailors snored around him.

CHAPTER FIVE

nthony approached the two guards standing at
the door of the governor's house in Brussels.
One guard stepped in front of him. Anthony
pulled out his letter of introduction and showed him the
governor's name and Don Francés's seal.

'I have a letter of introduction from the Spanish
ambassador in Paris addressed to the duke.' The guard
nodded, turned, and knocked three times on the heavy
oak door. The door opened and a young officer in white
hose and a red tunic beckoned him in. 'I have a letter of
introduction.' The officer took the letter.

'Come this way,' the officer commanded and led
Anthony down an ornately decorated hallway. He opened
the door at the end of the corridor onto a large plainly
decorated room. 'Wait in here!' There were benches down
either side of the room and at the far end was another
door with an empty chair beside it. The officer walked
down to the door at the far end, knocked, entered, said a
few words Anthony couldn't hear and came back out of
the room, closed the door and sat down in the chair. He
must have left the letter in the room. Anthony looked
around. On the left, there were three men sitting and two
standing. They were all well dressed and talking in
Flemish. Anthony's Flemish was virtually non-existent,
but they were saying something about new taxes.
Opposite them sat a stunningly beautiful, but gaunt
woman, plainly dressed, with three very thin children
sitting to one side of her. Her children were silent and
their heads bowed. The door opened and two well-
dressed men walked out. The officer stood up and went
into the room. After a minute, he came out again and

beckoned the group of five men over. They went into the room and the officer shut the door behind them. There was a space on the bench, on the other side of the beautiful woman. Anthony approached it.

'Would you mind if I sit here?'

'Please do,' the beautiful woman whispered.

'My name is Antonio Foscari.'

'Mine is Barbara Kegel. I'm pleased to meet you Mr Foscari.'

'Just call me Antonio, please. Is your husband away fighting?'

'My husband died two years ago.'

'I'm sorry.'

'What brings you to see the duke, Signor Foscari?'

'Just business. I'm a wine merchant from Venice. What brings you to see the duke?' There was some muffled shouting from the duke's office.

'I have come to beg. I have no income and my children are starving. I am hoping the duke will give me a small pension.'

'Is he a generous man?'

'He does not have that reputation, no. But I once knew a very powerful man, and I hope I can persuade the duke to grant me a pension.' The duke's door opened again and the five Flemish men walked dejectedly out.

'The duke will see you now, Señor Foscari,' called the officer from the doorway.

'The lady was next,' Anthony replied.

'The duke wants you next. I shouldn't argue, sir.' Anthony stood and walked over to the door and was ushered inside. He stood in front of the grand desk of Fernando Alvarez de Toledo, 3rd Duke of Alva, governor of the Netherlands. There was a smaller desk behind the duke, facing a window. An older man had Anthony's letter of introduction open on the desk and was writing on another sheet of paper. He stood up and brought both pieces of paper to the duke.

'Thank you Garcia,' said the duke, turning Foscari's letter of introduction over in his hands and examining the seal. He then read the deciphered version. The duke looked up at Anthony.

'So you are a Venetian, Señor Foscari. A very good spy, by this account.' He opened a small casket on his desk and took out some coins. He counted out twenty and tossed them towards Anthony. 'Here are twenty pieces of gold. Infiltrate the protestant army. Come back when you can tell me where William of Orange is, and what he plans to do next. Do that and I may have another mission for you.'

'If I join the protestant army and am captured, how will your men know not to kill me?'

'They won't. Next.' The officer opened the door. Anthony picked up the coins, bowed to the duke, turned, and left. He went over to Barbara and pressed two gold pieces into her hand.

'I don't think he is in a very generous mood. Take these. Good luck, and I hope I'll see you again one day.'

Anthony left the governor's house and started walking, and thinking. He weighed his purse in his hand and smiled. His smile broadened as he remembered that Francis wanted him to assess the balance of power on both sides, so there was no problem with him spying on the Protestant forces. His smile drained away as he wondered how he would get reports back to Francis. He turned a corner and saw a tavern ahead, so he decided he would be better able to think through his plan with a good meal inside him and a bed for the night. He was soon enjoying some roast chicken and cabbage with a goblet of red wine. He had arranged a room for the night and was eavesdropping on the conversations taking place around him. The other customers were, in the main, Flemish, but there were some Spaniards too, sitting apart from the locals. He thought some more about his next moves. He thought it would be best to stay where he was for a week or two. He had more than enough money for that. He also decided to stick with the wine merchant cover and see what he could find out. He would spend his time learning Flemish, reasoning that it would be essential if he were to be effective in the Netherlands. He also wondered how he could go about infiltrating the Protestant forces. After a few days, he found his landlord becoming a little friendlier and more open with him. Anthony had told him he was working for a Venetian wine merchant and trying to discover what opportunities might exist in Flanders.

'Most of the wine comes in by sea. Ours arrives by cart from Antwerp. I could give you the address of our supplier there if you like? I know he gets deliveries from Italy, as well as Spain and France. I don't see why he wouldn't consider your firm, if you can undercut his current suppliers.'

'Thank you. That would be useful.'

'Your Flemish is coming on well now, sir. I could barely understand a word you were saying when you arrived.'

'Thank you. But there's still so much I don't understand. What does "Guezen" mean?' Anthony asked. The landlord leaned over the bar and whispered. 'Beggars.'

'The context seems odd, from the bits I've heard about these beggars.'

'Back in sixty-six, when the present troubles started,

a group of local nobility got together and raised a petition of grievances. They took it to the then governor Margaret of Parma. Seeing a couple of hundred people marching on the governor's house, she got a little alarmed. Her councillor reassured her with the words "Fear not, madam, they are only beggars." Well, the term stuck.'

'That makes sense now. Thank you.'

'You might hear about the Sea Beggars. William of Orange commissioned privateers and by the end of sixty-nine they had almost a hundred ships,' the landlord said even more quietly.

'That sounds like they might be a bit of a threat to my wine trade. Have they affected the trade much?'

'Not so as I've noticed. I heard they'd captured or sunk several Spanish ships, but I'm sure Italian wine would get through. Anyway, since the duke took over from Margaret, they've been on the back foot, so to speak. I heard they are laid up in La Rochelle, Emden and Dover now.'

'That's interesting background. But it's the wine trade that interests me. I would like that address of your wine supplier in Antwerp.'

Anthony didn't want to spend his diminishing resources on a horse or a stagecoach, so he walked to Antwerp, resting overnight in a tavern in Mechelen. The following day, he reached Antwerp by midday and went straight to the port. During his walk, he'd done a lot of thinking. He quite liked the idea of becoming a Sea Beggar. He had enjoyed the sea crossing to France, and hadn't been seasick, as many of the other passengers had been. If he was to infiltrate the protestant forces, he thought that he might as well sail around, rather than march or ride all over the place. So he decided that he'd better get some training in sailing. He wandered about the port, looking for a ship that might suit him. Perhaps he could learn the ropes as a fisherman. He approached a Dutch fishing boat and called out for the captain.

'What do you want?' asked the captain from the deck.

'I'm looking for work. Do you need crew?'

'You done much fishing?'

'No, but I'm a quick learner.'

'We got no room for learners. Try the Sea Breeze down yonder,' the captain said, pointing. 'Old Jansen's looking for crew, and he ain't too particular.' The captain laughed and started shouting at his own crew again. Anthony walked down the quayside in the direction he had pointed. He soon found the Sea Breeze. It was smaller than the other ship but looked sturdy enough.

'Are you Captain Jansen?' he called to a man with grey hair and beard, and a weather-beaten face.

'I am who's asking?'

Anthony cupped his hand to his ear as if he hadn't heard while he cursed himself and thought. If I'm going to join the rebels, I'd better not be Catholic.

'My name's Standen.'

'Where are you from? Your Flemish is quite good, but you ain't from around here?'

'I'm English. I was working in the wine trade until the Spanish clamped down on the English merchants. I'd fallen in love with a Dutch girl, so stayed on. Now I'm out of work, she left me, and I can't get home. I'm told you need crew.'

'You done any fishing before?'

'No, but I'm a quick learner.'

'All right, step aboard lad! We ain't going anywhere for a few days until we've repaired the nets. We'll get you started on that, then I'll show you the ropes.'

Captain Jansen introduced Anthony to the rest of the
crew, which comprised a first mate called Ernst and two
crewmen, Didier, and Christof. The boat was forty-five
feet in length and thirteen feet in beam at her widest. It
had one mast with a tan-coloured gaff sail and two
foresails. There were hatches in the wooden deck, below
which were holds for the stores, principally barrels of
fresh water, salt, beer, bread, flour, butter, bacon, peas,
firewood and bait for when they were line fishing. There
was another hold for the fish and barrels for packing
salted fish. An enclosed area in the forward part of the
boat provided some accommodation and a small range for
cooking. There were three bunks, one for the captain's
exclusive use. When at sea, two men would be on watch
at all times, and two men off watch. When they were
fishing, everyone was working. Toilet arrangements were
a wooden bucket.

Over the next six months, Anthony learnt the
difference between halyards and sheets and booms and
yards. He learnt a dozen knots and how to splice rope. He
learnt to steer and to throw the lead line and measure the
depth. He could throw the log line and count the knots in
the rope, as it ran through his fingers, as he counted to
twenty. He developed calluses on his hands and feet. His
muscles grew as he pulled in nets full of fish or hauled up
sails. His face grew tanned from the long days at sea, and
the salt spray no longer stung his eyes as badly as at it
had at first. They spent several weeks at sea on each
voyage. When they had time to talk, he developed his
new cover story. He had been thinking about the point at
which he would become a Sea Beggar. What would make
him attractive as a Sea Beggar, and what would not. So he
played down the wine trade to a brief interlude and

embellished his fighting experience in Scotland for the protestant cause. He talked about making money through language teaching and also became a fencing instructor. As they chased the fish around the North Sea, they stopped at several ports to offload their catch, load fresh stores and drink. They had put into Willemstad, Scheveningen, Harlingen, and then one evening, they tied up to the quay in Emden.

'I heard that Emden is one of the Sea Beggar harbours. Is that right, captain?' asked Anthony.

'Ay, it is. See those two big black-hulled vessels over there?'

'Yes.'

'Them's Sea Beggar ships. You thinking of signing up?'

'It would be an adventure, at least if that's all right with you. I wouldn't want to leave you short handed.'

'All right with me, lad, I'll get another hand soon enough. I'd reckon you'd be out of your mind, though. You've seen what fishing's like. It's a hard living, but at least the fish don't fight back.'

'Who's the boss?'

'A gentleman called William Bloys van Treslong. Good luck, Standen, here's your pay.'

The first thing Anthony wanted to do after six months, mainly at sea on a cramped boat, was have a night in a bed, a decent meal and a drink. He looked around the fine city until he identified the best-looking tavern and booked a room. He arranged for a bath tub and hot water to be taken up to his room. After a good soak and scrub, he could no longer detect the aroma of fish on his skin. He went down to the bar, had a meal and a couple of goblets of wine. Then he went back to his room, took off his clothes, washed them in the bathtub and hung them up near the window to dry. He laid down on his bed and fell into the sleep of an exhausted fisherman.

The next day, he put on his only slightly damp clothes and set off for the quayside. He went to the two ships that Captain Jansen had pointed out to him. The quayside was busy with men loading stores onto the ships. There were several nationalities represented, including a couple of Englishmen who were just putting down a barrel. Anthony waited until one of them looked up.

'Excuse me. Who do I have to speak with to sign up?'

'Captain Bloys.'

'Where do I find him?'

'In his cabin, probably. Ask him over there, he's the officer of the day.' Anthony went over to the officer indicated. He tried English at first.

'I'm looking for Captain Bloys, I'd like to sign on.' The officer looked him up and down.

'Follow me.' The officer replied in accented English. The officer led the way up the gang plank, over towards the stern and through a doorway into a corridor off which there were several cabins. At the end of the corridor he knocked on a door then opened it.'

'Young Englishman here wants to sign up, sir.'

'Very good, show him in.' The officer stood aside and waved Anthony to go in. Then the officer saluted, closed the door, and left. The captain's cabin ran the full width of the ship and windows ran across the stern. The captain was sitting behind a desk writing, with his back to the windows. Looking up from his letter, he asked, 'What's your name?'

'Standen, sir, Anthony Standen.'

'And where are you from, Standen?'

'England, sir.'

'Tell me about yourself. Where you were born, what you do, and why you want to join us.' The captain spoke very good English.

'I was born in East Molesey near Hampton Court. My father is a lawyer. He wanted me to go into law, but I didn't have the aptitude for it, or any interest in it. From growing up playing with the children of diplomats, visiting the palace, I developed a love of languages, and found I had a great gift of picking them up easily. I also wanted to travel and see the places they had talked about. I…'

'What languages do you speak?'

'Latin, Ancient Greek, French, Italian, Spanish, German and I'm learning Flemish, sir.'

'Interesting. Carry on.'

'After school, I started teaching foreign languages. There wasn't much money in it, so I also started working with a fencing instructor at the palace. I did odd jobs for him and after a while became an assistant fencing instructor. Then I sought more adventure and heard that they were hiring mercenaries in Scotland. So I went up there for a while, fighting for the Protestants, sir. I wanted to travel abroad, so I went back south and got a job as a clerk for a wine merchant who sent me to work in Paris. It was boring work, if I'm honest, sir, and I still wanted adventure. So I headed for the Low Countries. I got a job on a fishing boat, which gave me the taste for the sea.'

'And why do you want to fight the Spanish?'

'When I was young, in Bloody Mary's reign, I saw the Islington Martyrs being burnt at the stake. It's a sight, sound and smell that's never really left me, sir. When I heard what the Spanish Inquisition was doing here, sir, I resolved I'd do what I could to stop it.'

'So, by your account, you're quite handy with a

sword. What sort of fighting did you do in Scotland?'

'I spent some time with muskets and artillery in the lowlands. Then there was some close quarters fighting in the highlands, sir.'

'So you can load and fire muskets and cannon, is that right?'

'Yes, sir.' Anthony thought, well a cannon is only a big musket. He'd seen it done, and was sure it must be the same principle.

'And your time fishing. Who with?'

'With Captain Jansen, sir, on the Sea Breeze. We put in here yesterday, sir.'

'Well, you do sound like you might be useful to us. We need as many good men as we can get. We do tend to get through them. We have quite a mishmash of a crew from many countries, and a good interpreter will be a great asset.' The captain stood and shook hands. 'Welcome aboard. That's the last time we shake hands. From now on you salute me, and anything else that moves on my ship.' He crossed to the door and called the officer of the day over. 'Lieutenant, allocate Standen a hammock, then put him to work. Then come back to my cabin.'

'Yes, sir,' said the officer and saluted. So did Anthony.

Twenty minutes later, the lieutenant returned to the captain's cabin.

'Lieutenant Jansen, do you know a Captain Jansen, master of a fishing boat called Sea Breeze?'

'He's my uncle, sir. I used to go fishing with him often as a boy.'

'Well, he's here now. Apparently Standen has been crewing for him. See what he thinks of him and check out his story.' Captain Bloys summarised Anthony's story, then Lieutenant Jansen saluted and left on his mission.

Throughout the winter of 1571–1572, Anthony sailed with the Sea Beggars. Despite his time fishing, he found that he still had a lot to learn. The Orange Avenger was a much larger ship than Sea Breeze. It had two masts and square-rigged sails, which meant a lot of climbing the mast to dizzying heights in order to furl or unfurl the sails. He found the first gunnery exercise deafening and one of his English crew mates, a Cornishman called Walter, had to save his life. Anthony had been standing too close to, and immediately behind his cannon, when it was about to be fired. He hadn't considered the distance such a cannon would recoil, and Walter dragged him aside just in time. He and Walter were scrubbing the decks after the gunnery exercise.

'You saved my life, Walter. Nobody has ever done that before.'

'Perhaps you've never stood behind a cannon about to be fired before.'

'No, I haven't, but thank you. I hope I can repay you some time.'

'I hope you don't have to, but if you do, then I'm sure you will. We're shipmates and our lives are in each other's hands. Whereabouts in England are you from?' Walter enquired.

'Here are three halfpennies, Son. Spend it wisely. That's half a day's wage for most men. We shall need to catch the flood tide around four o'clock, and I should have finished my business by noon, or thereabouts. So be sure you are back here before the bells strike two. Keep to the main streets and avoid the back alleys. Stay in crowds. If you should get lost, ask directions to Gray's Inn. When you get back, ask Thomas here if I've returned, and if I haven't, Thomas will let you into our rooms.' Thomas nodded. 'Do you understand, Son?'

'Yes, Father.' They set off together through the gate and turned right on Gray's Inn Lane. When they reached the main street, Holborn, they stopped. Edmund pointed.

'My business is over there, in Chancery Lane. Remember what I've told you, Son, and I'll see you by two o'clock at the latest.' He squeezed his son's shoulder and walked across the road.

Anthony surveyed the scene. The general tide of people seemed to be to the left, towards the sun, so heeding his father's words, he followed the crowd. He passed a fine church on the right, with a bell tower, and noted it was called Saint Andrews. Shortly after that, he crossed a bridge and paused to watch the River Fleet flow towards the Thames. Then he followed the crowd again and after forking left, soon found himself in a large field with many carts and market stalls. He ambled past the stalls. There was one with cloth, the next had vegetables. The one after that was laden with pots and pans for sale. There seemed to be nothing much to excite the attention of a young boy. Further on he came across several butchers' stalls, where the vendors, whilst not attending to customers, were waving cloths to keep the flies from settling. Beyond them was a pie stall.

'Fresh meat pies, straight from the oven. Lovely fresh pies!' cried the woman behind the stall.

'How much is that one?' Anthony asked, pointing at the largest pie on the stall.

'A penny, love. Beef and onion.'

'Oh, I only have a halfpenny. Will that do?' it was not exactly lying, not sinfully anyway, Anthony knew that you had to haggle.

'Would you rob a good Christian woman, boy? I could give you this one for a halfpenny. Just as fresh, pork and apple.' It was a smaller pie, but Anthony handed her one of his halfpennies and took the pie. 'Lovely fresh pies!'

Anthony moved on, taking a bite from his pie. There was a large crowd gathered at the far side of the field, just in front of a church. Munching his pie, he walked over to see what the attraction was. He worked his way around and through the crowd until he got to the front. There were large bundles of reeds set around four stakes, two men tied to each of three stakes, and a single man to the fourth. A man with a blazing torch set the reeds alight to cheers from the crowd. As the flames rose and a wall of heat hit them, the crowd pressed back. Anthony dropped the remnant of his pie as the smell of burning flesh filled his nostrils. The single man embraced the stake he was lashed to and screamed out, 'Lord, into thy hands I commit my spirit. Lord bless these, thy people, and save them from idolatry.'

'What crime have these men committed?' Anthony asked the man standing beside him.

'Crime, boy. They're heretics now. Too slow, or unwilling to change back from the reformist religion to the old religion again.'

Anthony pushed his way back out of the crowd and began running back the way he had come, the smell of burning human flesh clinging to him.

As the bells of Saint Andrews struck two o'clock, Edmund passed through the gate of Gray's Inn. He poked his head through the open window of the lodge.

'Is my son back, Thomas?'

'Yes, Mr Standen. I let him into your rooms about an hour ago. He was as white as a sheet.'

'Oh, any idea why?'

'Not exactly, but they were burning the first batch of the Islington martyrs, sorry, heretics, this morning, you know, out at Smithfield.'

'No, I didn't know.' Edmund rushed through the courtyard and up the second staircase on the left. He opened the door and found Anthony sitting at the table with his head in his hands. He looked up. His eyes were bloodshot.

'Oh, Father, they were burning men. I can't get the smell out of my head, or the screams. They say they were heretics, but they looked like us. Why, Father, why?'

'I'm sorry, Son, I didn't know or I would never have brought you.' Edmund took a chair next to Anthony and wrapped his arm around him.

'They didn't sound like heretics, Father. One cried out to God, like Christ, from the cross, begging for our forgiveness. So, why burn them?'

'Well, its history, and I know you prefer languages and fencing.'

'Yes, Father, but I think perhaps I should learn some history,' said Anthony, wiping his eyes.

'So you should. You won't make a living from

languages. It vexes me that you won't take an interest in law. It's what puts bread on the table. Anyway, I will try to be brief. The father of Queen Mary died the same year that you were born. King Henry died a Catholic, but he had broken from Rome in order to divorce Queen Catherine and marry Anne. Are you following me so far?'

'I remember why I detest history, but go on, Father.'

'Well, there was a man living during Henry's reign, in Germany, a Professor called Martin Luther. He taught that the practice of rich men buying absolution from sin was wrong. He also thought that the Holy Bible was the true source of God's word, rather than the word of priests. He thought that it should be available to people in their own language, rather than only in Latin. Unlike you, few people can read and speak Latin. A lot of people agreed with him. Henry allowed a translation of the bible to be made in English, and used in church. Nevertheless, it was under the young King Edward that reformist or Protestant doctrine became the rule. Do you remember how we had to take mass in secret when you were a boy?'

'Yes, Father.'

'Well, Edward began burning Catholics as heretics, and it became very difficult for many of the old religion to gain advancement. When King Edward died, Mary was crowned queen amid mass rejoicing. Most people had remained Catholic, and we could now follow our religion openly again. She married King Philip of Spain, and if they have a child, the succession will have been assured, and Catholicism will continue. Apparently, however, the rumours earlier this year about a pregnancy were false.'

'Is there anything so bad about a bible in English?

Should rich men be able to buy salvation? I'm sorry if I offend you, Father, but I don't see why this Protestantism is so bad. Should men be burnt for this?'

'My dear, dear boy, you do not offend me, far from it. You are quite right. And I have heard that the pope is intent on reforming certain corrupt practices within the church.'

'If Queen Mary dies and they start burning Catholics again, shall we become Protestants, Father? I mean, we'd still be worshiping God and Jesus, wouldn't we?'

'We would certainly have to be very careful. And you can become a Protestant if you wish, with my blessing. I'm not sure I can speak for your mother, though. But for myself, it's a very hard thing to change, not so much one's faith, because you are right, but those rituals that have governed one's daily life since childhood.'

'Do you know what I like most about the old ways, Father?'

'No, what?'

'Incense. I can't get rid of this smell.'

'Anthony, I said where in England are you from? You seem a little distant.'

Anthony shivered a little and then told him about his childhood. He reached for his lost St. Christopher when he spoke of his mother. He retold the lies he had told to Captain Bloys about how he had come to be in Flanders. He then enquired into Walter's background. 'I'm from Falmouth in Cornwall, saltwater in my veins. I had a choice, either be pressed into naval service for years, or come here and be paid well as a mercenary. I chose the latter. The more I learn about the Spanish, though, the less I feel like a mercenary. It's inhuman some of the things I've seen them do.'

They talked about England and both got a little homesick. It occurred to Anthony that he hadn't seen his home and family for over six years. He started to miss his parents and his younger brothers, and hoped he would see them again soon, once he had proved himself.

In March they spent the night at anchor, in the channel between the island of Wieringen and the mainland. Anthony was struggling to get back to sleep. The temperature had dropped dramatically in the last hour, and his shivering was keeping him awake. He peered over the edge of his hammock to see if Walter, Karl, and Joseph, the other men in his gun crew, were sleeping. They appeared to be. You must get used to it, I suppose, he thought. At that moment, Lieutenant Jansen rushed down the steps onto the gun deck and shouted.

'All hands on deck to weigh anchor.' Anthony clambered out of his hammock, colliding with Walter, who was doing the same.

'What do you think's up, Walter?' he asked.

'No idea, mate. We just does as we's told.' They rushed on deck with the rest of the crew, and forward to the anchor capstan. Through the first glimmer of morning twilight, they saw ice forming in the sea all around them. They put all their strength into gradually turning the capstan, and slowly but surely the anchor was raised. But it was a race they were losing. Even as the anchor was pulled free from the ice, some of the crew were high in the rigging, unfurling the sails. The wind filled the sails, and Orange Avenger leaned a few degrees. They started to move, ice grinding at the hull, but had barely covered a hundred yards before she ground to a halt, stuck fast in the sea ice. There was silence for a few minutes before more orders were barked out. The sails were furled again. Captain Bloys and Lieutenant Jansen were talking on the quarterdeck when a shout rang down from the mast.

'Soldiers.'

Everyone ran in the direction the sailor was pointing, transfixed. In the growing light, the shore of the mainland, about a mile away on the starboard side, was swarming with redcoats. Anthony estimated there might be four or five hundred of them. Orange Avenger had a crew of ninety. He watched in horror as the soldiers began making their way across the ice. The ship now sat embedded in its own ice island, connected to the mainland by a steadily widening ice bridge.

'Man the guns, starboard side. Open the armoury. Break out cutlasses,' shouted Captain Bloys. Everyone started running. Walter grabbed Anthony by the arm, and they both ran down to the gun deck. They saw Karl and Joseph at a cannon half-way down the starboard side and ran to it. They slotted into their practised roles. Karl was ready with a glowing match cord and a pouch of priming powder. Anthony, Walter and Joseph all heaved on the blocks and tackle to run the cannon out of the gun port. He pushed the packet of gunpowder down the barrel. Walter used the ramrod to force it right down and Joseph loaded the cannon ball. They peered through the gun port at the swarm of Spanish infantry getting steadily closer.

'Open fire!' shouted Captain Bloys.

A jet of flame erupted from the muzzle of their cannon and the cannon reared. Walter dunked the swab on the ramrod into a bucket of water and pushed it down the barrel to cool it. Then they began the loading and firing process all over again. They could see Spaniards lying on the ice, but most of them were still advancing towards them. They had fired half a dozen volleys at the advancing troops, and between the booms of their own cannon they heard the crackle of Spanish infantry musket fire, and the thud of musket balls hitting their heavy oak hull. 'Change to canister shot!' After they had fired the next volley, two crewmen arrived at Anthony's gun with a bucket of tin canisters, each packed with musket balls. They loaded one of the canisters and Karl aimed the cannon. They waited for the flash of their cannon. Anthony turned and saw Karl lying on his back with a hole in his forehead. He pulled the glowing match cord from Karl's clenched fist, sighted along the barrel and put the match to the touch hole. Through the smoke from the muzzle, he saw dozens of soldiers fall; crumpled to the ice. They kept firing volleys of canister shot, each time having to sight the gun lower at the advancing soldiers. As the ice bridge widened out to join the island of ice around the ship, the soldiers began to fan out. 'All hands on deck!' Anthony grabbed a cutlass from the pile at the bottom of the companionway and ran up onto deck, just ahead of Walter.

'Look!' shouted Walter, pointing to a grappling hook which had just landed on the deck ahead of them. The rope attached pulled it back, and it caught on the gunwale. Anthony lept forward and slashed at the rope with his cutlass. Dozens of grappling hooks were landing on the surrounding deck, faster than they could cut the ropes. Redcoats were clambering over the gunwale and drawing swords. One advanced towards Anthony. His sword was longer than Anthony's cutlass. He parried the Spaniard's thrusts but couldn't reach him with the cutlass. On the next thrust, Anthony stepped aside and brought his cutlass down as hard as he could on the soldier's sword arm. The blade cut deep and the Spanish sword fell to the deck. Anthony dropped his cutlass and picked up the sword. He felt much more comfortable with this, familiar weapon. Two more soldiers advanced towards him and Walter. The taller of the two went for Walter. Anthony parried his opponent's lunge and struck home with his own sword, which pierced all the way through the Spaniard's torso. The soldier crumpled to the deck and Anthony dropped too, as he tried to retract his sword. At his side the other soldier had parried Walter's cutlass and had a dagger in his left hand. As he drew it back, Anthony launched a kick into the soldier's left knee which cracked and the soldier fell to the ground.

'Thanks,' yelled Walter as he slashed the fallen soldier's throat. Hand to hand fighting was raging all around them as Anthony pulled his sword free. Side by side he and Walter advanced towards the quarterdeck. Glancing over the gunwale he saw piles of muskets where the Spaniards had dropped them in order to climb the boarding ropes. They felled another four soldiers between them as they advanced. A Spanish officer was just pulling himself over the gunwale as Anthony ran him through. The officer fell on deck and Anthony saw the pistol tucked in his belt.

'Wheellock. Nice.' He took it in his left hand. Ahead of them he saw a furious sword fight between Captain Bloys and the Spanish commander. A slash caught the captain on his right hand and his sword fell to the deck. The Spanish commander placed the tip of his sword against Captain Bloy's chest and shouted.

'Surrender your ship, captain!' Anthony cocked the pistol and aimed. He fired, and the Spanish commander dropped to the deck. With the crack of the pistol, those not immediately engaged looked round. The fall of the Spanish commander seemed to drain the fight out of the soldiers and encourage the crew of Orange Avenger in equal measure. Within ten more bloody minutes the Spanish had surrendered.

Whilst the ship's surgeon and his orderlies attended to the wounded, and the crew took it in turns to guard the remaining Spanish soldiers, Anthony and Walter were swabbing the decks.

'Have you killed a man before, Walter?' he asked.

'No, have you?'

'No. We killed rather a lot today, didn't we?'

'It is what we're here for. And they were trying their best to kill us. I thought they'd do it too. They got Karl, Lieutenant Jansen and maybe twenty others. Joseph lost an arm.'

'I didn't know about Jansen. You're right of course. It just feels so wrong, a sin.' Anthony longed for the solace of confession, penance and reconciliation.

'Shut up and keep scrubbing. Here comes the master. We signed up and now we just follow orders.' Master Bakker stood over them.

'Standen, the captain wants to see you.' Anthony put his scrubbing brush down, stood up, and followed the Master to the captain's cabin.

'Standen, I take it you heard we lost Lieutenant Jansen.'

'Yes, sir.'

'We also lost almost a third of the ship's company. We need a new lieutenant. We're a multi-national crew, and it's a difficult task to communicate at the best of times. So I'm appointing you acting lieutenant.'

'What, me, sir?'

'Yes, you. You can take Jansen's cabin. He should have a spare uniform in there. I think it'll fit. Don't look so surprised. If it wasn't for your quick wits and steady aim, they'd be looking for a new captain. You did well today. Now I want you to shadow Master Bakker. There's nothing about this ship and her crew he doesn't know, and I need you to learn it, fast.'

The day after the battle the sun shone, and the ice began to clear. Anthony was at Master Bakker's side as new attempts were made to break the ship clear. From the deck they surveyed where the ice appeared to be breaking up, and where it was not. They estimated, from the wind direction, what course they could sail to clear the channel and reach open sea, and where the ice would prevent them. Then they concluded that a small party with axes and some gunpowder charges, put down onto the thickest ice still gripping the hull, might break them free. The prisoners were allowed to take their wounded back across the diminishing ice bridge. Anthony was ordered to lead a party of six, down onto the ice, and plant the charges under direction from the master on deck.

'That will do. Back up the rope ladders men. Lieutenant Standen, when the others are all on board, light the fuse then get back up here as fast as you can,' called the master. When he saw the last man clamber on deck Anthony lit the fuse and ran back across the ice. He was just clambering over the ship's side when the chain of four small charges detonated. The master gave the orders for sail to be unfurled and the Orange Avenger began to nuzzle her way free.

An hour later they were in open sea and heading south southwest to where they planned to rendezvous with the flagship and the rest of the fleet. On the voyage Anthony learnt much from Master Bakker. He learnt the quantities of provisions required per man at sea, the amount of gin required to keep the water drinkable, and how many broadsides a barrel of gunpowder would deliver for different sizes of cannon. He learnt the arts of navigation, the use of a quadrant to measure the altitude of the pole star, and how to turn that into latitude. He even wished he had paid more attention to mathematics at school, because suddenly he saw a use for it.

Eventually the lookout shouted "Sail" from the crow's nest. An hour later they were close enough for Captain Bloys to determine the flag signals. It was the flagship of Admiral de la Marck and his fleet of twenty-four ships. After another hour the fleet had shortened sail and Captain Bloys was rowed across to the flagship. When he returned, he called a meeting with Bakker and Anthony in his cabin.

'Exciting news, gentlemen. The admiral has received dispatches that the Spanish garrison have abandoned Brielle to deal with an uprising in Utrecht. We are to make best speed for Brielle.'

On the 1st April 1572 the Sea Beggars fleet dropped anchor in the harbour of Brielle. Anthony was in one of the first boats to row ashore, as was Captain Bloys, with Walter and three other crewmen pulling at the oars. Behind them another fifty boats approached the town. Anthony gave the order to ship oars, and the boat glided the last few yards to the wooden jetty, where a group of locals were waiting to welcome them.

'Are there any Spaniards left here?' Captain Bloys asked.

'Two dozen men were left, and they returned to their barracks when you sailed into the harbour,' replied a tall man who stood at the front of the group.

'Good. Take me to the barracks would you. Standen

you stay here and help the other boats tie up. When the admiral arrives, give him the news and ask him to send an armed party to the barracks, where we will accept the Spanish surrender. Fifty men should be enough.'

'Yes, sir.' Captain Bloys followed the tall man and most of the other locals off towards the barracks whilst two stayed behind with Anthony and the boat crew. The next boat to pull up at the jetty carried a man wearing the most enormous panned trunk hose and a large ruff.

'You there. Who are you, and where did I see Bloys going?' shouted the elaborately dressed man as he climbed onto the jetty.

'I'm Lieutenant Standen of the Orange Avenger, sir. Captain Bloys has gone with locals to the barracks. I'm to wait here for Admiral de la Marck and give him a message, sir.'

'I'm Admiral de la Marck, lieutenant. What's the message?'

'The Spaniards left only two dozen men here, and they returned to barracks when they saw our fleet arrive. Captain Bloys requests that an armed party of fifty men be sent after him, then the Spanish surrender can be taken, sir.'

'I'll take the surrender, thank you very much. Out of my way!' The admiral, his lieutenant and four sailors pushed past Anthony and walked down the jetty towards the town.

'I'll show you the way, Admiral,' called one of the locals that had been left with Anthony, as he rushed off after them. When they were out of earshot Walter whispered to Anthony.

'So he's our admiral.'

'God help us,' whispered Anthony back.

92

In the following days Anthony was kept very busy. Two thirds of the Sea Beggar crews were moved to the abandoned garrison buildings. Although basic, the conditions were better than living on board and the garrison was far better placed to reinforce defensive positions if Spanish forces were sighted. Lookouts were positioned at the headland to provide warning of any ships, and further lookouts were placed at the edge of town. The other men remained on the ships engaged in maintenance tasks and provisioning. Rotas were organised to see that men had a fair amount of time on all tasks. Anthony found a woman in town who was happy to do his laundry, and make some small alterations to Jansen's uniform, so that it fitted him better. The admiral set up headquarters in the garrison commander's office. Anthony, like most of the other fleet officers spent time on board and in the garrison, by rota, ensuring that the fleet was ready to sail and fight when needed, and that the town was well defended.

On the 8th of April a rider arrived with news that the city of Vlissingen had declared support for William of Orange. According to the report, the people had taken great encouragement from the events in Brielle, and had driven the garrison out of the city. A Spanish fleet had appeared approaching the city, but a drunkard offered to climb the city ramparts for a few jugs of beer, and fire a cannon at the approaching fleet. He was taken up on the bet and he did just that. The Spanish fleet turned and sailed back the way they had come. Almost every other day a rider arrived with news that another city or town had declared for Orange. There was considerable jubilation amongst both the fleet and the townspeople. By the middle of June all the cities and major towns of Holland and Zeeland had declared for their William of

Orange, with the exceptions of Amsterdam and Middelberg. There was a sense of victory, the taverns were busy, and the fleet were lauded as heroes.

On Sunday 22nd June, Anthony was the officer of the day in the admiral's outer office when a rider arrived.

'I have a letter from William of Orange for Admiral de la Marck.'

'Thank you, I'll take it to him. Please rest and take some refreshment in the wardroom. I'll let you know if there will be no reply.' Anthony showed the messenger into the wardroom, where a few junior officers were having lunch, then went back and knocked on the admiral's door.

'Come in.' Anthony entered and saluted. The admiral was with Captain Bloys and Captain Jansz de Graeff. 'What is it?'

'A messenger has arrived with a letter from William of Orange, sir.' Anthony handed the letter to the admiral. The admiral opened it and started reading.

'Who the blazes does he think he is? He congratulates us on our magnificent victory, then he goes on to say that he "requires us to be tolerant" and "leave priests unmolested". Has he never seen what the inquisition have done?' screamed Admiral de la Marck as he screwed the letter up and threw it into the corner of the room. Anthony hesitated then asked,

'Will there be a reply, sir?'

'No there damn well won't. Get out!' Anthony saluted, left and closed the door behind him.

On Tuesday 8th July, Anthony was again on duty when a column of fifteen men, in absolutely filthy and torn friar's habits, were marched into the garrison courtyard. Their escort consisted of twenty well-dressed townspeople

carrying pikes, and two on horseback.

'Who are you?' Anthony asked the horseman at the head of the column.

'I'm the mayor of Gorkum with prisoners for the heroic Sea Beggars.'

'Who are the prisoners?'

'Priest scum,' said the mayor. Anthony bit his lip. He heard a door open behind him and footsteps.

'Welcome, Mayor,' said Admiral de la Marck. 'We will deal with them. Lieutenant Standen call the guard and have this rabble locked in the cells. Can I offer some refreshment for you and your good men, Mayor? What are you waiting for, lieutenant?'

'Yes, sir.' Standen saluted and marched off to the guardroom.

The following afternoon Anthony was talking with Captain Bloys in the courtyard.

'Four more prisoners arrived this morning, all priests,' said Captain Bloys. 'The admiral interrogated them all personally. Apparently they were all asked in turn to swear that they would abandon their belief in the real presence of Christ in the Blessed Sacrament as well as belief in the papal supremacy. They all refused to abandon their—' Bloys stopped as the admiral strode across the courtyard ahead of the nineteen prisoners guarded by crew from the admiral's flagship. They were heading for a large barn where grain was stored. Bloys and Anthony followed them. As they entered the barn, they saw that it had already been prepared. Benches ran the length of the barn and ropes with nooses had been slung from a beam above.

'Master de Vries, string them up. Adjust the ropes individually so that each one will hang with their outstretched toes just an inch above the floor. I don't want a long drop. I like to see them dance,' laughed Admiral de la Marck.

'Admiral, this is expressly against Prince William's orders,' shouted Captain Bloys.

'I don't recognise the authority of that upstart. Are you ready, Master de Vries?' The master nodded. 'Remove the benches!' Admiral de la Marck smiled as the priests writhed and their faces turned blue. Captain Bloys turned on his heels and marched out of the barn. Anthony fell on his knees vomiting.

It was several days later when both Anthony and Captain Bloys were onboard Orange Avenger. Anthony had been reliving the scene in the barn over and over. He thought of Walsingham's orders to gather intelligence on the forces of both sides. He thought too of the Duke of Alva's gold pieces and his mission to find Prince William and discover his plans. He paced the deck thinking of the Catholics he had killed himself. He knocked on the door of the captain's cabin.

'Enter!'

Anthony went in and closed the door. He saluted.

'Sit down,' said Captain Bloys softly.

'I'm sorry to bother you, sir. I admire you immensely, but I don't think I can serve under Admiral de la Marck.'

'Lieutenant Standen, you do realise that I should have you court marshalled for those words.'

'Yes, sir, but—'

'But I'm not unsympathetic to your point of view. The man is something of a monster, but he is the admiral, for now. I have my ship, my crew and my country to consider. I owe you my life and my ship. You must hold your tongue, you know. If you can't, it would be better if you went.'

'Prince William sounds like a very honourable man, sir. I should like to meet him.'

'He is, I met him once. I will write you a letter of introduction to him. I have heard that he is marching with an army towards Mechelen.'

'Mechelen. That's between Brussels and Antwerp isn't it, sir?'

'That's right. It's about a hundred and thirty miles from here. Will you go?'

'With your permission, sir.'

'I'll write you that letter.' Captain Bloys took a sheet of paper from a pile on his desk and began to write. 'I'll miss you, lieutenant. You have been a valuable member of the crew and a fine officer. I had my doubts about you at first, how wrong can one be.'

CHAPTER SIX

1572 – 1576, Flanders

Two weeks later, Anthony walked through the city gates of Mechelen wearing his old clothes. The grand bell tower of St. Rumbold's Cathedral was the focal point of the city, surrounded by streets with fine half-timber buildings, many of them four stories tall. A river ran through the city centre. He pulled out his purse and weighed it in his hand. Then he went looking for a tavern to rest.

The following day, feeling much better, he explored the city. There was no evidence of Spanish control and the people were excited by the rumours that Prince William was on his way. He found a shop selling stationery and bought some quills, a penknife, ink, a dozen sheets of paper and some sealing wax.

'I hear that Prince William is on his way here,' he remarked to the shopkeeper.

'So have I. They say it'll be late August before he gets here.'

'Not till then. Do you know if it's possible to get a letter sent to Paris?' Anthony asked.

'That's one thing we can thank the Holy Roman Empire for. In the market square, you'll find a building called Thurn and Taxis. They operate a mail service right across the empire. There are offices in every major city of the empire, and beyond.'

'Is it available to anyone, or only for government use?'

'Anyone with money. My grandfather told me it used to be for official use only, but in 1506 Philip of Burgundy stopped paying for it, so they opened the service to the paying public. It's been that way ever since.'

'Thank you,' said Anthony, paying the shopkeeper. He located the Thurn and Taxis building, then went back to his room in the tavern. He sat down and drafted a brief letter to Walsingham explaining what he had discovered so far. Then he concealed its contents in a much longer, innocuous letter addressed to Robert and used the date, 2.7th July 1572, placing a small dot between the two and the seven to show that every ninth word of the innocuous letter would reveal the enciphered message, confident that Robert would deduce the cipher. He signed it Anthony, folded it and folded it again. He used a candle to melt some sealing wax onto the join, then blew on it until it solidified and addressed it to Robert Clark, 26 Rue St. Honore, Paris.

Throughout August, Anthony explored Mechelen and the surrounding area, waiting for William of Orange to arrive. His purse was running low, and he thought about finding work. He wondered when he could expect a reply from Walsingham. It might take a rider a week to reach Paris. So he might expect a reply before the end of the month. He had given an account of the Protestant forces, from what he had learnt in the Sea Beggars, but he knew little about the Spanish forces. At some point, he would have to infiltrate them. When, where, and how could he do that? He stopped outside a very imposing four-story stone building. The brass plaque read 'Governor's Residence'. He knocked on the door. A plainly dressed, middle-aged man opened the door.

'I would like to see the governor, please,' Anthony

said.

'Governor? Where have you been these last weeks? The governor and his men have all gone. The mayor has moved in now.'

'Well, could I see the mayor then?'

'What about?'

'I'd rather tell the mayor.'

'He's out, and isn't expected back for another hour.'

'Can I wait?'

'I suppose so. There's a few waiting already. Come this way.' The man led Anthony down a corridor. There were rectangular patches on the walls that were a lighter shade than the wall. He saw hooks above them. Perhaps paintings had been removed. He silently counted his paces as they walked. The man opened a door on the right and showed him into a waiting room. Three men sat on the right-hand side of the room. There was a large window opposite them. Straight ahead was another door. 'Sit here with the others. As I said, the mayor will be an hour or so.' Then the man turned and left, shutting the door behind him. The three seated men watched Anthony silently as he paced about the room. After a few minutes, he also sat down. The three men began talking. They each had their own stories about the recent events. How the heroic Sea Beggars had fought off the Spaniards in Brielle. Anthony suppressed a smile. How they had driven the Spaniards out of Mechelen, wielding their carving knives. How their businesses had been crippled by the Spanish taxes. Eventually the waiting room door opened again and a well-dressed man with a mayor's chain of office around his neck strode in. He took a key from a pocket in his doublet and opened the other door.

'Who's first?' the mayor asked.

'I am,' said the man nearest to the mayor's office.

'Come in then.' The man got up and followed the mayor inside. Anthony also stood as they went in and peered after them into the office.

'I can't wait any longer. I've got things to do,' Anthony said, in his best Flemish, and left.

That night, when all was quiet in the streets, he returned to the governor's house. There was a little moonlight, but the house itself was in darkness and there was no sound to be heard. He looked up and down the street, then took out his lock picks and started work. He was a little out of practice, but it wasn't a complex lock and he was soon inside. The corridor was completely dark. He paced the distance to where the waiting room door should be and felt for the handle. The door opened with a slight creak. He stopped and listened. He could hear nothing except his own heartbeat. Inside the waiting room, there was some moonlight shining through the window. He walked over to the office door and tried the handle. The door was locked. He got out his picks again and soon had it open. He listened again, but there was no sound other than an owl hooting outside. Thankfully, there was also a large window in the mayor's office. He tiptoed across to the cupboard he had seen earlier and tried the door. It was locked. He felt for the keyhole and soon had the cupboard open. The cupboard was, as he had hoped, half-full of papers, in separate piles tied with ribbon. He took a few piles from the top shelf and went to the window. These are in Flemish. He put them back and selected some from the middle shelf and went to the window. Flemish again. He put them back and felt around on the bottom shelf. There were only three bundles, covered in dust. He took one over to the window. It was in Spanish. He put it on the desk and collected the other two piles from the shelf in the cupboard. He stopped as he heard steps from the floor above and a window being opened. He looked at the window and saw something fall, then a splashing sound. He heard the window close, then footsteps. Somebody had emptied their chamber pot. The footsteps stopped, and all was silent again. As he felt around on the desktop for the bundles of papers, he felt a box. He tried to open it, but it was locked. He picked the lock and felt inside. It was half-full of coins. He took a handful and put them in his pocket. He stuffed the bundles of papers inside his doublet and locked the box. He locked the cupboard and crossed back to the office door. He put his ear to the door and heard nothing, so made his way back through the waiting room and down the corridor, locking each door behind him. He opened the front door and peered out. There was still no sign of movement. He crept out, locked the front door behind him. and made his way back to the tavern.

In the morning, he checked his pocket. There was enough money to keep him going for about a month. He started reading the papers. The first two bundles were legal documents. The third bundle looked more promising. It contained correspondence, and some of it was enciphered. He sat down at his table, took a sheet of paper and his pen and tried to decipher it. After two hours, he was making good progress with the ciphers. He had reached that point where it would all unravel very quickly from here. Once the cipher was broken, he read the documents, although he struggled to understand why they had been enciphered in the first place. They seemed to be production targets and taxation strategy. He dropped his pen on the table, stood up, and paced around the room. Two things were evident. They planned a massive increase in food production and a commensurate increase in taxes. He doubted that the Spaniards would be planning for a proportional increase in the civilian population. He sat down again. *I know the provisions required for a hundred sailors per day, so if a soldier requires about the same, then over a year that's, no, that can't be right. He checked his sums. Yes, it is. That's an extra 50,000 soldiers by next year.* He looked at the taxation strategy. If the price of meat and grain stays roughly the same as it is, then there's practically none of King Philip's money paying for this. It's all being raised through local taxes.

One hot morning, towards the end of August, Anthony came downstairs for breakfast to find three men he didn't recognise as residents, eating as if they hadn't eaten for weeks. He greeted them in Flemish, but they didn't answer.

'They're French,' said the landlord as he carried in another tray of food and beer. 'Your usual, Anthony?'

'Yes please, Amand.' Turning to the Frenchmen, he addressed them in French. 'Do you mind if I join you?' They were too busy eating, but one nodded and Anthony sat down. When they had their fill, he tried to converse again. 'What brings you here?'

'We're refugees from Paris, arrived last night. There are thousands of us, all over the city.'

'What made you leave Paris?'

'To save our skin. We're Huguenots. On the eve of St. Bartholomew's Day, the slaughter started. First, the king's men killed Admiral Coligny and other Huguenot leaders, then they started slaughtering anyone who might be a Protestant, of any sort. Ordinary people joined in. It was my neighbours who chased after me. They got my wife.'

'My god! Was it all across Paris, or confined to a small area?' Anthony asked.

'Paris, all across France, more like. On the road, we met refugees from Rouen. The streets were ankle deep in blood there too.' they said.

Anthony feared that there might be a reason he hadn't received a reply to his letter yet.

The following day, Anthony was taking a walk and worrying about Walsingham. Without his help, he might never earn Queen Elizabeth's pardon and never see his family or his homeland again. If Walsingham was killed in Paris, he could try to contact Sir Henry, or even Cecil, perhaps. There might be a way of continuing his espionage career, and earning a pardon. Or he could spy for the Spanish. That seemed hardly likely to help him see his family again, though. In the meantime, he could try to find work, perhaps in the wine trade. Or he could just employ his talents as a thief. Given the number of men he'd killed, stealing shouldn't matter much, in the final reckoning. It was easy and paid well. A crowd cheering shook from his thoughts him. He walked toward the cheering and saw a great column of cavalry and infantry entering the city. Prince William had arrived at last. Anthony couldn't get close, but followed the crowds. Eventually, he got to the front of the crowd just as they were turning into the street where the governor's house stood. He saw the mayor talking to William. From what he could make out above the noise, the mayor insisted that Prince William move into the house for the duration of his stay. The mayor followed William in, accompanied by the senior officers and some local dignitaries. Anthony felt inside his doublet for his letter of introduction, but remembered he had left it concealed in his room. *I should let him get settled in, and come back tomorrow*, he thought.

The next day, after breakfast, Anthony went to the governor's house, showed the sentry his letter and was taken to the office he had burgled a week or so ago. Prince William of Orange sat behind the desk and looked up as Anthony entered.

'Your Highness,' Anthony said as he bowed. 'I served with your Sea Beggars and have a letter of introduction from Captain Bloys van Treslong.' Anthony handed the letter to Prince William, who opened it and read it. He turned the page and continued. It was quite a long letter. He then put the letter down and looked up. His gaze seemed to bore into Anthony's soul.

'It seems I owe you a great deal, Lieutenant Standen. Captain Bloys is a good man, unlike de la Marck. I didn't think he was this bad though.'

'I haven't known him very long at all, Your Highness, but I think he may be deranged, possessed by demons perhaps.'

'I shall certainly have to see what I can do about an admiral who ignores my orders. In the meantime, I should like to get to know you better, lieutenant. I have some things to deal with now but they are putting on a lunch for me today. Come back at noon and we will talk over lunch.'

'Your Highness,' said Anthony as he bowed and left.

Much to Anthony's astonishment, and to the mayor's obvious annoyance, Anthony was seated on the prince's left and the prince's aide-de-camp was on his right. The mayor was seated to the right of the aide-de-camp.

'Lieutenant, you have seen a lot of death. I saw it in your eyes this morning.'

'I have Your Highness, and that is why I left Captain Bloys, with his permission, and wanted to see you. I have seen savage cruelty of Catholics to Protestants and Protestants to Catholics. That is why your orders to spare the priests seemed so remarkable.' Prince William leaned a little closer to Anthony and whispered,

'I remain a Catholic myself, but even though I have kept my faith, I cannot accept that monarchs should rule over the souls of their subjects, nor deny them their freedom of belief and religion.' Anthony was silent for a minute, gathering his thoughts.

'Your Highness, I have waited so long to hear such thoughts. When I was young, too young, I saw Protestants burnt at the stake in the reign of Queen Mary. The smell has stayed with me ever since.'

'In the summer of 1559, I was with the Duke of Alva in Paris. We had been sent as hostages whilst a treaty was being negotiated after the Spanish French war. King Henry II of France began discussing with me his secret understanding with Philip II for the violent extermination of Protestantism throughout the Christian world. Since Alva knew about it, Henry assumed he would have told me. That was my defining moment, as the burnings must have been for you.' The conversation buzzed around them, but Anthony ate in silence for a while. The prince talked with his aide-de-camp. When that conversation finished, Anthony spoke again.

'Your Highness, I should very much like to continue in your service. I have discovered some papers, Spanish papers, which reveal something important. Could I speak with you alone after lunch?'

'Come with me after lunch, we will speak in the office.'

'Please sit down, lieutenant.' Prince William said as he lowered himself into a walnut chair with plain red

upholstery, a high, carved back and curved armrests, behind a large oak desk inlaid with a leather writing surface. Anthony bowed and sat in a plain chair with a lower backrest and without armrests, facing the prince. 'What is it you want to tell me?'

'Your Highness, I found some Spanish documents. They appeared to be quite ordinary financial documents, but they contained food production targets and taxation strategy. The food production requirement for Flanders indicated a rise over the year to support an additional fifty thousand men.' Anthony paused to let Prince William take it in. 'The taxation document suggested that, if you factor in the pay for that number of men, almost all the additional men are to be paid for out of local taxes.'

'That is astonishing, lieutenant. You have thought that through very well, it does makes sense. This is very worrying, but vital to know. It was foolish of them to leave these documents and not to have enciphered them.'

'Oh, they were in cipher, Your Highness. I deciphered them myself.'

'You deciphered them. How did you do that?' Anthony's head tipped back, and he gazed at the ceiling for a moment. He had run away with himself.

'Well, languages have always fascinated me. I read that Eastern scholars had analysed the frequency with which letters occur in a text. So I made a study of it myself and read more of the Eastern texts. It was difficult, but I broke the Spanish cipher.'

'Where did you get these Eastern texts?'

'My father was a lawyer at court in London. I used to play with the children of diplomats visiting court, which is how I learnt to speak foreign languages. There was once an emissary from Constantinople, and he helped me.'

'Extraordinary! And where did you find these Spanish documents?'

Anthony paused.

'There, on the bottom shelf of that cupboard, Your Highness, covered in dust.'

'And what were you doing in here?'

'I came to see the mayor when I arrived from Brielle, Your Highness. The mayor was called out of the office, so I had a browse around. I found the documents, and with my talent for languages, and knowledge of ciphers, I thought it might be helpful to you, if I took them and deciphered them, Your Highness.' Anthony smiled.

'Lieutenant, there is much of your story that, frankly, I don't believe. But there are elements that I do believe. Do you still have the documents?'

'I do, Your Highness.'

'Bring them to me. I would like to see them myself. Then we will think about how you can help me some more.'

'These are the enciphered documents, and here are my deciphered copies, Your Highness,' Anthony said, placing the papers on Prince Willam's desk. The prince picked each one up in turn and browsed through them.

'They look genuine enough. Now are you part of a Spanish deception to make me believe that we are hopelessly outnumbered, or…?'

'No, Your Highness. I wouldn't do that, it's—'

'You wouldn't deceive me?'

'I believe in you, Your Highness. I believe you will reign with tolerance for all faiths. I want to help you.' While Anthony spoke, Prince William looked straight in his eyes.

'I advise you not to gamble at the card tables,

lieutenant. I can see when you're lying and also when you're not. You are easy to read. You do want to help me. These documents are genuine, and you do have some very useful skills. I face a rapidly growing enemy. We are also growing, with many Huguenots joining us, but not in these numbers. So I need your unusual skills, lieutenant. I want you to infiltrate the Spanish forces. I don't know how. You'll have to work that out. I want you to gather more information on the Spanish numbers and deployments. I want to know about their movements against us, before they move.'

'If I do obtain such information, Your Highness, how will I get it to you, if I am with the Spanish?'

'We have agents in many places. They observe and listen, but they don't deliver anything like this,' Prince William said, picking up the papers. 'I will give you the name and location of our agent in Brussels. I will also give you a code word, so that he will know you are genuine. If you uncover something else like this, give it to him and it will get to me.'

'What if I'm not in Brussels, Your Highness? What about the other agents?'

'I can't afford to risk our entire network of agents. Brussels is the Spanish headquarters in Flanders, so you are likely to pass through. If you are moving elsewhere, tell our agent, and he may give you details of another agent, if your information is valuable enough.'

'Talking of value, Your Highness, will I be paid for this work?' There was a knock at the door, Prince William acknowledged, and his secretary came in.

'Your Highness, a dispatch rider has arrived with messages.' The secretary placed the messages, all bearing the House of Orange wax seal, on the desk.

'Thank you. I have some dispatches written. Here

they are. Seal them, would you, then give them to the rider.' Prince William took letters from his desk drawer and handed them to the secretary. The secretary bowed and left. 'Yes, the agent will be instructed to pay you for your information. Now all you have to do is work out how to infiltrate the Spanish forces. Do you think you can do that?'

'Yes, Your Highness, I think I can,' Anthony said, stroking his beard as he gazed at the pile of dispatches the rider had brought.

When Anthony left the governor's residence, he went to the Thurn and Taxis building to see if a reply had arrived from Walsingham. He was handed a sealed letter, which he took back to his room in the tavern to open. It was a letter from Robert dated 28th August 1572. It was all about Robert's children, how they were getting on in school and their attempts at painting. It finished with how his youngest daughter was learning to talk but had trouble pronouncing words containing certain letters. Anthony picked up his pen and started underlining every tenth word. The message read *we are all well excellent work need more on the yellow and red F W*.

FW Francis Walsingham. So they are alive. He is pleased with my report but wants more on the Spanish. So everything is pointing to me joining the Spaniards. I know how, I just don't know where and when, but it had better be soon. Now for some shopping. Anthony screwed up the letter, picked up his canvas bag, and went downstairs. He poked his head into the kitchen. The cook was busy, and Anthony threw the screwed-up letter into the fire. Then he picked up a metal spoon with a long handle, dropped it into his bag, and left.

He went next to the stationery shop and bought every

colour of sealing wax they had, then to the cathedral, where he had seen men working on replacing some lead roof tiles. He asked if he could buy some lead from them and they happily obliged. He noticed they had some thick leather gloves and bought one of those too. He then found a pottery where he was able to buy some clay and plaster of paris. Finally, he went to the gunsmith and bought a pouch of gunpowder, some wadding, a few spare pieces of pyrite and a dozen balls for the wheellock pistol he had acquired in the battle of Wieringen. He went back to the tavern to think through his next moves.

At breakfast the next morning, Amand told him that Prince William's army had left the city at sunrise, leaving a small garrison behind. The gossip was that the Duke of Alva was striking back hard against the rebellion. Anthony wondered what to do. He daren't risk getting too close to Alva in case he recognised him as the Venetian spy he hadn't seen for almost a year. He decided to stay where he was and see what more news might arrive. He needed to know where the opportunity would arise to infiltrate the Spanish army. Otherwise, he could chase about all over Flanders, achieving nothing, and Amand did cook an excellent breakfast.

Throughout September, Anthony picked up snippets of news. Prince William had visited his brother, Louis, who had held Mons since March. Then later Prince William had headed north towards Ghent. On the 19th September, he learnt that Alva had laid siege to Mons and two days later, he learnt that on the 19th Alva had allowed Louis to leave Mons with full honours of war. It seemed that Alva was pushing the rebel army north, back into Holland and he was now heading towards Mechelen. So Anthony wouldn't have to find the Spaniards. They were about to find him.

Charles Neville, 6th Earl of Westmorland, now a captain in the Spanish army, was riding at the head of his platoon towards Mechelen. Beside him rode Sergeant Augusto Sanchez.

'Do you think we will be paid when we have captured the city, captain?'

'I don't know, Sanchez. I know the men are very restless, and I haven't been paid either.'

'Are you married, captain? I have a wife, five sons and four daughters. I haven't seen them for six years. It's too much to bear, and there doesn't seem to be any reward for our loyal service.'

'Yes, I'm married. My wife's name is Jane. My only son died in childhood, but I have four beautiful daughters. I haven't seen them for, well, it must be three years now.'

'Pay or no pay, the men are going to get very drunk and have a very good time when we finish fighting in Mechelen, captain. You know what I mean?'

'I can't blame them Sanchez, I can't blame them at all.'

On the 29th September, the Spanish army advanced towards Mechelen, led by the Duke of Alva's son, Fadrique. The small garrison put up a valiant fight in the suburb outside the city walls, during which Fadrique received minor injuries, and the remaining garrison retreated back within the city walls. The garrison continued to fire at the Spaniards from the ramparts throughout the following day, but when the heavy artillery was seen approaching, the position appeared hopeless. The garrison fled that night.

Anthony had observed events carefully. When he saw

the garrison creeping out, he grabbed his canvas bag, went to the kitchen and loaded it with some bread, meat and beer, then went to the cathedral. Many local people had taken shelter in the cathedral, but Anthony went to the staircase which led up the bell tower, and climbed to the top. He grabbed hold of one of the bell ropes and pulled it all the way up. Then he got out his knife and sawed his way through the thick rope. He tied one end to one of the timbers and coiled it up on the floor. Then he pulled up a thinner rope from the smallest bell, cut it and coiled it up so that he could sling it around his neck. From the tower, he had an excellent view across the city and beyond, in all directions, but there was only one staircase leading up. If the Spaniards came up, he could either fight or use the rope to climb down the outside of the tower and hope the Spaniards were too busy on the ground to look up. He then settled down to wait and watch.

On the 1st October, the Catholic bishop had the gates opened and the choir and people sang psalms of penitence. Fadrique was not impressed and unleashed his troops in an orgy of slaughter, pillage, and rape. Anthony watched the slaughter from the tower, powerless to do anything. Well, there wasn't really anything he could do. After two days and a night, he sensed a gradual easing of the fury. That night, he loaded his pistol and stuck it through his belt, slung his canvas bag around his neck, and crept down the staircase. He kept stopping and listening, but there was no sound coming up the stair, only the screaming and shouting from outside. When he got to the ground floor there were some candles still burning, and in their dim light he found bodies strewn all about him and the tiled floor thick with blood. The clothes of the younger women had been torn from their bodies. He couldn't find a sign of life within the cathedral. He slipped out of the vestry door into the night. He waited in the graveyard until daybreak, then slipped out onto the street. He made his way cautiously towards the governor's house, sticking to the side of the street in shadow. He heard a girl's scream from a narrow alleyway to his right. He crept into the alleyway and, sticking closely to the wall, edged towards the source of the screaming, now muffled. Ahead of him, he saw the girl on her back with her legs towards him. One Spanish soldier, wearing the uniform of a captain, was behind her with his knees on her shoulders, his left hand over her mouth, and his right hand holding a knife to her throat. Another soldier, in a sergeant's uniform, was kneeling between her legs and pulling down his breeches. Two muskets were lying on the ground between the girl and Anthony. He pulled the pistol quietly from his belt and aimed at the soldier with the knife. As he cocked the pistol, the man with the knife looked up.

'Drop the knife!' Anthony whispered. The soldier dropped the knife and took his hand from the girl's mouth. The other soldier started to turn around. 'Don't move a muscle!'

'Can, can I get up now, sir?' the girl asked.

'Don't get in my line of fire. Roll over to your right until you reach the wall, then get up and follow the wall towards me.' The girl followed Anthony's instructions, and the soldier backed off, holding his hands in the air. As the girl passed Anthony she said, 'Thank you, sir.'

'Find somewhere safe if you can,' Anthony replied. The soldier, with his breeches around his knees, went to pull them up. 'You were anxious enough to get your breeches off. Now take off everything, now! And you. And the boots.' When the soldiers were completely naked, Anthony said quietly, 'Off you go, run away.' As they disappeared down the alleyway, he went over to the piles of clothes, selected the garments that he thought would fit him best, and rammed them into his bag. Then he made his way back to the graveyard. He thought he should be an ordinary soldier, so he used his knife to cut the insignia of rank from the Spanish uniforms and changed into the one that fitted him best. He discarded his old clothes.

Anthony made his way towards the governor's house. When he was about fifty yards away, he came across a shop that appeared ransacked and deserted. It would afford a good view of his target, so he pushed the door, which was ajar, and entered. The shop had indeed been ransacked, and an elderly, dead man lay crumpled where he had fallen. Everything that was valuable and portable had been taken. A clock which was valuable but not easily portable was ticking. Anthony found the key and wound it. Then he pulled an empty crate over to the window as a makeshift stool and observed the governor's house. All day he watched, noting the times the sentry was relieved and the people who came and went. He saw riders come, take documents from their saddlebags, show their documents to the sentry and enter and leave again a few minutes later. When he was confident that the current sentry was two thirds of the way through his watch, and looking bored, Anthony stole out of the shop and walked confidently up to the sentry.

'I've been sent to relieve you,' he said.

'Is it time already?'

'Time flies when you're enjoying yourself.'

'Very funny. All your's then.' The sentry walked off towards the garrison, and Anthony took his place. A few officers came and went and then a rider arrived. He tied his horse to a rail, showed Anthony his documents, and Anthony opened the door for him. When the rider came out again, Anthony asked, 'How do you get a cushy job like a dispatch rider then?'

'Cushy! Riding through hostile country on your own, with anyone free to take potshots at you. It's the most dangerous job in the army.'

'It can't be as boring as this. I'd give it a go.'

'You must be mad, but the sergeant is always looking for new riders. We lose plenty.'

'Where do I find him?'

'At the garrison. Ask for Sergeant Lopez.' Shaking his head, the rider untied his horse, mounted and rode off. Anthony looked around, and as nobody was about, marched off at a brisk pace towards the garrison.

'I'm looking for Sergeant Lopez.'

'Over there in the office on the end of the stable block,' replied a sentry at the garrison gate. Anthony walked over to the office, knocked on the door and entered as ordered.

'What do you want?' asked the short, dark-haired man behind the desk.

'I want to volunteer to be a dispatch rider, sergeant.'

'What's your name?'

'Pompeo Pellegrini, sergeant.'

'Italian, eh? Good soldiers the Italians. How do you ride?'

'Like the wind, sergeant.'

'Good, we always need dispatch riders. Come with me.' The sergeant stood up and walked round to the stable. He led Anthony over to a stall with a large black stallion in it. 'Let me introduce you to Lightning. He's just come free.'

116

'Free?' said Anthony, stroking the horse's mane.

'He returned here last night, still carrying his rider, musket ball in his back. He's a good horse, and very fast. Well, he seems to like you. Let's go and get the rest of your kit.' Sergeant Lopez led Anthony to a store room and took a set of black leather saddlebags, embossed with the royal coat of arms, from a rack. 'Take these.' Sergeant Lopez handed the saddlebags to Anthony and led the way back to his office. 'Here's a map with important landmarks and the major towns and cities. You can read I take it?' Anthony nodded. 'And here are some dispatches for Brussels. Deliver them, then wait for your next dispatches.'

'Will they be to deliver back here?'

'They'll be for wherever they need to be delivered. It could be Madrid, for all I care. Well, what are you waiting for? On your way!'

'Yes, sergeant.'

Anthony remembered the road from Mechelen to Brussels, from when he had walked to Antwerp. When they got to a wooded section, he reined Lightning in, and they went off the road into the woods. Anthony dismounted and tied the reins to a branch. He collected fallen branches and twigs, opened one of his saddlebags, and pulled out his canvas bag. From the bag he took out his pistol, the gunpowder pouch, his penknife, a water flask, and the plaster of paris. Next, he took the dispatches from the other saddlebag and placed them on a nearby rock. He mixed some plaster of paris with water and carefully sliced the wax seal off one of the documents, which he set down carefully on the rock. He covered the impressed seal with the plaster of paris mixture and left it to set. He stacked the twigs in a pyramid shape, opened the priming pan on his pistol, and scattered the gunpowder grains from the pan into the pile of twigs, adding a little more gunpowder from his pouch, until he was satisfied the fire would take. He tied the pouch securely and put it back in the canvas bag. He then held the pan of the pistol against the stack of twigs, cocked the pistol, and pulled the trigger. Sparks flew as the wheel spun against the pyrite. There was a small flash and fizzing sound as the gunpowder ignited amongst the twigs, and the twigs caught. Anthony blew on the twigs until they were burning well and then stacked against it suitable dry branches to make a good fire.

He munched on some bread and cheese and fed Lightning some carrots, that he had taken from a pile in the stables, as he had led Lightning out. He then got out his paper, pen and ink and began copying the dispatch. It wasn't too long, but was enciphered. He opened the other dispatches and copied those too. When he had finished, he tested the plaster of paris. It was set. He held the plaster cast over the fire until the wax ran out. He rubbed his fingers in some of his cheese and rubbed it around inside the plaster cast. Then he pressed some clay into the plaster cast and left it to dry. It was a long wait, but when he was satisfied that the clay was dry enough, he tentatively chipped away the plaster. Then he took out his leather glove and put it on. He got out his long-handled metal spoon and the lead. He hacked off a small piece of lead with his knife and put it in the spoon's bowl. He held the spoon in the fire until the lead melted, then poured it into his clay mould. He finished his lunch and fed Lightning some more carrots while he waited for the lead to cool. When it was cool, he chipped away the clay and examined his work. He had made his own government seal. He reached into his bag and took out the red sealing wax, cleaned the spoon with some leaves and then used the spoon again to melt some wax. He folded the dispatches and used his new seal to seal them again. He packed everything away, kicked the fire apart and stamped out the smouldering embers, untied Lightning and continued on his way to Brussels.

On arrival, he delivered his dispatches to the governor's house. He was told to return in the morning to collect new dispatches. He asked where he could stay and was given directions to the garrison. Instead, he went to a tavern, not the one he had stayed in when he was last in Brussels. He didn't want to be recognised. He tied Lightning up outside and went in to see if they had a room. He ordered dinner, and the landlord offered to send a lad to look after his horse. After dinner, Anthony sat in his room, at a table by the fire, deciphering the copies of dispatches he had made. He folded a large piece of paper and addressed it on one side to Robert in Paris. He then wrote out a summary of the two dispatches and recoded them using their date-based code. He put the innocent-looking letter inside the folded paper and sealed it with plain candle wax. He put the sealed document and the deciphered copies inside his doublet, screwed his workings into a ball and threw it in the fire. Then he headed out to the address of Prince William's agent in Brussels.

It was dark and took him a while to find the address in the moonlight. Anthony knocked on the door of the grocer's shop. A tall, fat, middle-aged man opened the door and stepped back when he saw Anthony's uniform. He tried to close the door but Anthony stuck his foot in the way.

'Do you have any pomegranates?' Anthony asked.

'Not until November,' the man said, relieved. 'Come

in my friend.' The agent led him to the back room and Anthony gave him the deciphered dispatches. He read them in the light of an oil lamp. 'These are excellent. Do you know where you are going next?'

'No. I have to go back and collect more dispatches in the morning. I'll know then.'

'Call by on your way. If it's necessary, I'll give you a contact at your next destination.' The man opened a casket on the table and gave him a handful of silver ducats. Anthony left and went back to the tavern. The following morning he paid the landlord's boy to take his letter to Robert to the Thurn and Taxis building and post it. Then he collected his new dispatches, passed by the grocers and collected the details for the agent in Ghent and some carrots for Lightning.

A few months into his service as a dispatch rider, Anthony was sitting on a rock in some woods on the outskirts of Heffen, just northwest of Mechelen. He was busy deciphering some dispatches. Lightning was grazing contentedly, and the small fire he had made for melting the wax to make a new seal was crackling and spitting as the flames ate into the damp wood on top. From the corner of his eye, he saw Lightning flinch, and in the same second he heard a twig crack behind him. He lunged for his wheellock which lay beside his saddlebags in front of him. He heard the release of a bowstring and an arrow tore his hat from his head and pinned it to a tree before him. As his right hand closed around the grip of his wheellock pistol, he heard a man shout in Flemish.

'Shoot son!'

Anthony's torso twisted, and he saw an emaciated man pulling an arrow from the quiver on his back. A boy of about thirteen, also just flesh and bone was aiming his drawn bow at Anthony. Anthony hesitated to shoot the boy, he fixed his gaze on the boy's eyes and saw his eyes close slightly as he released the string. Anthony flung himself to one side and felt the arrow fly past his left cheek. He rolled onto his stomach and levelled his pistol at the man who had not yet fixed his arrow.

'Drop the bows,' he shouted in Flemish. The man dropped his bow. The boy reached for another arrow from his quiver.

'I don't want to shoot the boy, but I will shoot you if he draws that bow.'

'Drop it son. I'm sorry, sir, I thought you were Spanish. They have taken everything we have and we are starving. Please spare the boy.' As the boy dropped his bow Anthony stood up, carefully keeping his pistol levelled at the man's chest. He walked slowly back to his saddlebags and pulled out a few carrots and some dried ham. He also took a couple of silver coins. He tossed the food and the coins to the man.

'Mark my face, sir.' Anthony said quietly. 'Go in peace, but remember well not to cross me again.' The man picked up the food and the coins.

'Thank you, sir.' With that, the man and the boy turned and ran off into the woods. That was too close, he thought. It really is a dangerous business carrying dispatches. He must be more careful.

Throughout the seasons, for the next few years, Anthony and Lightning repeated the same routine, criss-crossing Flanders. He visited scenes of slaughter on a scale that made Mechelen mild by comparison, Naarden and Leiden were amongst the worst. He was constantly on the watch for locals, or Protestant troops who might assault him. Several times he felt the whistle of a musket ball or sometimes an arrow fly past him. Whenever he was riding through woodland or past outcrops that might conceal an assailant, he urged Lightning into a gallop. He kept the metalwork on his pistol brightly polished and placed it in front of him whenever he was resting or deciphering documents. Every few moments he glanced at the pistol to look for the reflection of any movement behind him. In November 1573 he read a dispatch saying that the Duke of Alva was to be replaced by Luis de Resquesens y Zuniga. Other dispatches confirmed his earlier conclusions that King Philip had drawn the purse strings tight again.

Throughout 1575, most of his work was between Brussels and Breda, a good two days' ride to the north. He learnt that peace negotiations were in progress, but that King Philip would not accept any concessions to Protestantism. Catholicism could be the only faith. The peace talks fell through.

If the Spaniards had kept records of when dispatch riders collected and delivered their messages, and if they had examined the average times taken, then they would have been surprised that Anthony took on average an hour longer to deliver his messages. But they did not, they had other matters on their minds. Equally, if Anthony had paid more attention to the soldiers he met, and his fellow dispatch riders, he would have noticed how thin they were getting, whilst he was eating heartily on the profits of his work.

On Sunday 4th November 1576 he was in Antwerp. He had made his delivery, entrusted the copies to the agent in Antwerp, and taken his swollen purse to the tavern. He ate a good dinner and drank his wine, observed by a group of Spanish soldiers. Anthony went out the back of the tavern to relieve himself, and woke up lying in his piss the following morning, with the back of his head caked in congealed blood. His purse had gone, so had his bag, and so had Lightning. He felt in his pocket. He still had his lock picks, penknife and the lead seals he had cast. His hand reached for his St. Christopher. He remembered that it was long gone, and he began to doubt the luck that it might have brought him. He staggered into the street. Buildings were burning, soldiers were running amok and looting wherever they could. There was a difference. This time the Spanish officers were not directing the action, they were victims of the mutineers too. Anthony staggered his way out of the city, keeping to the backstreets, and began plodding his way towards Brussels.

A penniless Standen closed the tavern door behind him. It was the third tavern he had tried, since arriving back in Brussels, that wouldn't offer him a room on credit. The sun was setting, and he sat down dejectedly on the ground, resting his back against the tavern wall. He pulled his cape tightly around him and shut his eyes.

'Why, is that Antonio Foscari, the wine merchant?' Anthony opened his eyes and looked up into the beautiful blue eyes of Barbara Kegel.

'Barbara?'

'Yes. You look a little down on your luck, as indeed I was when we met. Are you in trouble?'

'If you call having no money and nowhere to sleep, in trouble, then yes I am. Otherwise I am alive at least. You look even more beautiful than when I last met you. Did you get the pension?'

'Yes, and our house is nearby. Occasionally I take in lodgers to supplement my pension, so come and stay with us. It's just the children and I at present.' She offered her hand to help him up.

'I'm afraid, as I said, I have no money.'

'Don't worry about that. You were very generous to me when I was in need. Besides, you are rather handsome yourself, in a very dishevelled sort of way.' She smiled and squeezed his hand as she helped him stand up. She led the way to a pleasant-looking, two storey, detached, brick-built house on a corner. There was a glow of oil lamps shining through the front room curtains. She opened the door. 'Please come in. Hopefully Paul, he's the eldest, will have put Margaret and Simone to bed.' She opened a door off the hall way and led him into the front room. A fair-headed blue-eyed boy of about eight was sitting on the floor in front of a log fire. 'Thank you, Paul. Say hello to Signore Foscari. He's going to be our new lodger for a while.'

'Hello, Signore Foscari.'

'Hello, Paul. You can call me Antonio,' Anthony said smiling.

'Well done, Paul. Have you eaten?'

'Yes, Mother.'

'Very good, then run along to bed. I'm going to get Antonio something to eat. Give me a kiss.' Barbara bent down and her son kissed her.

'Good night, Antonio.'

'Good night, Paul.' Paul left the front room and closed the door. Anthony could hear the sound of his feet running up the wooden stairs.

'I have some bread and cheese, and some cold meats. Would that be all right? I have some beer too, if you'd like some?' Barbara asked.

'That would be wonderful, I'm starving. I've walked from Antwerp, the army were looting, it was awful.'

'I'll put some water on to heat and put the bath tub in

front of the fire. I hope you won't be offended, but you look as though you could do with a bath.'

'I'm not offended in the slightest, I know I could do with a bath, but is the water clean? My father said that King Henry closed down the bathhouses in Southwark because of an outbreak of syphilis. He said the water enters your body through your pores carrying disease if the water's dirty.'

'He didn't tell you that Flemish women, who offered the gentlemen additional services, not just a wash and rubdown tended the bathhouses. It really isn't dirty water that spreads syphilis you know. Anyway, my water is perfectly clean. I'll fetch out some of my late husband's clothes. You're a little taller that he was, but otherwise I think you'll find something. Do sit down at the table, I won't be long.' Barbara left the room and came back in a few minutes with a tray and plates of meat, cheese, some bread, butter, cutlery and a jug of beer. 'I ate earlier, so please tuck in. I'll go and fetch those clothes.' Anthony started to eat. He heard Barbara going up stairs. By the time he heard her footsteps coming down again, he had finished the food and was just draining the last of the beer. 'Here we are. There's a towel for you too.' Barbara draped a towel, some breeches, a shirt and a doublet over the back of the chair beside Anthony. 'Can I get you some more food, or beer?'

'No thank you. That was just right.'

'In which case, I'll clear these things away. Would you help me bring the tub and water through from the kitchen?'

'Of course.' Anthony got up and followed Barbara to the large kitchen. Along one wall was a large pot suspended over a fire.

'If you could take the bath tub through, and then

come back. I could use a hand carrying the water. There's some soap by the tub.' Anthony put the soap in the tub and carried it through to the front room. He put it down next to the fire, then went back to the kitchen. 'Put these on,' Barbara said passing him some leather gauntlets. 'It'll be hot.' She put some gauntlets on too and Anthony squeezed past her to get to the other side of the pot. He felt a thrill as he brushed past her. They lifted the pot down and carried it into the front room and poured the steaming water into the tub. Barbara put her finger in the water, and Anthony bent down and did the same. 'Is it too hot? It feels too hot.'

'No, it feels just fine.'

'Perhaps it's me then.' Barbara smiled at him, her eyes gleaming like warm sapphires. 'I'll leave you to it. Give me a shout when you're done and I'll show you to your room.' She smiled again and left.

Anthony got undressed and climbed into the bath. It was a little cramped but Anthony washed himself thoroughly, and felt refreshed. He climbed out and went over to the chair with the towel and clothes. As he passed the door to the hallway, he noticed it was ajar, and thought he was being watched. He towelled himself down and tried on the clothes. They weren't a poor fit, and with some longer hose the breeches wouldn't look too bad.

'I'm decent,' he called out. Barbara came in.

'There, you scrub up well,' she whispered. 'I'll wash your clothes tomorrow. Could you help me take the tub out and pour the water away?'

'Of course.' They carried the tub out and poured the dirty water down a gully in the floor. 'So who was the powerful man you knew. You obviously got the pension. You were half starved when we met in the duke's office, what was it, five years ago?'

'About that. It's a rather painful story for me to tell to a stranger, Antonio. Please don't think I'm rude. I may tell you, but I'll need to know you a lot better. I do hope you'll stay for a while; I think you're well worth getting to know. Come, follow me, I'll show you to your room.'

It was a few days later and branches of the elm tree scratched at the window pane. Light from the rising sun glistened in Barbara's jet-black hair, spread across the white linen pillowcase. Anthony gently brushed the hair away from her neck and kissed her.

'Has anyone ever told you how stunningly beautiful you are?'

'A few have,' she said without stirring.

'How many is a few?' She turned and pressed her finger to his lips.

'A lady must have a few secrets.'

'Talking of secrets, you haven't told me who the powerful man was. Was it the Duke of Alva?'

'No, not him.'

'So who was it?'

Barbara paused for a few heartbeats.

'Charles the Fifth.'

'Holy Mary!' exclaimed Anthony sitting up in bed.

'Not Mary, Holy Roman Emperor, to be precise. I was young and a singer. He took a fancy to me. We had a child, but they took the boy away from me on the day he was born. I haven't seen the boy since, and that was the end of the affair. The duke kindly wrote to Philip, telling him that I was a widow now, and he granted me a pension.'

'Are you telling me that King Philip of Spain is your son?'

'Of course not, don't be so bloody cheeky, I'm not

that old! My boy was of course illegitimate, but yes, he is a younger half-brother of King Philip. Much younger!'

'So who is your son?'

Barbara smiled. 'You talk too much, Antonio Foscari, wine merchant. But who knows, you may yet sire the half-brother or sister of Don Juan, Duke of Austria. Now do you want to try again?'

Anthony kept making excuses to himself for failing to send a message to Walsingham. He found some work with a nearby wine merchant and was able to pay Barbara his due board and lodging. Barbara tried to refuse, after all he never slept in his room, but he insisted he pay what was due. She seemed to grow more and more attractive with every passing hour. The long nights of winter turned to spring and rumours began to spread around the city that a new governor was to be appointed to replace Luis de Requesens, who had died suddenly. Anthony decided he really should send a coded message to Walsingham and find out what he was to do next, but he also resolved to enjoy every single minute he and Barbara had together.

Weeks went by without a reply to his message. One Monday morning in early May 1577, Anthony decided that he would be late for work. The rising sun's golden light gave Barbara's skin an irresistible glow. His gentle caresses gradually woke her, and they fell once more into the unison of lovemaking. At the most inconvenient moment, there was a loud banging on the front door. 'Open the door. It's your long, lost son. I've come to see you, Mother. I haven't got long, I'm the new governor.'

Anthony rolled off Barbara, leapt out of bed, and pulled his breeches on. Barbara jumped out of the other side and pulled her dress over her head. They heard the patter of a child's feet running down the stairs and then the sound of the bolt being drawn back. Anthony pulled his doublet on, opened the window and swung his legs out. Heavy footsteps were pounding up the stairs. Anthony jumped for the nearest stout branch. As he swung himself down, he heard a loud voice from the window.

'Round this side. A half-dressed man. Seize him!'

Anthony's feet had barely hit the ground when two soldiers rushed towards him, the tallest a few paces in front of the other. He used the first man's momentum to throw him on his back and the second one ran into Anthony's punch to his solar plexus, and fell breathless. Anthony ran in the direction they had appeared from. He turned the corner to see another bemused-looking soldier holding the reins of four horses by Barbara's front door. He kicked the soldier's feet from under him, climbed into the saddle of the best looking horse, a black stallion, and rode for his life.

CHAPTER SEVEN

1576 - 1580, Flight to Constantinople

'I chose well. May I call you Lightning?' Anthony asked, bent low over the stallion's neck, running the fingers of his right hand through the new Lightning's mane. 'You beauty, you absolute beauty,' Anthony gasped, to the drumming of the hooves on the cobbled street as they galloped out of the city. He barely had to caress the reins as Lighting's pounding hooves dodged potholes with a deftness he hadn't encountered in a horse before. Lightning seemed to sense Anthony's urgency, through only a featherlight touch on the reins. His hair flayed against his neck as the wind pummelled his cheeks, but despite the speed, it was as though he were flying on a magic carpet. They soon reached open country, and the cobbles gave way to turf. The fresh scent of crushed grass rose to refresh him as Anthony eased Lightning into a canter, the stallion whinnying, steam rising from his neck. Anthony glanced back over his shoulder. Two riders were pursuing him, but they were no match for Lightning and were falling steadily behind. He reached Leuven by noon, rode through the city and continued on the road towards Liege. When he found a stream with grassy banks and a good view of the road behind him, he stopped and let Lightning drink and graze whilst he took stock. All he had were the clothes he stood in. He felt in his pocket and found he still had the tools of his trade. Then he noticed the saddle bags. In one, he found a pile of documents tied together with a ribbon. He started looking through them.

Oh my lord, he thought. I've stolen the duke's horse. In the other saddlebag, he found a purse full of gold ducats. No wonder I'm being pursued, he thought. Is it the gold or the documents? Or is it that he didn't appreciate finding a man leaping from his long-lost mother's window?

From his years as a dispatch rider, Anthony had a good mental map of the country. Although sunny, it was November, and he needed to find some warmer clothing and shelter for the night. At least he had plentiful funds now. He calculated that he couldn't get as far as Liege by nightfall, but could probably reach Sint Truiden. He could buy some clothing there and find a tavern. No, he scolded himself. They'll ask about any strangers riding in on a black stallion. He could buy a fresh horse with this much money. Anthony imagined townspeople being questioned by his pursuers.

'Yes, he sold me this horse in exchange for a bay mare. He went that way. No, he was wearing a red cape.'

He decided that there wasn't any point changing horses, particularly when he was riding the best horse in Europe. Lost in thought, he looked back down the road. Then he got up, pushed the documents and purse back in the saddlebags, and mounted Lightning. 'Come on, Lightning, we need to go.' They galloped off towards Sint Truiden with six horsemen in pursuit.

He looked over his shoulder again after a few miles. He still had six pursuers, but he was stretching out his lead again. When he got to Sint Truiden, he bought some blankets, bread, cheese, and carrots. Then he set off again towards Liege. When dusk fell, he left the road and headed towards some farm buildings. There was an oil lamp glowing in the main farmhouse, but there were also a few outbuildings. He made a circular approach around a field to ensure he wouldn't be seen from the farmhouse. He passed a pigsty then came to a barn. He dismounted and opened the large barn door. He led Lightning into the barn and closed the door behind him. He selected a few bales of straw and arranged his blankets. He cut open another bale for Lightning and then lay down to sleep. Although he was dead tired, his mind continued to race. Where would he be safe from these damned duke's men? Could he stay ahead of them until he reached Buda? He'd be in Ottoman territory then, and they daren't follow. On Lightning he could cover, perhaps, fifty miles a day. Two weeks should get him there. It will take me through Austria, being pursued by the Duke of Austria's men. You can't say it's not a daring plan. He should probably change those fine leather saddlebags, with the Duke's crest, for something less conspicuous though.

A very weary Anthony, and an equally exhausted Lightning, plodded through the city gates of Buda. It had taken them sixteen days of hard riding, sleeping in barns, caves, clefts in rock, forests and sometimes in the open. He found a promising looking tavern, tied Lightning up outside, and pulled the last carrot from the carpet bags that had replaced the saddlebags. He stroked Lightning and fed him the carrot. Then he hobbled into the tavern. The local language was incomprehensible to him, but he tried English, French, Spanish, Latin and finally found that the landlord spoke quite good German. There were several rooms available, and they would take his horse to the stable and look after him.

'Would you like dinner?' the landlord asked.

'Yes please. But first I'd like a bath. Could you arrange for a tin bath to be taken to my room and some hot water?'

'Sir, we are not barbarians.' Anthony looked puzzled. 'There is a thermal spa a hundred yards down the road. It has been here for centuries, but the Ottomans have greatly enhanced the facilities. It will be open for at least an hour more. Your dinner will be ready when you get back. Where are you from?'

'I'm English.'

'I haven't had an Englishman stay here for months, and then two arrive in one day. Are you travelling together?'

'No, I've travelled alone. I didn't know there was another Englishman within a hundred miles.'

'Then while you are bathing, I will ask Mr Harbourne if he would like to dine with you, with your agreement?'

'That would be very pleasant, thank you.' Anthony hobbled back out of the door and made his way down the road.

The two men sat opposite each other around a table piled with meats and vegetables. They were both ravenous after their journeys, and after initial pleasantries, ate and drank until they were almost bursting.

'Well, Sir Anthony, this is an honour. What brings you here?'

'Just Anthony is fine. It's a long story. Maybe another day. What brings you here, William?'

'I'm a merchant. I'm making my way to Constantinople, or Istanbul, as the Ottomans call it. I'm on government business.'

'Government business, that is interesting. Do you mind me asking who sent you?' William flushed with pride.

'None other than the Principal Secretary himself.'

'I have been away from England for many years.

Who is that now?'

'Francis Walsingham. Have you heard of him?' Anthony almost choked on his wine.

'Is Robert Clark still working as his secretary?'

'Well, Walsingham's brother-in-law, Beale, handles most things.' Anthony's gaze dipped to his wine goblet. 'Robert Clark handles the more sensitive correspondence. He gave me a list of fifty words to memorise, each one equating to words I might need to use in respect of that side of my business. Cipher Clark I call him.' William laughed, and Anthony smiled. 'Is it a sensitive matter that brings you here?'

'In a way. I was working for Francis in Flanders, but it was the Duke of Austria's men that chased me here. Well, as far as Vienna, anyway.' As they drained their second flagon of wine and ordered the third, Anthony and William were becoming much more comfortable with each other. 'Since you have a code to correspond with Francis, you must have a way of getting messages to him. I really need to send him a message and find out what he wants me to do next. Can you help?' Anthony asked.

'Of course. By far the fastest and most secure way is by ship. I have cargo plying back and forth between Constantinople and London. The ships I use can do the round trip in between two and six months, depending on the wind and how many stops they have to make. I'm only travelling overland because I also had business in Paris and Geneva. Why don't we travel on together to Constantinople, and I can send your message out on the first England-bound ship? It will be a great relief to me to have a travelling companion.'

'I've heard a lot about Constantinople and will be honoured to accompany you,' Anthony replied, smiling.

Anthony and William rode side by side through the city of Sofia.

'Why are you doing this work for Walsingham, Anthony?'

'When I left London and travelled to Scotland with Lord Darnley, we did so without Queen Elizabeth's permission. I've become tarred with the same brush as Darnley, and am not welcome in my homeland. My aspiration is that by working for Walsingham he will persuade the queen to let me return.'

'I see. And what about after that? What other ambitions do you have?'

'Just the usual things, make my fortune, build a big house, marry a beautiful woman and have children.'

'How is it going?'

'Up and down.'

It was Christmas Eve, 1576. The journey south east from Buda had been much slower than Anthony's flight from Brussels. They averaged around thirty miles per day. They rode side by side, talking much of the time, except when negotiating the narrow mountain passes.

'What languages do they speak in Constantinople, William?'

'Turkish, Arabic and Persian.'

'Do you speak these languages, William?'

'Lord no. I can detect the differences between them, but they are complete gibberish to me, in the main. I've picked up some of the greetings, like As-Salaam-Alaikum, which means *peace be with you* in Arabic. But that's about all.'

'So do the Ottomans speak English?'

'No. We rely on the services of what they call Ottoman minorities: Jews, Greeks, Armenians and

Christian Arabs. On my previous visits, Abraham, a Jewish physician who speaks Turkish, Arabic and English, has accompanied me. He's a fine physician too, gave me a very effective tea to ease my gout. A janissary will also accompany us. They are very professional soldiers and bodyguards. The Ottomans don't trust westerners very much. For a fee, they give us freedom to roam in some places, but always with an escort.'

'Where will we stay?'

'They have always provided a room in the palace, the Topkapi Palace, for me. You have privacy in your room, but there will be a janissary on guard outside your door. I think the best thing will be if I ask for a second interpreter to assist you while I'm conducting the negotiations. He can bring you up to speed on the etiquette required. Bow the wrong way, or use the wrong greeting, and at best you would wreck the negotiations and at worst lose your head.'

'I certainly don't want to do either. And I would love to learn these languages, and the culture. We're going to be here at least three months, aren't we?'

'Almost certainly.'

'May I ask what your negotiations are about, William?'

'Well, since we are both working for Walsingham, I suppose it can't hurt. The Ottomans have been trying to spread their empire through the Mediterranean and have been fighting the Venetians and the Spanish. They seized Cyprus from the Venetians in 1571, but the following year a combined fleet of Venetians and Spaniards, under the command of your friend, Don Juan, Duke of Austria, decimated their fleet at the battle of Lepanto. Sokollu Mehmed Pasha is the Grand Vizier, that's the William Cecil of the Ottomans, and the fellow I'll be negotiating with. He says that by seizing Cyprus, they cut off one of the enemy's arms. By decimating their fleet, the enemy shaved off the Ottoman's beard. An arm won't grow back, but a beard grows back thicker. Walsingham wants three things. First, he wants to encourage the Ottomans to continue to fight the Spanish. He says that there is more in common between Protestantism and Islam than between either and Catholicism.'

'How can that be so?'

'Idolatry, for example, Muslims abhor it too. Secondly, he wants to help the Ottomans rebuild their fleet and rearm. And thirdly, he wants to make a great profit out of it, for the queen, of course. We have an abundance of tin and lead from the Catholic monasteries and churches. The tin is essential for gun making and the lead is for canon and musket balls. The Ottomans have been having great trouble getting hold of it. It seems to be literally worth its weight in gold.' As they reached the top of a hill, they stopped and stared in silence.

'There she is Anthony, Constantinople. The sea to our right is the Aegean Sea. The sea to our left is the Black Sea. The strait connecting them is the Bosphorus. The land across the Bosphorus is the continent of Asia. The magnificent dome with the four turrets is the Hagia Sophia mosque. The great palace to its left is the Topkapi Palace, our destination.'

Anthony sat at the writing desk in the room he shared with William in the Topkapi Palace. It was a light, airy room with a high ceiling, decorated with fascinating geometrical patterns. A frieze ran around the room with Arabic calligraphy in gold lettering against a black background. A rainbow of light, from windows with red, blue and green glass, played across the walls. The soothing sound of cascading water drifted in from the fountain in the courtyard. William had set off for his first meeting with the Grand Vizier, so Anthony pulled the Duke of Austria's documents from his saddlebag and started examining them. There were half a dozen enciphered documents and two documents not in cipher. One was a commendation for gallantry for a Sergeant Cortez. He read it with interest. It was written in a beautiful hand, and had the duke's seal in red wax. The other was a draft proclamation, presumably destined for the printers. Next, he set about the enciphered letters where the secrets would lie. The cipher hadn't changed since the last dispatches he had deciphered, so the work was quickly done. The difficult bit was summarising the information for Walsingham. The key points seemed to be that the duke had orders to concentrate more on the south, particularly Namur and Gembloux. He was also instructed to raise taxes further to finance an expansion of the fleet and ambitions in Portugal. Anthony also learnt that the duke's secretary was a man called Juan de Escobedo. Anthony wondered what ambitions Philip might have for Portugal. Anthony remembered from his school days that Pope Alexander the sixth had brokered a treaty between Spain and Portugal in which any new lands discovered west of a line running between the Azores and the Cape Verde Islands would belong to Spain, and any new lands to the east would be Portuguese. Perhaps Philip wanted it all. Anthony wrote out in plain text his message to Walsingham before encoding it.

Have had to leave Flanders. Now in Constantinople with Harbourne. Luis de Requesens died and has been replaced as governor by Duke of Austria. His orders to move south and crush Namur and Gembloux. Also raise taxes for expansion of fleet and ambitions in Portugal. Duke's secretary is Juan de Escobedo. Please advise new orders. Cannot return to Flanders.

Yes, that seemed to cover the key points. Anthony then thought about the bit he enjoyed the most, creating an innocuous letter positioning the words of the message within it at a fixed interval. He could ask if Robert has had any news from his cousin in Flanders. Does she live in Namur or Gembloux? He could use reference to an English duke and invent some mutual friends, Juan Requesens and Luis Escobedo. Hopefully, they are common names. He could moan about taxes, then say something about Portuguese and Austrian wines, perhaps. Fleet, yes he could mention the River Fleet. Anthony then set about composing his encoded letter.

There was a knock on the door, and Anthony opened it.

'Good afternoon, my name is Joseph. Mr Harbourne has gained the Grand Vizier's permission to appoint me as your guide in the etiquette of our hosts.'

'Do come in Joseph, I realise I have much to learn.' Joseph entered and the janissary guard closed the door and resumed his sentry duty outside. They both sat on the large cushions, in the Turkish style, since there was only one chair. 'I am very interested in languages, Joseph, and fascinated by this Arabic script. I believe you speak Turkish and Persian too, is that right?'

'Yes, Sir Anthony. There is little similarity, I fear. Which would you like to learn first?'

'I'm not sure how long we will be here. At least three months, I believe, and possibly a lot longer. I would rather learn one language well than three poorly. This Arabic script is so strange and beautiful that I would like to start with that. And do call me Anthony, please.'

'Thank you, Anthony. Arabic it shall be then. But first we should talk about Islam, and the surrounding aspects of etiquette. Islam and Christianity, like Judaism, are Abrahamic faiths. They both accept the scriptures of the Torah, or for simplicity, what you know as the Old Testament. As you will know, Christianity is based on the teachings of Jesus. Islam is based upon the revelations of Muhammed. He was born in Mecca in the 6th century after Christ. When he was forty years of age, he was visited by the Archangel Gabriel, and received revelations from God, or Allah. He began preaching the revelations he had received and gained a great following. His revelations were recorded in the Quran. Like Christianity, what we know of the prophet's teachings is what was written down, in some cases many years later. Muhammed never claimed to be anything more than a man who had received revelations from God, whereas Jesus claimed to be the Son of God. Islam recognises Jesus as a prophet but does not accept a Holy Trinity. There can be no splitting the one true God into three pieces. You have admired the Arabic script on the walls and the ceilings, and I dare say the geometric patterns?'

'Yes, they are exquisite.'

'But you have seen no portraits or landscapes. That is because it is a sin to imitate God by making figural images. Whereas the Arabic script is the word of God, that God has given to us via Gabriel and Muhammed, to be communicated in a very beautiful style of calligraphy.'

'What is calligraphy, Joseph?'

'Calligraphy is simply writing in a decorative style, as an art in itself. We will work on that too if you like.'

'Yes, I would like to learn more about this beautiful writing.'

'Where was I? Yes, I think if Jesus and Muhammed

had met, they would find they agreed about most things. I suppose the biggest difference is that Jesus was crucified in his early thirties and it was his disciples who spread the gospel. Muhammed lived to his early sixties and had to confront great opposition from polytheistic tribes in Mecca, and the surrounding Arab lands. The early followers of Muhammad faced persecution and Muhammed had to become a warrior as well as a prophet.'

'So whereas the crusades came long after Christ, for Islam, the fighting was there from the beginning,' Anthony stated, testing his understanding.

'Yes, but Muhammed, didn't start the fighting, although he did become very good at it, thanks to God, of course. Now we should look at etiquette. Many of the customs are my customs also, because they stem from the Abrahamic tradition. You should only eat and drink with your right hand. You should drink in slow gulps. Meat from cloven-hoofed animals is not to be eaten. Meat must be carefully prepared. I will not go into the prayer times and rituals, because you will not be required to perform them, but I will now show you how to bow.'

Joseph stood up and demonstrated, placing his hands together above his head and bowing from the waist. Anthony copied him.

As Anthony became more and more proficient in Arabic, Joseph suggested a guided tour of the city, and Anthony was quick to take him up on the offer. Followed by the janissary, they made their way through the palace courtyards. Anthony stopped beside a flower bed full of the most beautiful red and yellow flowers.

'Joseph, what are these? I've never seen such beauty in a flower.'

'They're called tulips. They are rather special, aren't they? Don't you have them in England?'

'No, and I haven't seen them in Scotland, France or Flanders either.'

After a few minutes of sniffing and gazing at the tulips, Anthony moved on. Joseph exchanged a few words with the janissary in Turkish and they made their way through narrow, busy streets to the Bosphorus.

'I'm going to take you on a short ferry ride across to Galata. It's where I live.' Joseph spoke with a boatman and then he and Anthony, followed by the janissary climbed into the boat. The boatman used a long pole to push his boat away from the quay, then hauled the sail up and they quickly built up speed towards the walled town on the other side of the narrows. When they got there, Joseph paid the ferryman, who steadied them as they stepped, in turn, up onto the gunwale of the ferry and hopped onto the quayside. The quay was bustling with laden wagons, some drawn by horses and others by donkeys, spurred on by the crack of whips and a cacophony of shouting. Anthony's attention was drawn to a tower dominating the quay.

'What's that tower?' Anthony asked.

'That's the Galata tower. It used to be the tallest building in Istanbul. It's used now as a lookout post for any fires that might break out. It's also used as a prison and a storage facility. Most of the buildings here, by the Bosphorus, are taverns and brothels. They are particularly well frequented by sailors, merchants, local bachelors and the janissaries.' They continued through narrow streets before stopping beside a church. 'This is a Greek Orthodox church. There are eleven Catholic, nine Greek Orthodox, two Armenian churches and twelve mosques in Galata. This used to be a Genoese colony in Byzantine times. When the Ottomans conquered Constantinople, Galata surrendered quickly and was rewarded with a large degree of autonomy. That's why we still have the Christian churches, the taverns and the brothels, and why there is such a diverse population here.' Joseph continued showing Anthony around Galata, ending at his own small house. He made some mint tea for Anthony and took a cup to the janissary who was standing guard outside.

'Do you live alone, Joseph?'

'Yes, I'm afraid my wife died in childbirth seven years ago. The child died too. It was our first, and only.' Anthony watched a single tear roll down Joseph's left cheek.

'I'm very sorry, Joseph.'

'I have my work. I make a living. Now if you've finished your tea, we'll cross back over the Bosphorus and I'll show you the other sights.'

Joseph showed Anthony the Hagia Sophia from the outside, since non-Muslims were forbidden to enter a mosque. Then they toured the Grand Bazaar, with its glittering displays of goods, vibrant colours, smells of spices, and cacophony of noise. He was taken to the great parade area, which used to be the hippodrome, and finally returned to the palace. William was in their room when Anthony entered, weary, but excited.

'William, have you seen the beautiful flowers in the fourth courtyard? They're tulips, Joseph told me. I've never seen anything like them before, have you?'

'Only on my visits here.'

'Have you ever thought about trading in tulip bulbs?'

'Why would I? I know nothing about flowers. Cloth has been my stock in trade, and now precious metals. Stick to what you know, that's my motto. I can't imagine anyone paying good money for flowers when they grow in every garden and meadow.'

'Not flowers like these tulips.'

'Stick to what you know.'

'I suppose you're right.'

It was another bright summer day in 1578, when William returned to the palace from a visit to the harbour. Anthony was in their room conversing in Arabic with Joseph.

'I'm sorry, Anthony, I've got a dreadful headache. Do you mind cutting short your Arabic lesson?' William asked.

'Not at all. Would you like me to stay with you, or shall I take Joseph up on his offer of another tour of the city?' Anthony replied.

'Could you stay please?'

'Of course. I'm sorry, Joseph, can we resume tomorrow?' Anthony asked, turning to Joseph.

'Certainly. Your Arabic is coming along very well. I shall see you tomorrow at the usual time.' Joseph got up from his cushion and left. William waited until Joseph had closed the door and he heard his footsteps receding. He put his finger to his lips and crossed to the desk where Anthony was seated. He bent down and whispered in Anthony's ear.

'We have our replies from Walsingham,' he said, handing Anthony a sealed document. 'Do you mind if I decode mine first? I want to see what he says before I have my meeting with Sokollu Mehmed Pasha this afternoon.'

'Not at all, after you.' Anthony replied, getting up to let William use the desk. William sat down, broke the seal on his document, and started reading. Half an hour later, he stood up.

'The queen wants a higher price for the metals. This might take a while,' William whispered. 'Sorry, the desk's all yours now.' William stood up, folded his letter and put it in his pocket. Then he went to his bed, kicked off his shoes, and lay down.

Anthony sat at the desk and started work on his letter. It was much longer than usual. He started drafting out the extracted, encoded contents.

Plot uncovered to kill Elizabeth. Mary still big problem. Write a plain letter in your hand pleading with her. You are not allowed home, destitute in Florence, need a position. Can she help? Send your letter via William to me. I'll deal with it. With luck she will recommend you to her friend in Florence. Resume your work for me there.

Anthony tore the papers into small pieces and put them in his pocket. He would dispose of them later in the latrine. He felt bad about spying on Queen Mary, who had knighted him, but he was Queen Elizabeth's subject, and it was her he needed to please. He started drafting the letter to Mary Queen of Scots.

It was late March 1579 before the next letters arrived from Walsingham. Queen Mary had provided a letter of introduction and recommendation for him to Francesco de Medici, Grand Duke of Tuscany. She beseeched him to do whatever he could on her behalf. William had also received confirmation that the new price for the metals was acceptable and instructions to agree to the exchange arrangements. William had a further meeting with Sokollu Mehmed Pasha, the Grand Vizier after which he came back to the room.

'Anthony, everything is settled. We can leave at last. The ship that has just arrived has the first shipment of tin and lead on board.'

'Excellent! I can't wait to see what Italy is like. When do we sail?'

'Tomorrow. But first we have been granted an audience with the sultan, Murad the Third. Come on, we mustn't keep him waiting,'

Anthony followed William to the room where they were to meet the sultan. They were, as usual, followed by a janissary. When they entered the room, the bright colours, the geometric patterns and the Arabic calligraphy on the walls, floors, and ceilings again entranced Anthony. He followed William's lead in bowing and saying As-Salaam-Alaikum and Wa-Alaikum-Salaam, the peace be with you greeting. The sultan looked about thirty years of age, elaborately dressed, with a huge white hat and a large black beard. His voice was deep and soft, but clear. He paused after every third phrase for the translator to speak. He talked about how he hoped they had enjoyed their stay in the palace, and that the business had reached a successful conclusion. There were breaks when the sultan left and they brought sweet mint tea in for them to drink until the sultan returned.

'Where has he gone?' Anthony asked William discretely.

'It's always like this, in our meetings. There are regular prayer breaks and also harem visits. The tea is refreshing, is it not?'

'Yes very.'

When the audience with Sultan Murad the third was complete, William and Anthony went back to their room. The janissary took up his post outside their door.

'The sultan seemed a very decent man, very sincere and devout. The number of times he stopped the meeting for prayers, as well as the other,' Anthony said.

'Very much so, he is a great sultan.' William pulled Anthony closer and whispered. 'When his father died, he had his five younger brothers strangled.'

'What!'

'Quiet!'

'Sorry,' Anthony whispered. 'I have younger brothers, and the idea of strangling them, well it appalls me.'

'He didn't do it himself; he had a janissary do it.'

'That doesn't make it much better, does it?'

'No, but there is power in the harem too, you know. Each wife wants her son to be sultan, and they'll do anything to make it happen. He saw it as defusing an almost certain attempt on his own life.'

'I think I'm ready to go to Florence now, William. Let's get out of here.'

The ship was being loaded with provisions for the voyage. The tin and lead had been offloaded and stacked on the quayside. The largest set of weighing scales Anthony had ever seen had been set up nearby. It consisted of a trestle which supported a wooden beam about twelve feet long, with notches in the upper surface. Buckets hung by rope from the end notches on either side of the trestle. The beam was horizontal and the buckets about three feet off the ground. Buckets of gold ducats were on the ground nearby, guarded by a dozen janissaries. Two viziers selected some samples of tin and lead and took them away.

'Where are they going with those, William?' Anthony asked.

'A forge, probably. They'll do a fire test to assess the quality.'

'What's a fire test?'

147

'They'll take a sample and dissolve it in aqua regia. It's an acid. Then they'll put the solution in a vessel and put it in the furnace. Different substances give off different colour flames. They'll also melt a sample to see how much impurity there is in the sample.'

'Are we going to test the gold?'

'Of course we are. But we don't need the furnace. I have a touchstone, and this.' From his pocket, William produced a dark stone and a pencil of pure gold. They went over to one of the buckets of gold coins. A Vizier accompanied them. He selected a sample at random and rubbed it on the touchstone. 'Now I'll rub my gold pencil on the stone beside it and compare the colours in the light. As you see, they are identical. So, the gold in the ducat is of the same quality as the pencil.'

'I've seen my father bite into a gold coin.'

'Yes, that's a good test too. Gold gives a bit. Pyrite feels gritty.' William put the coin between his teeth and bit. 'Yes, it's good.'

They watched the horses being put in canvas slings, ready to be hoisted onboard the ship, using a mainsail halyard. Anthony went across to Lightning and stroked him.

'It's fine, Lightning. You're not going to enjoy it, but you'll soon be safely onboard. I'll come and see you, and feed you every day. You're not going to like the voyage much either, but you'll be fine.'

Then the sailors who had led the halyard to the anchor windlass started hauling and Lightning was lifted. Another rope ran from the top of the sling to three sailors on the quayside who kept it taut, holding the horse away from the ship's side until Lightning was above the bulwark, then they let out the rope and Lightning was lowered into the ship's hold. As William's horse was being readied for the same procedure, the viziers returned from the forge. Everyone gathered round as one of the buckets of the giant scales was filled with tin. The beam tipped until the bucket was on the ground. When the bucket was full of tin, two janissaries started tipping gold ducats into the other bucket, closely watched by William. When the beam was horizontal again, the janissaries stopped adding gold. They took the buckets down, carried the tin over to a horse-drawn cart, and loaded it. They tipped the gold ducats into a wooden chest, with stout brass straps which had a padlock. The process was repeated over and over until all the tin had been taken and a dozen chests filled with gold and locked.

A ladder was leant against the beam, and a man climbed the ladder and moved one of the weighing baskets to a position half-way between the pivot and the position it had been in.

'William, why are they doing that?' Anthony asked.

'The agreement reached is that the sultan would pay the weight of tin with an equivalent weight of gold, but only half the weight of lead in gold,' Anthony smiled. 'What is it, Anthony?'

'You're an alchemist. You've turned base metal into gold.'

The voyage was mainly pleasant. A summer voyage across the Aegean, through the Greek islands and around the boot of Italy, was a far cry from fishing and fighting in the North Sea, winter or summer. William was anxious not to deviate too far from his route back to England but agreed to land Anthony at Civitavecchia, a port near Rome. Anthony was perfectly happy with this plan, as he'd always wanted to go there. It would be less than a week's ride to Florence from Rome, and he would explore the city a little and make his confession. It was many years since his last one, and he had a lot to confess. He and his horse were put ashore at Civitavecchia on the 12th of July 1578.

CHAPTER EIGHT

1580 - 1587, Florence

It was on another beautiful day in late July that he reached the crest of a hill and caught his first glimpse of Florence. It was magnificent. The city nestled in the valley of the river Arno, and spread over both banks, although the main city was on the opposite side of the river to him. The city had a massive wall with battlements running around the perimeter on both sides of the river. He could see a tower and city gate in the wall ahead of him. From there, he saw a road leading to a covered bridge with what looked like two storeys above the bridge deck. From there, the road led past a complex of grand buildings, one of which had a tall tower, and then to a domed cathedral. He urged Lightning forward, and they rode down to the city gate. He showed a sentry his letter of introduction and was given directions to the Palazzo Vecchio, which it turned out, was the building with the tall tower. He crossed the bridge, which had shops on either side, and rode up to the door of the palace. He dismounted, tied Lightning to a post, and presented his letter to a sentry. The sentry called to someone else who was given the letter and went off inside the palace.

After what seemed like an hour, the man who had taken his letter from Mary Queen of Scots returned.

'The Grand Duke will see you. Please follow me.'

'What about my horse?' Anthony asked, stroking Lightning's mane.

'He will be taken care of.' The man turned to one of the sentries. 'Take the horse to the stables and see it is fed and watered.' Turning back to Anthony, he continued. 'This way, signor, come with me.' They entered the palace, passed through a courtyard, and then went up a flight of stairs. They went into an extraordinarily grand hall. Anthony had thought that Hampton Court Palace was grand, but this was in a different class. Anthony stopped and gazed around him and up at the ceiling. 'It is the Hall of the Five Hundred, signor, where the council meets. The frescoes and the ceiling paintings are all by Vasari. This way, signor.' At the end of the hall, the man knocked on a door and opened it. This was a much smaller room, but elaborately decorated. There were no windows to provide views outside, but small windows admitted light just below the roof. 'Your Grace, here is the Englishman, Sir Anthony Standen.' The Grand Duke was seated at a table with all manner of spirit burners, crucibles, and porcelain jars, together with four large books. The Grand Duke turned to face them.

'Thank you, Vinta, that will be all. Sir Anthony, Queen Mary, was a good friend of my late wife's. She says in her letter that she owes you her life and that you are a master linguist. What languages do you speak, other than English?'

'Your Grace,' Anthony said bowing, 'Latin, French, Spanish, Italian, German, Flemish, Ancient Greek obviously, and Arabic.'

'Arabic, did you say? Can you read Arabic?'

'Yes, Your Grace.'

'Then you may be of some use to me. I acquired some rare books that may hold great secrets of alchemy, but they are in Arabic. Where did you learn to speak Arabic?'

'I have just come from Constantinople, your grace. I was there for almost four years, with little to do other than study the language. I was well taught by a Jewish physician.'

'The Muslims harbour great knowledge in mathematics, astronomy, medicine and alchemy. Will you help me with my books?'

'I would be honoured, Your Grace. Alchemy is the art of turning base metal into gold, is it not?'

'It is that, and other things too.'

'I have seen it, Your Grace.'

'What have you seen?'

'Base metal turned into gold, Your Grace.'

'Where man, where?'

'In Constantinople, Your Grace.'

'How was it done?'

'I only saw it from a distance. There were many coloured powders used, Your Grace.'

'What colours? Do you remember the colours?'

'I will try to, Your Grace. I have a good memory.' There was a knock on the door.

'Damn it, who is it?' The door opened and the man Vinta came in.

'An envoy has arrived from Rome to see you, Your Grace. He says it is urgent.'

'Very well, Vinta, I will see him in the reception room. Take him there and I will join him soon. Then come back and take Sir Anthony to one of the spare rooms. Give him everything he needs. He will be my wife's secretary. And you will help me with my experiments, Sir Anthony.'

For his first few weeks in Florence, Anthony worked as secretary to Bianca, the Grand Duke's wife, in the mornings, and assisted the Grand Duke in his laboratory in the afternoon. He discovered that Bianca had been the

Grand Duke's mistress. It had been Joanna of Austria, his first wife, who had been a good friend to Mary Queen of Scots. Unfortunately, she had fallen down the palace stairs only four months previously. She had been heavily pregnant, with a son, who was still born, and she died the next day. The Grand Duke had married Bianca just two months later, in secret, and the marriage had not yet been publicly announced. There were five of the Grand Duke's children in the palace. The eldest was Eleanor, she was thirteen. There were two other girls, Anna, who was ten, and Maria, who was five. There were two boys, Antonio, his son by Bianca, who was two, and Philip, his only surviving son by Joanna, was one. Anthony didn't think Philip was very well. He had an unusually large head and often complained of headaches. Anthony had once seen him suffer a seizure.

He read the Arabic books, and they were certainly great sources of knowledge. The first one he read was about mathematics. His time at sea had shown him that there was a useful purpose to mathematics, so he read more diligently than he had at school. One thing he discovered from this is that if he described twelve coloured powders that were used in a particular sequence to turn base metal into gold, which he couldn't quite remember, there would be almost half a million permutations of those powders. If Grand Duke Francesco was as passionate about alchemy as he seemed, this should keep them going for a very long time. He also discovered that the fourth book was about alchemy, and it was a long book, so reading that to him and transcribing it for him would also buy a lot of time. There was a book on medicine which he found interesting. He took particular interest in a chapter concerning poisons, their sources, effects, and antidotes.

Anthony did his best to befriend the Grand Duke's secretary, Belisario Vinta, and other members of the palace staff. He discovered that the source of the Grand Duke's wealth and power had come initially from the family bank, the Medici bank. In the first half of the 15th century, it had become the largest bank in Europe, making vast fortunes. In the second half, it had fallen victim to bad loans and bad managers, and finally collapsed. The Grand Duke was still an immensely wealthy man, from the money the bank had invested in the textile industry, his porcelain and stoneware factories, but most of all in his political power, and the taxation he was able to raise from the people of Tuscany.

Anthony learnt that aside from his alchemy, Grand Duke Francesco's great obsession was his rivalry with the House of Savoy. The House of Savoy had much nobler ancestry than the House of Medici, but Medici had much more money. To Anthony, it appeared to be rather petty. It seemed to be all about who sat closest to the pope, or the emperor, at official functions. But however petty it may have seemed to others; it was of the greatest importance to Francesco and his opponent, Emanuel Filibert. The battleground for this rivalry, he understood, was the diplomatic circle, where no expense was spared to impress foreign diplomats.

By night, Anthony explored the palace, which was connected to a newer palace, the Palazzo Pitti, by a secret walkway. He used his lock picks to get into rooms he hadn't been taken to, and to open locked cupboards and drawers. He found old correspondence to and from Mary Queen of Scots, but it was all between her and the Grand Duke's first wife, Joanna. There wasn't even any mention of the Florentine banker Ridolfi, who had been at the centre of a plot to assassinate Queen Elizabeth almost a decade earlier. He learnt his way around the two palaces very well and found his way into roof spaces above the ceilings of several of the important function rooms. He had seen Francesco stop his work in the laboratory sometimes and use a spy hole he had made to observe and listen to what was happening in the Hall of the Five Hundred.

Anthony accompanied Francesco and Bianca on visits to one of their villas, Villa di Pratolino, a short ride north of Florence. It was nearing completion and had been built for Bianca when she was still Francesco's mistress. It was now being made ready to host their official wedding. The guest list included all the local dignitaries and as many foreign diplomats as could get to the wedding by the appointed date, Wednesday 10th June 1579. Anthony was very happy to have been asked to attend in the capacity of an interpreter. The Grand Duke knew how easy it was to misinterpret someone's meaning, in a language that is not your mother tongue. He didn't want any mistakes on the big day.

The marriage ceremony was held on the terrace of the villa. The sky was clear, the sun shone, and the guests were crowded around to watch. When the service was over, and the couple had kissed, to raucous approval, there was an interval before the speeches. Groups of guests spread out down the gently sloping garden path. The path was wide and ran down from the centre of the villa, with fountains on either side and jets of cooling water forming archways over it. Because of the heat, the groups of guests formed clusters along this path. Waiters circulated with trays of silver goblets, followed by more waiters with flagons of wine, and yet more with trays of sweetmeats. Anthony also circulated, appearing to be fascinated by the fountains, but listening to the conversations.

'I don't think we've met. I'm Ferdinando, Francesco's brother,' said an elegantly dressed man to another.

'I'm pleased to meet you; my name is Matteo Zane. I am a Venetian diplomat. Your brother, the Grand Duke, has received me many times. He is a most generous host, and a very interesting man.'

'Yes, he certainly is. Although I wish his generosity extended just a little more to his adoring brother. You have had a long journey from Venice, Francesco is indeed honoured.'

'It was no trouble. A diplomat is on the road much of the time. I am on my way to take up a post as Venetian ambassador to Spain, in Madrid, as a matter of fact. Do you live in Florence, Ferdinando?'

'No. I live in my villa in Rome. I am a cardinal, involved in administration mainly. My passion is collecting art.'

'That must be a very expensive passion.' A bell rang, everyone fell silent, and the Grand Duke addressed his guests.

'My wife and I would like to thank you all for attending our wedding. We know that many of you have had a long way to come. Dinner is about to be served, so I will keep this announcement brief. I officially announce that from henceforth, my darling wife will be Grand Duchess. I also officially announce that our son, Antonio, although my eldest son, will be second in line to succeed me, as Grand Duke, after Philip, my son by my first marriage.' Anthony was watching Cardinal Ferdinando, whose face had turned slightly red, his nostrils had flared, and his fists were clenched. This struck Anthony as curious. Did Cardinal Ferdinando consider that having been born illegitimate, Antonio should not be second in line to succeed his father as Grand Duke. Perhaps he held out hope that disease or an accident might remove Philip and make him, as Francesco's brother Grand Duke. Well, art collecting is an expensive hobby, as Matteo Zane had said.

On Thursday 29th March 1582, Francesco's son Philip died. He was only four years old. The household went into mourning. For weeks, Francesco didn't go near his laboratory. He only attended to the most vital business and otherwise paced the corridors of the palaces, or knelt alone in his private chapel. His brother, Cardinal Ferdinando, came to see him. They met in private, in the Grand Duke's office. Anthony had followed them there from a discreet distance. Through the closed door, he heard muffled shouting concerning Antonio and the succession. When the shouting stopped, Anthony walked quickly away.

A few weeks later, the secretary, Belisario, came to find Anthony.

'Anthony, his grace would like you to join him in his laboratory. He is trying to get interested in alchemy again.'

'Of course, I'll go at once. I'll just pick up some of the texts I was translating.'

'Anthony, there is something you should know. His grace is not well. I think it's the shock. His face has fallen a little on the right side. His right hand is always in a sort of claw shape, and he drags his right foot a little. I just want to warn you. He is sensitive about it.'

'Thank you, Belisario,' said Anthony, stroking his

beard.

Anthony was reading from the Arabic text on alchemy whilst Francesco mixed yellow and green powders in a crucible, using his left hand.

'Anthony, I don't think you told me why Queen Mary of Scotland said she owes you her life.'

'Your Grace, I was in the employ of her husband, Lord Darnley, as Master of horse, and travelled with him to Scotland for their wedding. Queen Mary had a secretary called David Rizzio. I got quite friendly with him. He was from Savoy, born near Turin, he said. Well, poor David made a lot of enemies, including Darnley's uncle. One night I was passing the queen's apartments and there was a great commotion. A group of ruffians, including Darnley's uncle, pushed past me into the apartments, seized David and dragged him off. The queen was heavily pregnant with her son, James, now King James of Scotland, and I managed to put myself between her and the ruffians. The queen was very grateful, and I was knighted. You could say that I saved both the queen and future, now King James.' The Grand Duke cast his eyes downward. 'Oh, Your Grace, that was insensitive of me, so soon after the death of poor Prince Philip. I'm sorry.'

'No, it's all right. I was just wondering. Eleanor is thirteen now, and I should find her a suitable husband. Do you think you could broker a marriage with King James? How old is he now?'

Anthony thought for a moment. 'He must be around sixteen now, Your Grace. What a perfect match. I can draft a letter to Bishop Ross suggesting it.'

In June 1582, Matteo Zane, the Venetian ambassador to Spain, came to visit the Grand Duke on his way back to

Venice from Madrid. Anthony was keen to know what Matteo had learnt, but couldn't think of a way to approach him directly. He went to find Belisario.

'Who's the fellow that just arrived? I saw him from my window. He looks familiar but I can't think where I've seen him before.'

'That's Matteo Zane, the Venetian ambassador to Spain. He was at the wedding.' Belisario replied.

'That's right, I saw him there talking to his grace's brother. Does he come here often?'

'Whenever he can. He likes fine wine, and his grace pays him generously for information concerning the House of Savoy. They'll be enjoying some wine this evening over a private dinner.'

Anthony wandered around the palace looking for the butler. Eventually, he found him supervising the laying of a small table for two in the Sala di Clemete VII on the first floor. It was a very warm day, and he noticed that the windows were open. He made his way up the stairs to the second floor. Directly above the Sala di Clemete VII there was the Loggiato, an open gallery. There was nobody around. He could hear the clink of plates being laid from the window below. He settled down and waited. Eventually, he heard Matteo's voice.

'Your Grace is very kind. It is good of you to see me.'

'Nonsense, Matteo, I enjoy your visits. Here, have some wine. It's a Sangiovese. I think you'll like it. Do you know what King Philip is doing with this additional taxation he has levied on us?'

'He's levied it on everyone, Your Grace. A lot of it went to pay for the conquest of Portugal.'

'But that ended last year.'

'Yes, Your Grace, but he is also building a great armada of the most powerful ships yet built. Nobody seems to know exactly why. There are many theories, of course. Some say he will invade England and depose Queen Elizabeth, putting Queen Mary of Scots on the throne. Others say it would be much easier to invade Ireland as a stepping stone. The English fleet is strong too, in their own waters. This armada is certainly a far larger fleet than would be required to seize the Azores. The Dutch Sea Beggars are still a great thorn in Spain's side, and so are the English pirates, so the armada may be to wipe both of those threats away and secure the Spanish sea routes to Flanders and the Americas.'

'And what is your view, Matteo?'

'I have good information that strategies have been made for all of those possibilities. My assessment is that King Philip doesn't yet know himself. He constantly changes his mind.'

The conversation drifted away to other subjects. Anthony listened until the end. He waited for the room to be cleared below, then he quietly made his way back to his room and began drafting a message to Walsingham.

Months went by, with little for Anthony to report. He continued reading and translating the Arabic books. From reading the book on medicine, he became convinced that Francesco had probably suffered a blood clot to the brain, and that he was likely to suffer another, which may prove fatal. He was not richly rewarded for his duties, but his purse was growing. If Francesco dies, what then? He wondered. The book recommended garlic and turmeric as helpful medications. He had tried turmeric when in Constantinople, and knew that it was plentiful in India. The Italian diet was already quite rich in garlic. He collected together his transcriptions and set off for the laboratory.

'Your Grace, I have translated these passages from one of your books in Arabic, the one on medicine. I think you should read this.' Francesco took the paper that Anthony handed to him and began to read.

'I see. You think this may be the cause of my illness. What is turmeric?'

'I came across it in the east, Your Grace. It is an orange/yellow powder made by grinding the roots of a plant called curcuma longa. It is grown in India.'

'I will make enquiries and purchase some. Orange/yellow, you say. Wasn't one of the powders you saw used in the transmutation of lead into gold orange/yellow?'

'Yes, Your Grace.'

'Well, that's it, man. Don't you see? You were in Constantinople. This turmeric may be the missing ingredient.'

'You may be right, Your Grace. It hadn't occurred to me.'

'This letter arrived for you, Anthony. Perhaps it may concern King James and Eleanor.' Anthony took the letter, opened it and began reading.

'No, Your Grace, although it is from Queen Mary. She was most distressed to hear of Joanna's death, and sends her condolences. She is desperately short of money and in great fear of her life. In short, she asks if you might be able to help her.'

'I suppose it might help advance the prospect of James taking Eleanor, if I help his mother.'

'Indeed it might, Your Grace.'

'I shall see to it. Where should the money be sent?'

'She is held in Sheffield castle, Your Grace.'

'Very well, I shall get Vinta to make arrangements. I suppose the guards will take their share?'

'Most probably, Your Grace. But the letter suggests

that she is permitted her own servants and small luxuries. She is also in poor health and needs medicines.'

'I shall be generous.'

Anthony continued to help the duke with his alchemy whilst studying the Arabic books in his spare time. The alchemy was once more interrupted by the death of Anna in February 1584. It was not until early in 1585 that a reply arrived from John Leslie, Bishop of Ross, and Mary's ambassador.

'Well, what does it say?'

'He has made every endeavour on your behalf, Your Grace. It seems that King James treads a very difficult path between the Scottish lords, Catholic and Protestant. He dare not at this time take a Catholic wife without fear of losing his delicate grip on the Scottish throne. He does, however, say that when he is more secure, he will give every consideration to the proposal.'

'Eleanor turns eighteen next month. How long does he expect me to wait? No, I must find her another husband. The Duke of Mantua seems interested. I shall invite him to the villa.'

In September 1585, a coded letter arrived from Walsingham. He was very pleased with the intelligence Anthony had obtained from the Venetian. In the meantime, it had been learnt that King Philip had agreed to finance the Catholic League. This had provoked Queen Elizabeth to sign a treaty with the Dutch, providing six thousand infantry and a thousand cavalry to fight the Spanish in Flanders. It had been a long and difficult decision, with Walsingham in favour of the treaty and Cecil against it. But now it was done. England was officially at war with Spain. Anthony was to divert all his resources to gaining more intelligence on the armada.

How was he supposed to do that? Matteo didn't visit on a regular basis. Though it had been three years since his last visit. And there were other diplomats. He could go to Madrid himself, but he'd lose the opportunity to eavesdrop on visiting diplomats here. And how would he profit from it? It was an easy life here. Money, a home, he could meet someone, marry, settle down, only a part of him still missed England.

Throughout the next year, Anthony worked with Francesco on his alchemy. The turmeric had arrived, and it did seem to be improving his health, but they hadn't yet found the right formula for turning lead into gold. There was always hope, though. Francesco's brother Cardinal Ferdinando was now a frequent visitor and taking great interest in his elder brother's health. Anthony was spending more time exploring the city, and had made a number of friends, mainly girls. Whenever Anthony sinned, which was becoming quite often, the solace of Catholic mass and confession was readily available. Life was good.

It didn't seem like a particularly significant day. Francesco was away in Rome, and Anthony was wandering through the palace a little bored. He hadn't been to visit the girls he knew in the city since his last confession. The feelings he had for them were shallow, physical, and temporary. He was wondering where Barbara was now, when he heard shouting coming from a room a little further down the corridor. The door was open, and he stopped outside. Inside the room, the Grand Duchess Bianca was trying to calm her stepdaughter, Maria.

'I know it's your birthday, and I'm sorry your father isn't here. That isn't my doing. He's away on business. Don't you like the beautiful doll's house he had made for you?'

'I hate it, I'm not a baby anymore.' Maria screamed as she picked the doll's house up and threw it against the wall. 'And you're not my mother. She died. My brother Philip died. My sister Anna died. Everybody dies.' Maria dropped to her knees and cried.

'Come and find me when you've calmed down,' Bianca said, turning to leave. Anthony stepped aside as she left. 'Perhaps you can talk some sense into her, Sir Anthony.'

'Do you mind if I come in?' Anthony asked.

'If you want. I'm afraid I'm not good company today,' replied Maria.

'I heard. So, it's your birthday today. How old are you?'

'Twelve, and I've already outlived all of my siblings except Eleanor and my half-brother, Antonio. Do you believe in God and heaven, Sir Anthony?'

'Of course, and you should call me Anthony. Can I call you Maria?' Maria nodded. 'You're going to ask me who created God and the Devil, aren't you?'

'Yes, why not?'

'Shall we go for a walk? I always feel better when I go for a walk. It clears my mind and helps me think.'

'I'd like that. Do we have to take a guard with us if we go out?'

'No, you'll be quite safe with me, I promise. Let's go to the park. Shall we get some bread from the kitchen and feed the ducks?'

'I think I'd like that.'

Francesca was sitting on a bench by the lake in the park. It was such a beautiful day in April. The spring flowers were bursting into life, the birds were singing and she had decided to do her sewing in the sunshine instead of cooped up in the house with her mother. She looked up from her sewing as a tall, handsome man and a girl approached. They stopped by the lake's edge. The man took some bread from a bag he was carrying and tore off a piece for his daughter. They both began feeding the ducks. Above the quacking of the ducks, Francesca could hear their conversation. She had probably been about the same age as the girl when her own father had died five years ago. It had been hard since then.

'So, who did create God and the Devil?' asked the daughter.

'That was a question I kept asking when I was a child. I got quite a few beatings for it, especially when I asked our priest. The official line seems to be that God has always existed, and that you just have to take that on faith, if you don't want to be burnt at the stake. So please keep what I have to say to yourself. I tried to figure it out myself, because I couldn't see how something could always exist. Surely something, or someone, must have created God and the Devil, but then what, or who, would have created the creator? Then one day, after a very long walk, I thought if the Devil is the opposite of God, then what if they sprang from absolutely nothing? What if nothing, at the beginning of time, split apart into the Devil and God, rather like the way that a credit balances a debt? Together they balance, add up to nothing, but broken apart, they exist as a debit and a credit. That way, I could see why both God and the Devil have to exist. Do you see? Why would a benign God create the Devil, unless God couldn't exist without the Devil?'

'I've never heard it explained like that before. So God went on to create heaven and earth, and the Devil created hell. Is that it?'

'Well, something did, and I haven't come across an idea that seemed better.' Anthony suddenly became aware of being watched. He turned and saw a beautiful girl smiling at him from a nearby bench. She had jet-black hair, like Barbara, but honey brown eyes. Her smile was similar, her lips full and inviting, but she was very much younger. 'I'm sorry, I hope we haven't disturbed you?' Anthony asked.

'Not at all. I have been quite entranced listening to you and your daughter. It made me a little sad, thinking about my own beloved father, who was taken from us when I was around your daughter's age. I raged against God then. I wish I'd had you around, back then, to calm me, rather than our priest and his platitudes.'

'He's not my father. The Grand Duke is my father,' Maria said indignantly. Francesca dropped her sewing and leapt up from the bench. She curtsied.

'Your Highness, I didn't know. Please forgive me,' Francesca pleaded. Anthony stepped over to her and picked up her sewing.

'I'm afraid your sewing seems to be in a bit of a mess. Can I help? I'm quite good at stitching. I learnt to sew when I was a fisherman.' Anthony asked, gazing into Francesca's eyes.

Anthony went to the park every day that he could, hoping to meet Francesca again. Unfortunately, Anthony's free time was usually in the morning, and Francesca's free time was more often in the afternoon. When he slept, Anthony dreamt of Francesca. Barbara's beauty seemed a distant memory, and his ambition to prove his worth to his father faded away. In its place grew a compulsion to build a large house for Francesca and the family they would have. Chance could not keep Anthony and Francesca apart for very long. After a fortnight of near misses, Anthony and Francesca met by the lake once more and he found that Francesca felt the same love for him as he felt for her. They arranged meeting times, and Anthony found a hiding place in an old tree where they left each other notes, if they failed to meet. They walked in the park and sometimes Anthony smuggled her into the palace. Francesca had never seen anything like it. They made love for the first time in one of the guest rooms.

'I'm going to make a great fortune one day, and marry you, and buy us a big house in the country, not as big as this, of course, but big enough. People will look at us as we ride by in our carriage and say, "there are Lord and Lady Standen." I want to make you very happy, my darling. We can have lots of servants to look after us and our children. I want us to have lots of children, do you? I so hope you do.'

'Yes Anthony, I do. But I don't need a big house, or servants, or a carriage. A big house would be lovely, but I'd be just as happy with you living in my mother's house.'

'It would be rather cramped, don't you think? No, we must have a big house. You'll see, it will be like heaven on earth.'

In September 1586, Anthony received another coded letter from Walsingham. A plot had been uncovered which implicated Mary directly in another plot to assassinate Queen Elizabeth. Mary had been moved to Fotheringay castle and put on trial for treason. A steady trickle of Jesuit priests into England was fast becoming a flood. The Catholic menace had to be stamped out. Any intelligence he could gather on priests making for England would be useful.

Anthony was troubled enough by the Catholics he had killed, but at least they had been trying to kill him and his friends. To turn his talents against the church and its priests seemed an unconscionable step. He thought again of the priests he had seen hung, the Martyrs of Gorkum. He thought also of the rape and slaughter he had seen committed by Catholics. Francesca, the girl he was now in love with, was Catholic. He hoped to marry her and build a big house in England, where they could raise a family one day. The queen who had knighted him was on trial for treason. Any minute now, the four horsemen of the apocalypse must surely ride in. He should make his confession again tomorrow.

In October 1587, Anthony was in his room translating some new Arabic texts which Grand Duke Francesco had bought when there was a knock on the door. Before he could speak, the door opened and Belisario burst in.

'Anthony, terrible news from the villa. His grace has had another stroke. Her grace has called the physician, but she has asked you to take your translations of the medical book there. She hopes it may help the physician. Take the turmeric too.'

'Of course.' Anthony collected the medical book translations, ran to the laboratory to collect the turmeric, stuffed everything in a bag, and hurried to the stable. He saddled Lightning and galloped across the city and out through the north gate on the road to Villa di Pratolino. He reached the villa in half an hour. A few servants were standing in a huddle outside. Anthony dismounted and ran up the steps and through the open front door. He heard voices from upstairs and ran up the stairs to the Grand Duke's bedroom. There were two bodies on the bed. Francesco and Bianca. Cardinal Ferdinando was giving the last rites to Bianca. Francesco wasn't breathing, and his eyes were closed. Bianca's face was red and swollen. Her breathing was very shallow. Anthony suddenly realised there was a man standing behind him.

'I am the physician, Giorgio Ascari. I am afraid you are too late.'

Bianca convulsed, opened her eyes, and stopped breathing. The physician stepped forward and closed her eyes. Cardinal Ferdinando walked across to Anthony.

'Sir Anthony. Thank you for getting here so quickly. Bianca told me she had called for you. She had high hopes for this powder. Sadly, it was already too late.'

'What happened to the Grand Duchess? It must have been very sudden.'

'I think she died from grief. Isn't that right, Doctor Ascari?'

'Well, it is possible. The redness and swelling is very odd,' said the physician, stroking his beard.

'Let us arrange a prompt burial, in case it was some sort of plague. I will make the arrangements,' said Cardinal Ferdinando. 'Sir Anthony, I will not be needing your services any longer. I shall be taking over my poor brother's duties and moving into the palace. You may stay on for a while until you find somewhere else.'

'I thought Antonio was to succeed the Grand Duke?' said Anthony.

'That will be all, Sir Anthony. Leave us please, I have burials to organise.' The cardinal left the room. Anthony turned to the physician.

'Doctor, the redness and swelling, the convulsions,

these are all symptoms of arsenic poisoning, aren't they?'

'Cardinal Ferdinando is a powerful man and even more powerful now. I think we would be wise to keep our conjectures to ourselves, don't you?'

Anthony rode back to the palace. He went straight to the Grand Duke's office, looked around him and got his lock picks out. He was soon in the office and went to the desk drawer, in which he knew Francesco kept his purse. Anthony quickly opened it and took half the contents of the purse. Then he locked up, went to his room, and composed a message to Walsingham. He encoded it, sealed it and addressed it to Robert. He rode to the Florence office of Thurn and Taxis and posted his letter. Then he went and found a room in a tavern, just around the corner from where Francesca lived with her mother. He had no intention of staying under the same roof as a poisoner, cardinal, or no cardinal. He would rather be near his love.

Anthony enjoyed some secretive weeks of passion with Francesca before a reply from Walsingham arrived at the Thurn and Taxis office. His new instructions were to go to Rome and hang around in taverns near the seminary. He was to look out for Englishmen studying at the seminary, find out who they were and their plans. Any intelligence on when they intended to land in England and at which port would be helpful. The message came with three hundred crowns to cover expenses. He bade one last, passionate farewell to Francesca and set off on Lightning for Rome.

It took him six days to reach Rome, at a more leisurely pace. He stopped in Siena, Perugia and Assisi. It was a slight detour but Anthony felt he couldn't miss seeing St. Francis's home town. He enjoyed the beautiful

Italian countryside and architecture, but he couldn't avoid the thought that he may just be delaying the time when he would be spying on fellow English Catholics. He stopped in Spoleto and Rieti before finally arriving in Rome on Thursday 16th November 1587. Anthony made enquiries and was directed to the English College on Via di Monserrato. He found a tavern nearby and took a room, which had a view of the college. He spent several days watching the comings and goings of students. He followed some of them, to see where they spent their free time. There was a tavern in Piazza Farnese that seemed to be popular with the students so Anthony spent his lunchtimes and evenings eating and drinking there.

On the third day he was there, two men sat at a table to his right and began speaking English. They appeared to be in their mid-forties. They ordered lunch and some wine.

'So Charles, you have a command again, congratulations! When is it you leave for Flanders?'

'In a week's time. I have some things to do before I take up my command under the Duke of Parma. And you, Robert?'

'In around a week I will make for Madrid. Claudio has offended King Philip in some way and I have to go to conciliate. There are more priests to be ordained next week and I would like to see them safely on their way to England before I leave for Madrid.'

The lunch arrived, and the conversation ended. When they had finished, they stood up and turned to go. As they did, the one called Charles glanced at Anthony and froze. He quickly composed himself and they walked away towards the English College. Anthony was slightly surprised by the reaction, but finished his lunch.

When they were about a hundred yards away from

the tavern Charles whispered to Robert.

'That fellow on the table to my left, the one eating alone. Did you get a good look at him? Would you recognise him again?'

'Yes, I think so, Charles, why whatever is it. He isn't English is he? We should be more careful.'

'No, he's Dutch I think. He spoke Dutch to the heretic wench, and Spanish to us. Whatever he is, he ruined my life. I was in Flanders, back in '72, commanding a troop under Fadrique, the Duke of Alva's son. We had seized Mechelen from the rebels. I was with my sergeant teaching a heretic wench a lesson when I found myself staring down the barrel of that fellow's pistol. He forced us to let her go, and then he…'

'Then he what Charles?'

'He forced us both to strip naked and run. We were the laughing stock of the Spanish army. I was never allowed to live it down. I lost all credibility and was relieved of my command. That Dutchman ruined my life. I want to know his name. Will you help me, Robert?'

Anthony sat at the table and wondered what to do next. He now knew that there were English priests soon to head for England. He knew that the ringleader was Robert, and there was an English soldier called Charles, who was going to fight with the Spanish in Flanders. He could give a description of them both, but that was about it. Walsingham would want more, so what should he do? He could go to the English College and try to enlist as a trainee priest. Robert saw him at the table beside them. If he knew he was English, he'd know he overheard their conversation. He'd wonder why he didn't just say there and then, he wanted to be a priest. Perhaps he could break into the college at night and look for a register of names.

That might work. But he didn't know the layout. Perhaps he could try to get a job there as a cleaner or odd job man. Maybe he could just watch the college and wait for a group to leave, then follow them. But all the way to the coast? They would probably leave in pairs, anyway. He was still wondering what to do when Robert walked back to the table.

'Do you mind if I join you?' Robert asked in English.

'Not at all,' Anthony replied before he realised he had answered in English.

'So you are English?' Robert said, sitting down. 'My name is Robert Persons. What is yours?'

'Anthony Standen, Sir Anthony Standen.' Anthony was cursing himself. This fellow was several steps ahead of him. He had been taken completely by surprise. It was reminiscent of the time when he was beaten up by Captain Rodriguez and his men, except this Robert Persons was using brains rather than brawn.

'What are you doing in Rome, Sir Anthony?' Robert asked.

'It's a long story.'

'I have plenty of time, I'm interested. Why not start at the beginning?'

So Anthony did. He told Robert that he was a Catholic and had served as Master of Horse to Lord Darnley. He talked about saving Mary Queen of Scots, then how he was out of favour with Queen Elizabeth and had to flee the country. He said he had been fighting for the Spanish in Flanders and had seen terrible sights.

'So you see, I'd had enough of fighting. I decided to come to Rome and find peace. I thought I might train as a priest.'

'I see. Do you know what the English heretics do with priests these days? They are hung, drawn and quartered. Around ten a month at present.'

'It needn't be like that. There could be religious tolerance. I know it can be so. I have seen Protestants burnt at the stake in Queen Mary's reign. Isn't that right?'

'There is only one true religion. The church of Jesus Christ, the universal religion, the Catholic faith.'

'As I told you, I am a good Catholic, and I have come to train as a priest.'

'Well you have come to the right place. I can help you. Do you know the English College on Via di Monserrato?' Anthony nodded. 'Then meet me there tonight, about nine. I have some things to do now but will introduce you to the college tonight. But now I must go.' They both stood up and shook hands. Then Robert walked off, his robe flicking from side to side, his head leaning very slightly to the left.

Later that afternoon Robert Persons and his friend Charles Neville met in a quiet backstreet near the English College.

'Charles, his name is Sir Anthony Standen. I'm certain his story about being a Catholic and fighting in Flanders is true. Well, you can verify that anyway. I think he is one of us, but I can't understand why he didn't approach us yesterday. If he isn't one of us, then he's a danger to the whole movement.'

'Leave him to me, Robert. I'll deal with him.'

'I arranged for him to meet me at the English College at nine tonight.'

'Excellent, Robert, I'm rather looking forward to this. This time I'll have the jump on him.'

It was dark, with just a little moonlight as Anthony

walked to the English College. There was nobody about. Then he thought he heard footsteps behind him. He looked around, and a man was directly behind him with a club in his raised right hand. Anthony stepped in close and used the momentum of the assailant's attack to throw him onto his back. Anthony kicked him in the groin, then got behind him and applied a choke hold. He kept the pressure on until the man went limp, then he released it. When the man came to, he started to struggle and Anthony reapplied the choke hold until he went limp again, then released it.

'I can keep this up all night if you want, or just finish you off. Now tell me who you are and why you attacked me.' Anthony said softly.

'Damn you to hell,' Charles rasped. Anthony applied the choke again.

'Actually, I can't wait all night, somebody might come along. So you will answer my question with your next breath, or it will be your last. Do you understand?' Anthony began to apply the choke hold again, and Charles nodded. Anthony eased the hold. 'Your name?'

'Charles Neville, 6th Earl of Westmorland.' Anthony was surprised but remained ready to apply the choke again.

'One of the northern rebels. You're lucky to have a head at all. What interest do you have in me?'

'You don't recognise me do you. But I'll never forget your face.' Charles gasped. 'The last time I saw you, you were pointing a pistol at me in Mechelen. You ruined my life.'

'That was you, about to rape that girl?'

'Heretic wench!' Anthony reapplied the choke and held it for a count of thirty. Then he got up. Charles was still breathing but unconscious. Anthony took a circuitous route back to the tavern, making sure he wasn't being followed. When he got to his room, he drafted a message to Walsingham.

Cover blown. Robert Persons head of operations. Party due to head for England. Charles Neville heading to Flanders. What next.

Then he encoded it, sealed it and addressed it to Robert Clark, c/o 26 Rue St. Honore, Paris. Anthony posted it at the Thurn and Taxis office and then lay low for weeks, hardly leaving the tavern except to visit the Thurn and Taxis office when he considered that a reply might be due. On the second visit a reply had arrived. He took it back to the tavern and decoded it.

Travel to Bayonne on the French-Spanish border. By the time you get there, our agent will be there. Visit the Cathédrale Sainte-Marie de Bayonne each day wearing a red scarf. Our agent will wear a green scarf.

Three weeks later he rode into Bayonne. He found a room in a tavern and after a bath, some food and a rest, he went to the market. He found a red scarf and bought it. Then he went to the cathedral. He walked around it several times before going inside. He walked slowly down the aisle, looking around for a man, or woman with a green scarf, but there were none to be seen. He turned around and left the cathedral.

'Are you Sir Anthony?' He turned around. A stocky man of about thirty, with long blond hair smiled at him. He was wearing a green scarf.

'Yes, who are you?'

'My name is Tom Lawson. Shall we take a stroll?' They walked to a corner of the graveyard where there was nobody about. 'Walsingham sent me. We are certain that the Spanish will launch their armada this year. He needs to know every detail of it. How many ships, how well armed, how many crew, how experienced the officers are, and their orders. We are to cross into Spain tomorrow and find that information. The Spanish are likely to intercept any post directed to England or our embassy in Paris. Therefore, I am to be your messenger.'

'How's your Spanish?'

'Not as good as yours, I'm told, but I've passed myself off as an Austrian speaking Spanish before. I've done this sort of work in Spain several times now. Where shall we start, A Coruña?'

'That's a sensible place to begin, a good part of the armada will be there. But some of it will be in Lisbon, some in Cadiz. No, let's go to the heart. We ride to Madrid.'

CHAPTER NINE

1587 - 1588, Spying on the Armada

The ride to Madrid took them ten days. They entered the city in late January, 1588. Anthony assumed the identity of a Spanish wine merchant, and Tom was his Austrian assistant. They found a tavern a few streets away from Government House and booked two rooms.

'How are we going to go about bribing officials, Sir Anthony? Here is all the money Walsingham sent, eight hundred crowns. Will it be enough?'

'We will not bribe anyone. It's too dangerous. It has burnt me in the past, and I know an easier way.' Anthony opened his saddlebag and pulled out some expensive paper he had bought in Burgos. He got out some quills, ink, and his penknife. He started writing himself a commendation for gallantry, modelling it on one he had seen when he was a dispatch rider in Flanders. He used the fine calligraphy he had learnt in Constantinople, and embellished it with citations of his extreme courage under fire, and his record of exemplary dispatch riding, which bore no equal in all of Flanders. Searching through his bag, he found a signature of Don Juan, Duke of Austria, together with his wax seal, that he had torn off a document he found in Lightning's saddlebags, all those years ago. He copied the signature and prised off the seal with his knife. He used a candle to melt a little wax on the back of the old wax seal and then set it on his commendation. He passed it to Tom. 'Tomorrow I'm going to see if I can get a job as a dispatch rider again. I will make copies of all dispatches before I deliver them. Then we'll decipher them and you can deliver the relevant ones to Walsingham.'

'That's incredible! How will you open the dispatches and then seal them again? They might not come off as cleanly as that did just now. And how will you decipher them?'

'Have you met Robert Clark?'

'Walsingham's special secretary?'

'Yes. He taught me.'

The following day, Anthony went looking for a market. He selected some cheap clothing that would fit him, and some second-hand shoes. He went to a small park and distressed the clothing in some soil. Then he went back to the tavern and changed into his purchases.

'My god you look a state, Anthony,' said Tom.

'Wish me luck, I'm off to Government House job hunting. If I'm successful, I'll be in uniform so I won't come back here. After you've had breakfast, wait for me in that olive grove outside the city gate. The one through which we entered, on the road from Burgos. Do you remember it?'

'Yes.'

'Bring lots of paper, the pens and ink. Buy some lead, and every colour of sealing wax you can get, oh, and some plaster of paris, a full water flask, and a long-handled metal spoon. We'll also need a thick leather glove. When you get to the olive grove, start collecting firewood. Bring a flint and a steel. Have you got all that?'

'Yes, and good luck.'

Anthony went to Government House, waited and watched. He saw dispatch riders coming and going. When he saw one that had just come out of Government House and was about to mount his horse, Anthony approached him.

'Hello, I used to be a dispatch rider in Flanders. Since then, I've fallen on hard times.'

'I've got no money for a beggar. Be off with you!'

'No, it's not that. I thought I might gain employment again, dispatch riding. Where's your sergeant?'

'Over in that building.' He pointed towards a smaller building with a stable block. 'Ask for Sergeant Gomez.'

'Thank you,' Anthony said, and walked over to the stable building. He found a sentry standing by the door of the building. 'I'm looking for Sergeant Gomez. Is he here?'

'Yes, have you got any identification?'

'I have this commendation from my service in Flanders. I'm looking for a job now. You seem to be very busy.'

'We are. Seems all right,' said the sentry, reading Anthony's commendation. 'Third door on the right down the corridor.'

'Thank you.' Anthony went down the corridor to the door and knocked.

'Come in.' There was a desk in front of him with a stout man sitting behind it, reading. Behind him, on the wall, was a large wooden board with a map of Spain painted on it. Holes had been drilled into the board at town and city locations, and there were about a dozen wooden pegs with coloured stripes on them in the holes. 'What is it?' the stout man said, looking up.

'I'm looking for work, sergeant. I was a dispatch rider in Flanders from '72 until '76. Then I was wounded and fell on hard times.'

'I can see that. Do you have your discharge papers?'

'I have this, sergeant,' said Anthony, handing the

sergeant his commendation.

'I knew the duke. He was a tough man. Half-brother of the king, by some slut.' Anthony clenched his right fist behind his back, not saying a word. 'He didn't write many of these. So if you were all right for him, you're all right for us. Let's get you kitted up and out of those rags. I'm Sergeant Gomez, Private Pellegrini.'

Sergeant Gomez took Anthony to a storeroom and picked some uniform clothing from a shelf and handed them to Anthony.

'Try these on.' While Anthony was changing into the uniform, Gomez took some boots out of a cupboard and put them on the floor next to Anthony. 'Yes, they look like they'll be a reasonable fit. Try the boots.' Then Gomez took a wooden box from a cupboard. 'There's a pistol in here, standard issue matchlock. Steel and flint here for making a fire to light the match, flask of gunpowder and some lead balls. There's a stick of lead and a mould for making more balls if you need to. Is that all clear?'

'Perfectly, sergeant. We were always being shot at in Flanders. It's not the same within Spain, surely?'

'You'll be surprised. There might be the odd spy about, but mainly it's the taxes.'

'Taxes, sergeant?'

'The tax is so high that the peasants will shoot you for the meat on your horse, particularly in the mountains. I dare say they'll eat you, too. The run to the north coast is the worst, crossing the Picos de Europa. We lose a lot on that run, but it has to be done. Let's get you a horse.' They went across a courtyard to the stables. 'You can have this one. His last rider called him Lucky.'

'Is he, lucky that is?'

'The horse is, the rider wasn't.' Gomez took a pair of

leather saddlebags with the royal crest embossed from a peg and handed them to Anthony. 'Right, you know where your horse is. Bring your saddlebags and your gun back to the office and we'll get you a map and your first dispatches.' On the way back along the corridor to his office, he opened a door to a large rectangular room with six bunk beds. There was also a table and benches on the two long sides. 'This is the rider's mess. If you're here waiting for a job, you can take any bunk that's free. A jug of ale and some food will be brought to the table at meal times.' He closed the door again, and they went back to his office. He looked through a pile of dispatches and studied the wooden board. 'Well normally I wouldn't give a new recruit the Coruña run, but it's the most important run at the moment and all my riders are out. Anyway, you're an old hand.' He moved one of the coloured pegs on the board to the Valladolid hole. 'Perez should be there by now. So take these dispatches to the admiral's headquarters in Coruña. It's in the port. Here's a map. Bring the reply back here. Any questions?'

'No, sergeant.'

'Right, on your way. Good luck.'

Anthony went back to the stables and saddled his horse. 'Well Lucky, I hope you're going to be lucky for me.' He attached the saddlebags, put the gun case in one and the dispatches in the other, and rode out of the stables. He urged Lucky into a canter when he reached the road to A Coruña. When out of sight of the building, he turned towards the Burgos road. It was, in fact, only a minor diversion, as Burgos was to the northeast and Coruña was to the northwest. He found Tom waiting for him in the secluded olive grove.

'Did you get everything, Tom?'

'Yes, it's all here.'

'Excellent. Start making the fire and get it lit. I'll make the plaster cast of the wax seals.' Anthony went through the routine he had learnt from Robert Clark. While he waited for the plaster casts to dry, he began opening the dispatches. 'Tom, when you're happy with the fire, start copying out these dispatches. I'll do these two and you do those.' They worked quickly and quietly. When they had finished, Anthony melted some lead and poured it into the plaster cast. When it had cooled, he broke the cast used the new lead seal to reseal the dispatches with the red wax. 'Tom, take these copies back to your room in the tavern. Buy a metal box from the ironmongers on the way. Make a second copy of each, and put the second copies in the metal box and put it on a ledge I found in the chimney above my fireplace. Make sure you pay innkeeper well for our rooms and that he'll keep them for us while we're away. Then get the first copies back to Walsingham and return as soon as you can. If I'm away when you get back, have a look in the box. If I've had new dispatches, I'll copy them and put a 2 at the top. I'll put them in the box, ready for your next delivery. Is that clear?'

'Yes, but why the second copies?'

'Because I want to decipher them myself, so that I know Walsingham is getting everything he may want. If it's just routine stuff, we may need to resort to other methods.'

Charles Neville, 6th Earl of Westmorland, had fought his way back from disgrace to command seven hundred English Catholic fugitives serving Alexander Farnese, Duke of Parma. They were garrisoned in Antwerp, awaiting the arrival of the Spanish Armada. Their army numbered 30,000 men. The Duke of Guise also had

12,000 men waiting in Normandy to assist them. The armada would soon sail up the English Channel, crushing the English privateers, gathering the massed Catholic forces and landing them on English shores. It could not be long now before the heretic Queen Elizabeth was brought to justice and English Catholics would be free again. He would recover his confiscated lands, and best of all, he would hold his darling wife Jane again, and his four beautiful daughters. He might even have grandchildren by now. He knew the size of the Armada, and that nothing could stop them now.

When Anthony arrived back in Madrid for the fourth time from Coruña, he was exhausted. They had shot at him several times in the mountains, as predicted, and only by hard riding and Lucky's speed had he survived unscathed. He had gathered some good intelligence from the dispatches he had copied. He had discovered that the total strength of the Spanish fleet was 127 ships of all sizes. Twenty were warships or armed merchantmen and four were galleasses or super-galleys. The largest ships were about a thousand tons. He had also found references to Admiral Santa Cruz's earlier plans for the armada requiring no less that 510 ships, of which 150 must be galleons, 40 heavy transports and 320 auxiliary craft. The number of sailors required to man them would be 30,332 and 65,000 soldiers would be ready for the invasion.

Anthony reported for duty to Sergeant Gomez, who looked Anthony up and down and examined his horse, Lucky.

'I think I've squeezed as much out of you as I can on the Coruña run for a while. You can take the Escorial run for a week or two to recover.'

'Escorial?'

'El Escorial. It's the king's new palace and monastery at San Lorenzo, half a day's ride northwest of here. You can't miss it, it's huge. Take these. They've just arrived for the king from Flanders.' Anthony took the dispatches, mounted Lucky, and rode off. When out of sight, he turned and headed for the tavern to find Tom. He took off the uniform items that identified him as a dispatch rider and hid them in the stable. He found Tom in the bar.

'Tom, I'm going up to my room. Bring me a flagon of ale, please, I'm exhausted.' Ten minutes later, Tom gave a coded knock on Anthony's door and Anthony let him in. 'Thank you, Tom, I really needed that,' he said, downing half the ale in a few large gulps. 'I've got some documents here for the king from the Duke of Parma. I'll need you to get them to Walsingham in double quick time. Can you help me with copying them out?' As they worked, Anthony let out a whistle. 'These are pure gold. Santa Cruz proposed a plan for the armada to establish a base in Ireland or Cornwall, but Parma wants to invade Kent from Flanders under escort from the armada. But whereas Parma had thirty thousand men available last year, now disease and desertion have reduced him to eighteen thousand. I may carry dispatches to and from the king for only a week or two, and we need to make the most of it. Can you think of some way you can relay these on, from Bordeaux perhaps, and get back here for the next lot?'

Tom stroked his beard for a moment. 'Yes, I'm sure I can.'

Around noon the following day, Anthony emerged from some woodland on a hill above San Lorenzo. Gomez had been right. The palace was enormous. It was a monstrous block of grey, with a domed tower in the front centre and a turreted tower in each corner. From his vantage point, he could just make out a subdivision into perhaps a dozen internal courtyards. He rode down to the palace, presented his credentials to the sentry at the guardroom and was directed to the courier's stable block. They took his dispatches from him and rushed off to the king. They showed him to the messroom where he could get some bread and cheese and ale. After an hour, the king's secretary arrived with some dispatches for him to take back to Madrid.

The next few weeks were critical. Document by document, he discovered that Admiral Santa Cruz had died and been replaced by the Duke of Medina Sidonia. He learnt that the king's direct orders to the duke were to sail up the channel and rendezvous with Parma's forces in Flanders. The armada would then escort Parma's army to land on or near the Kent coast. There was to be no divergence from these orders and the armada was to avoid conflict with the English navy in the channel.

The day after he had passed on the king's direct orders to the armada, Sergeant Gomez judged Anthony fit for the Coruña run again. Anthony realised what incredible good fortune it had been for him to have been assigned to the Escorial run at just that time. God really must be on the English side.

On Wednesday 20th March 1588, Anthony delivered dispatches from Government House in Madrid to the Admiral's House in A Coruña. He had copied it in the much-practised way before resealing it, and gave the copy to Tom. They had been working a faster system of delivery since late February in which Tom would deliver the copies to another of Walsingham's spy masters, Anthony Bacon, in Bordeaux. Tom would then ride back to Madrid for the next dispatch, whilst Bacon sent a messenger to London with the first dispatch. It ensured a faster supply of intelligence back to London.

As Anthony rode out of the city, he looked back from a hill overlooking the harbour. He decided he had a little time and stopped to let Lucky graze on the grass. He took his saddlebags down and got out some paper, pen, and ink. He sat down on the grass and put his saddlebags on his lap to rest the paper on. He started sketching the harbour. He had done little drawing since he was at school, but he remembered that his tutor, Mr Dobson, had said you must spend nine tenths of your time looking at the subject and one tenth drawing. Mr Dobson had thought he was quite a promising artist. He tried to draw, as accurately as he could, the size of the ships, the rigging and the number of gun ports. It might be of no use to Walsingham, but it would make a nice souvenir.

'What are you drawing?' asked a girl's voice. Startled, Anthony turned to look at her.

'The harbour. It's quite a sight, isn't it?'

'Yes, I've never seen so many ships. Do you think they're full of gold?'

'Possibly.'

'If you've finished, you can draw me if you like.' She sat down on the grass, ran her fingers through her hair and looked towards the harbour. 'My name's Anna, what's yours?'

'Antonio.' He wondered why he'd used that alias. He was Pompeo Pellegrini at the moment. He started drawing her.

'I'm thirteen now. My father wants me to marry a banker. They have lots of money, he says, but I prefer artists and musicians. Artists can make a lot of money too, I expect.'

'I think they can if they're very good. They're worth more dead than alive, you know, artists,' murmured Anthony, drawing quickly.

'How do you mean?'

'Well, when an artist dies, his paintings become much more valuable, or so I'm told.'

'Why is that?'

'I don't know. I suppose that because they won't make any more paintings, they become rarer and more valuable.'

'How old are you?' Anna asked.

'Much too old for you.'

'I don't know, I could have it both ways.'

'How do you mean?'

'I could enjoy you while you're alive, and sell your paintings for lots of money when you die,' Anna said, stroking her hair.

'You're very romantic.'

'I know. My father says I'm much too romantic. Have you nearly finished yet?'

'Almost, just a bit more shading here. There.' He handed his drawing to Anna.

'It doesn't look anything like me.'

'No, you're right.' Anthony stroked his beard. 'It looks like someone else.'

'She's very beautiful as well, though,' Anna said, handing the drawing back. 'Does she have a name?'

'Yes, Francesca,' Anthony said, staring at the drawing.

'Well, I can see I'm going to have to find another artist,' Anna said, getting up. 'Adios Antonio!'

On the first day of June 1588, Anthony and Tom were sitting in Anthony's room in the tavern.

'The armada has sailed, Tom. I saw them go. We've done all we can. It's up to Walsingham now. What's the news from London?'

'They're delighted with the intelligence we provided; it was everything they could possibly want.'

'So they should be. The last dispatch you delivered had the king's orders to the overall commander, the Duke of Medina Sidonia, with precise details of what to do in any eventuality. He doesn't leave anything to the initiative of his commanders.'

'What now then, Anthony?'

'Well, I'm going to disappear as far as Sergeant Gomez is concerned, and take a well-earned rest in Madrid. You find out from Anthony Bacon what Walsingham wants us to do next.'

'What do you hope our orders will be? It's been a long time since you left England, hasn't it? Do you miss the old country, Anthony?'

'I think so, but it might be my family I miss. I think that must be it, because France and Spain are quite beautiful countries, and I can mix in like a native, so I guess it is my family, but I'm in no rush to get back.'

'Why not?'

'Well, I'm not welcome. The queen was very put out that I went to Scotland with Darnley without her permission.'

'Surely after this, that will change. You gave Walsingham everything he wanted. What more could they want?'

'You're right, Tom, it's not just that. I need to make a success of myself. I need to make a fortune and show my father that I'm a success. I was knighted by Mary Queen of Scots, you know, but nobody recognises it. The trouble is, every time I make a bit of money, I lose it again. I want him to be proud of me, Tom, like he's proud of my brothers. And mother, too, I want her to be proud. Then I intend to build a large house and marry. I need to make my fortune. That has to be my top priority. But first I think we've earned a good meal and a flagon or two of wine, don't you? Let's go downstairs.'

While he was waiting for Tom to get back, Anthony found a tailor and had himself measured for a fine new suit of clothes. He was expecting to be richly rewarded for his work. He had agreed with Tom that if anybody asked, he had, in fact, bribed secretaries within Government House and the naval bases to make copies of the dispatches. The bribes had of necessity been very large, and Anthony had borrowed heavily to make them. If they declared what they'd actually done, and that it had cost them nothing, what could they expect their reward to be? He had agreed that Tom would get a third share.

He went back to the tailor's after a couple of days and tried on his new clothes. There were some minor alterations required, but he left the tailors feeling like the nobleman he should rightly be. He was passing a tavern near Government House that was busy with customers sitting outside in the warm June sunshine when he heard a shout.

'Hey, Foscari, I never forget a face or a name. Come and join us.' Anthony turned. It was Don Francés de Alava, the Spanish ambassador to Paris who had thought he was a Venetian spy. What was it, twenty years ago? Anthony went across to the table where Don Francés was seated with another impressive-looking man. They shook hands and Anthony sat down facing Don Francés. The other man introduced himself as Don Juan de Idiáquez.

'This fellow, Juan, is probably the best spy the

Venetians have ever had. I came across him when I was our ambassador in Paris. Of course, he wasn't able to fool me. I caught him red handed trying to bribe my secretary. Initially I had him beaten up, but later I decided to turn him to working for us. Isn't that right, Foscari?' Anthony smiled and nodded. 'Well, you wouldn't believe the information he was able to get me on the English and the French. High quality stuff. The fellow can even walk through locked doors. He's expensive, of course, but well worth it.'

'So what are you doing here in Madrid?' asked Don Juan de Idiáquez.

'The doge wished me to advise on how likely I thought it was that the armada would be successful. Unfortunately, I was too late. I am informed the armada has already sailed.'

'You are well informed,' said Don Juan de Idiáquez.

'We may have need of your services again,' said Don Francés. 'How should we contact you?'

'I am based in Paris again. The Venetian embassy there uses a wine merchant, Lavigne, as a letter drop. If you have a message for me, have it addressed to me and delivered there.'

'Yes, I know the place,' said Don Francés. 'Do have a goblet of wine.' Don Juan remained silent with the palms of his hands pressed together and his fingertips resting against the tip of his nose. Finally, he spoke.

'Actually, Signor Foscari, I think there is something you could do for us now. We are interested to know the intentions of Henry, King of France. He has made serious concessions to the Huguenots. Perhaps you could gather some intelligence for us. Would fifty ducats now and fifty more on receipt of suitable intelligence on his intentions, particularly with respect to the Duke of Guise, be sufficient inducement?' Anthony's thoughts tumbled for a few seconds. It might be some time before he received new orders from Walsingham, and he could make some money from the Spaniards. Whatever he discovered might also be valuable to England. He could see no harm in spying on the French, only profit.

'Yes, I think so,' said Anthony. 'How shall I communicate with you?'

'I will give you a letter of introduction to our agent in Bordeaux. He has been striving to gain such intelligence, but sadly, he cannot walk through locked doors. You may have more success.'

CHAPTER TEN

1588 - 1592, Bordeaux & Spain

On the twelfth day of June 1588, Anthony arrived in Bordeaux. He took out the letter of introduction to the Spanish agent and looked at the map drawn on the back. He located the address and knocked on the door. Two knocks, count to five, and then four more knocks. A middle-aged man with short cropped hair and high cheekbones opened the door and invited him in. Anthony handed him the letter and was led through to a sitting room.

'Please sit.' Anthony pulled a high-backed chair out from a table and sat down. The man paced the floor, reading the letter. Then he sat down and turned to Anthony.

'There have been some recent developments, news of which will not have reached Madrid yet. Henry Duke of Guise has marched into Paris and forced King Henry to flee. Henry… sorry, you look perplexed, you're not alone in that. This affair is becoming known as the War of the Three Henrys. The King of France is Henry III. When he was young, he flirted with Protestantism and called himself a little Huguenot. His mother kept him in check and he became a good Catholic, plotting St. Bartholomew's Day, for example. Yet he has become an appeaser of the Huguenots, and an opponent of the Catholic League. He is more interested in the arts than war or hunting, and his sexuality is, well, let us say ambiguous. He has not produced an heir, nor as far as we know any offspring at all, so his heir is his cousin King

Henry III of Navarre, a Protestant. So these are the three Henrys. Henry Duke of Guise, founder of the Catholic League. Henry King of Navarre, who, God forbid, could be a stoutly Protestant king of France, and the current King Henry, who swings both ways, as it suits him, in more ways than one.' The man chuckled. 'Sorry I haven't introduced myself. I'm Maurice. What's your name?'

'André Sandal,' replied Anthony. 'They have sent me to spy on the king of France. I understand you have had little luck.'

'Not for the want of trying. I've tried bribing servants, but it hasn't got me very far. A kitchen maid could tell me what his likes and dislikes are at the table. I could have him poisoned if I received the order. But what his plans are, I haven't discovered. Now that they have displaced him from Paris, it might be easier.'

'Do you know where the king is now?'

'I'm afraid not. But now that Guise has taken Paris, I suppose he will have inherited some staff that may have been left behind during the king's flight from Paris. A secretary may have been visiting a sick parent, for example, and come back to find his master gone. There may have been papers left behind.'

'It's a bit of a long shot.'

'Yes, but I don't know what else to suggest.' Maurice shrugged.

'Very well. Paris it is then. Is there some sort of introduction you can give me that will get me an audience with the Guise Henry?'

'Oh yes, that's easy. There have had to be many code words and secret signs established for the Catholic League. I'll write you a letter.'

It took eight days of hard riding to reach Paris. As

Anthony entered the city and saw Notre Dame, he thought about how much had happened in the twenty-one years since he first saw the cathedral. He'd killed and nearly been killed. He'd loved and lost. He had come very close to making his fortune, then had it snatched from him. He rode to the Louvre Palace, dismounted, and presented his letter to one of the sentries.

'Wait here, sir, I'll get someone to take this to the duke.' The sentry marched off. Anthony paced back and forth, gazing up at the palace, admiring the immaculately manicured gardens, and wondering where his latest adventure was going to take him. He desperately hoped he would make his fortune and be able to build a big house and settle down with Francesca. After an interminable wait, the sentry came back. 'This way, sir.' The sentry led him through the palace corridors with their high, ornately decorated ceilings. After the palaces he had stayed in, in Florence and Constantinople, Anthony was difficult to impress, but this was indecently decadent. He was shown into a room with impossibly impressive chandeliers and exquisite furniture. 'Here he is, Your Grace.' The sentry bowed, the duke nodded, and the sentry turned and left, closing the door behind him. The duke was perhaps a few years younger than Anthony, finely dressed, and bore a deep scar on his left cheek. Sitting beside him was a very attractive woman, who Anthony assumed was the duchess. Anthony bowed to them both.

'Your Grace, Your Grace.' The duchess chuckled. The duke spoke.

'A simple mistake to make, Monsieur Sandal. May I introduce Charlotte de Beaune, Viscountess de Tours. My lady is the appropriate form of address. We are friends, very close friends. How can I help you?'

'Could we speak in private, Your Grace? I mean no offence my lady, it is just routine business, tedious business.' Anthony smiled at them both.

'I shall be in the music room, darling. Call me when you have finished,' Charlotte said, standing up. She walked across the room to another door and went into an adjoining room, closing the door behind her.

'There, we may speak freely. What is your business, Monsieur Sandal?'

'I am working for Don Juan de Idiáquez.'

'King Philip's first minister. You have my full attention, Monsieur Sandal.'

'I have been sent to spy on King Henry and in particular to discover what his intentions are towards Your Grace. Other spies have tried before me, and got nowhere, but since you seized Paris, the king has gone into hiding. We wondered if there might be any clues here that may help us locate him. A member of staff left behind perhaps, some papers, anything that might help.'

'No need. He will be hiding in the Château de Blois. It's about 120 miles southwest from here between Orleans and Tours. I do not know how you will get in. He will have tight security.'

'Leave that to me, Your Grace.' Anthony bowed and left.

'You can come back now, darling.' the duke shouted. Behind the connecting door, Charlotte took the old hearing trumpet from her ear and placed it back in the piano stool. Then she opened the door and rejoined the duke.

Anthony arrived in the city of Blois a few days later. He found a tavern, took a room and lay down on his bed to think about his next moves. He was fairly confident that if he could get into the chateau, he would be able to move around by night fairly easily, but it would be better if he became familiar with the layout first. If he could get some sort of job in the chateau, however menial, he could take it from there. Of course, if he could get a better job, he could add to the fifty ducats he would collect from Don Juan. What might Walsingham pay to discover the plotting going on in the War of the Three Henrys? He pictured his big house, in East Molesey perhaps, and he saw Francesca playing with their children on the lawns. No, he must focus on the present. One step at a time, first the fortune.

The next morning at breakfast, when the landlord, Alfonse, was clearing away his plate, Anthony asked for his advice.

'Alfonse, I don't suppose you know of any vacancies at the chateau, do you? Clerical, translator, Master of Horse? I'm quite versatile.'

'You could try asking Jaques. He works there in the kitchens; he comes in here most Fridays. I'll introduce you, if you're still here.'

'Thank you, Alfonse, I'd be very grateful.' Anthony pressed a few francs into the landlord's hand.

When Friday came, Anthony was sitting in the bar drinking wine. A tall, dark-haired man in his early twenties came in and asked at the bar for a goblet of wine. Anthony saw the landlord whisper to the man and point in his direction. The landlord winked at Anthony and the young man came over.

'Hello, Monsieur Sandal. Alfonse says the wine's on you tonight. How can I help?'

'Yes, do sit down and have some. I understand you work at the chateau, and although I'm all right at the moment, I need to find some work soon. Do you know of any vacancies?'

'What sort of vacancy?'

'Well, preferably something indoors. My back's not up to gardening these days.'

'They are short of waiters. I work in the kitchens and the food's gone cold by the time it gets to the dining room. They're always complaining. Not my fault I told the butler, you need more waiters.'

'Do you think you could get me an interview with the butler?' Anthony asked.

'Mind if I help myself to another wine?' Anthony waved his hand at the flagon. 'Yes, I think so. Have you got good references?'

'Oh yes, I have excellent references.'

'All right, I'll speak to Monsieur Lambert, the butler, on Monday. Come and ask to see him on Monday afternoon. If I clear it with him, he'll tell the gatehouse to expect you.'

When Jaques had gone, Anthony went to his room and pulled out some paper. He thought about the great Parisian houses he had broken into when he was working there, and the documents he had copied. Some names and signatures stuck in his mind, and he set about writing himself some excellent references.

The interview with Monsieur Lambert, the butler, had gone well. In fact, he seemed to think that with such excellent references, Anthony might be after his own position. The first few weeks were testing. He started with the advantage of having spent many years in royal palaces, Edinburgh and Florence. He knew how a place was set and the correct way to serve. But he did struggle with the speed required and carrying heavily laden trays. He bribed a waiter to give him a few tips, saying he was out of practice. Once he got through the first fortnight, he settled into the routine well. He shared a dormitory in the attic with the lower-ranking male staff, and had been issued a uniform. Simply by waiting at table, one thing had become absolutely apparent. The power behind the throne was the king's mother, Catherine de Medici. He had become familiar with the layout of the chateau, but hadn't started searching locked rooms at night yet. Sleeping in a dormitory with five other men made it awkward to sneak out in the middle of the night. Eventually, he hit upon the idea of using his days off to pretend to head into town, but sneak back and hide in one of the storerooms. Then he was able to steal out at night and pick the locks to enter locked rooms. He took a particular interest in Catherine's drawing room. Unfortunately, he found nothing in her correspondence that indicated what might be intended for the Duke de Guise. However, whilst searching her room, he did hear an owl hoot, and it seemed to be coming from the fireplace. He went over to the fireplace and looked up. He could hear the owl hooting clearly and could see part of the moon. The idea occurred to him that if he could hear the owl, the owl could probably hear him.

He relocked the desk drawers and left the drawing room, locking it behind him. Then he counted his paces down the corridor to the servant's spiral staircase and climbed to the floor above. He paced out the same number of steps back along the corridor and discovered that the room directly above Catherine's drawing room was a guest bedroom. He went up another flight and found that the room two floors above Catherine's drawing room was a storeroom, a different one to the one he had been using to hide in, on his days off, but similar.

He noticed, over a few weeks, that Catherine had

regular guests, mainly exquisite young noblewomen. They would go to Catherine's drawing room and be there for hours. If the visits coincided with one of his days off, he let himself into the guest bedroom, if unoccupied, or the storeroom when it was, and listened to the conversation via the chimney. In the summer, when the fire wasn't lit, he might as well have been in the room with them. Catherine referred to these young women as her L'Escadron Volant, her Flying Squadron. Catherine was telling them who to have affairs with, and what information she wanted. They were telling her all their lovers' secrets. How clever, he thought.

Throughout the summer and autumn, Anthony gathered piecemeal intelligence from his chimney eavesdropping. There was nothing yet that he could take back to Don Juan de Idiáquez and claim his fifty ducats. Then, in early December, as he was passing through the dining room, he saw another Flying Squadron spy arrive. He recognised her as the Duke de Guise's mistress, Charlotte de Beaune. He served her lunch, hoping he wouldn't be recognised, but she scarcely gave him a glance. After lunch, when they retired to Catherine's drawing room, Anthony told Monsieur Lambert that he was feeling very ill. Then he went upstairs and let himself into the unoccupied guest bedroom.

'The Catholic League has taken almost all of France. Henry is being treated like a puppet. He has been forced to make Guise Lieutenant General of France!' screamed Catherine. Regaining her composure, she spoke more quietly. 'You must lure him out of Paris, bring him somewhere nearby, Orleans, for example. You will find a way.'

'What then, Your Majesty?' asked Charlotte.

'Then the royal bodyguard will deal with him.'

Anthony had heard enough. He slipped back to the dormitory, changed out of his uniform, collected his belongings and left the chateau. As he crossed the courtyard, he was oblivious of Charlotte watching him from Catherine's drawing-room window.

'That man crossing the courtyard. I've seen him before. He came to see Guise,' said Charlotte.

'I will have him followed,' replied Catherine.

Anthony rushed back to the tavern, collected together the things he had left there, and paid his bill. He saddled Lucky and set off on the road south. As he rode, he wondered whether he could trust Maurice to deliver his news to Don Juan and collect his fifty ducats. Perhaps Maurice would take his money and not return, but somehow, he doubted that. Don Juan would probably require Maurice to return to his post in Bordeaux, and whilst it was a lot of money, it wouldn't be enough to cross Don Juan for. It took him five days hard riding to reach Bordeaux, and by the time he got there he had decided that if the news was to get to Madrid in time to be of any use, it was definitely time for a fresh rider to take on the remaining nine days riding; he was exhausted. Anthony dismounted outside Maurice's house, tied up Lucky and knocked on the door with the two knocks, count to five, and then four more knocks code. Maurice opened the door and Anthony went in. He was half-way through telling Maurice his story when the coded knocks were rapped out on the door again.

'That'll be the messenger from Madrid,' said Maurice, as he got up and opened the door. Maurice was flung to the ground as six soldiers stormed in. Anthony didn't even have time to get up before a musket was levelled at him. 'You've been followed, you damn fool,'

Maurice shouted, before a soldier thrust the butt of his musket into Maurice's stomach.

'You two search the house,' ordered the French officer in charge. 'The rest of you take these prisoners to the castle.' With that, Anthony and Maurice were frog marched to Bordeaux Castle. They were strip searched and then locked in separate cells. Anthony had lost almost everything, including his lock picks. He looked around his cell. There was a small slit of a window, which let a little light and air in, but was too narrow for even a three-year-old child to squeeze through. There was a small fireplace in the corner which looked as though it hadn't been used for years. He examined the chimney. It was black with soot and far too narrow to climb. There was a rickety wooden bed with a filthy straw mattress. He lay down and closed his eyes. He was awoken by voices; the officer and the remaining soldiers had returned. He heard footsteps and then the sound of a key turning in a lock, not his cell lock, though.

'You're first, up you get. Right, who are you and who are you working for?' the officer asked.

'You'll get nothing out of me,' Maurice snarled.

'Really? Bring the cutters, sergeant.' Moments later, Anthony heard a scream. 'Right, lop off another finger, sergeant. Little finger on the right hand this time, I think.'

'No!' screamed Maurice. 'I'll tell you what you want. We're working for Don Juan de Idiáquez. He's first Secretary of State for King Philip of Spain. I've been trying to get information to support the Catholic League in your wars of religion, with little success.'

'And the other one, who's he?'

'His name is André Sandal, also working for Don Juan. He only arrived about six months ago. He went to Paris to find out from the Duke of Guise where your king might be hiding.'

'He had more success than you. Fortunately for us, he came up against a superior spy, and was followed.'

'What are you going to do with us now?' asked Maurice.

'Well, first you're going to tell us all your codes and ciphers, and then we will find out how large a ransom King Philip will pay to have you returned.'

'Yes, of course, I'll give you everything.' Anthony listened for half an hour as Maurice gave the officer all the details of the ciphers and codes the Spanish agents used, as well as the locations and names of the other Spanish agents in France. He already knew how simple the Spanish ciphers were to crack, but he recited over and over in his head the details of the Spanish agents. It might be of value to Walsingham, but they'd no longer be agents by the time he got to tell him. When the officer had finished with Maurice, the soldiers left, locking the cell door behind them. Anthony walked over to his cell door and called through the barred grating.

'What are you going to do with me?' The officer turned and came back to Anthony's cell door. 'Nothing. We have what we want. We don't lop off fingers for pleasure, you know. We have standards.' He then turned on his heels and walked away.

For days, weeks, and months, the same things happened every day. Meals, if you could call them that, were brought into his cell on a tray. There was always a second guard outside the door. His bucket was taken away to be emptied and brought back half an hour later when his tray was taken away. The tray, spoon, and goblet were all wooden. There was nothing he could fashion into a lock pick. His bucket was wooden with a rope handle. He paced up and down his small cell for exercise. He started to spit on his finger and rub his finger tip in the soot of the chimney and put a mark on the wall for each day he had been imprisoned. That way, he could keep track of what day it was. Without anything positive he could do, Anthony fell into despair. When his thoughts turned to Francesca, as they often did at the beginning, he felt a cold hand squeezing his heart. Having lost the small fortune he'd worked so hard to get, he found thinking of her smile and her sparkling eyes too painful to bear. Instead, he imagined his brothers excelling in their legal careers. Perhaps they'd be married with children by now. He pictured his nephews and nieces giving immense pride and pleasure to his father and mother. He wondered whether they ever thought about him. If they could see him now, rotting in prison, he imagined their thoughts, "I told you so, son, you should have gone into the law. I said you'd never get anywhere with languages, and drawing, and fencing." That's what Father would say. Why wouldn't he, he was right. Look at me, what an abject failure I have become.

'We should have had word of the ransom by now,' Maurice called to him from his cell one day.

'I guess we're not as valuable as we might have hoped,' replied Anthony. 'It looks rather bleak, doesn't it?'

By Anthony's reckoning, it was the 1st March 1591. They had been imprisoned for three years and almost three months. His hair reached almost down to his waist. His door was unlocked, and a guard brought in his tray. He was also carrying a sheaf of papers. As he put the tray down, he dropped the papers, and they scattered across the floor. The guard uttered an oath and bent down to pick up the papers. Anthony used his foot to push some of them under his bed. He glanced at the cell door, but the second guard was standing outside as usual. After the guard had left, he picked up the papers from under his bed. They were notices concerning a curfew, which were presumably to be posted up around the city. He hid them under his mattress until his tray had been collected and his bucket returned.

Then he got the papers back out again. He had five of them, and they were blank on the reverse side. He hid four and then used his dampened finger to write in soot on the back of one.

Deliver Anthony Bacon for big reward. Captive in Bordeaux Castle. Please help. André Sandal.

Then Anthony folded the message into a paper dart and waited, looking out of his window for a suitable person to pass by the castle. After an hour, he saw a young man riding by, whistled and threw the dart. The young man stopped, looked up, and caught the dart as it passed him. He unfolded it, read it, smiled, and put it inside his doublet. Then he rode on. Anthony tried the same tactic at weekly intervals until he had used all five sheets. Then he waited.

On the 9th April, his cell door was unlocked.

'You have a visitor.' A handsome, well-dressed man walked in. The cell door was locked again.

'Monsieur Sandal, I'm Anthony Bacon. How can I help you?'

'My name isn't Sandal. It's Sir Anthony Standen.'

'Good lord. You provided all that incredible intelligence on the armada. How did you end up here?'

'That's a long story. Did it help, with the armada I mean?'

'Very much so. The armada was totally defeated. Storms did the rest.'

'Do you think you can get a message to Walsingham and raise a ransom to get me out?'

'I'm afraid Walsingham died last year. I'm working for my uncle now, William Cecil, Baron Burghley. But yes, I'm sure we can get you out, you're too valuable to be left rotting in here. The Marshal de Matignon is a friend of mine. He may be able to help. I think you are rotting by the way, you stink to high heaven.'

'I'm sorry about that. The facilities here are rather basic,' Anthony said, pointing at the bucket. They talked for almost twenty minutes until the guard came back and said that their time was up.

'Chin up, my friend, we will get you out of here, and then you shall have a long bath and a haircut. There is also an excellent tailor near my house.'

Within three months, Anthony was a free man again, but without a penny to his name.

Anthony took a few weeks to recover his health after his long incarceration. He stayed at Anthony Bacon's house and they became good friends. They were both excellent linguists, although Bacon's Spanish was mediocre. Anthony's tales of his adventures fascinated Bacon.

'But what am I going to do now, Anthony? I have got to make some money, one way or another,' Standen asked.

'I could use your help. We believe that King Philip is building a new armada, and we need to know what is happening. Could you use your contacts to find out?'

'Back to Spain then?'

'Yes. I can advance you twenty ducats to cover expenses,' Bacon replied.

The next day, Anthony set off from Bordeaux on the road towards Madrid. The ride took ten days, during which he considered his options. He had learnt, from considerable experience, that he was most convincing in his deceptions when most of his story was true. He had also learnt that if he lived a lie long enough; it became sufficiently true to pass as truth. So he decided to return to Don Juan de Idiáquez, and report back to him on the failure of his mission to spy on the King of France. When he rode into Madrid, he went straight to Government House, and asked if Don Juan could be told that Anthonio Foscari had returned from France to see him. To his surprise, the messenger came back and led him to Don Juan's office.

'Sit down, Foscari, I am intrigued. After the Duke of Guise's assassination, I didn't expect to see you again. What happened?'

Anthony told him the whole story of his meeting with the Duke of Guise and his mistress, Charlotte de Beaune. He related how he had infiltrated the chateau as a waiter and had observed and overheard Catherine de Medici plotting with her Flying Squadron of female spies. He described how he had learnt of the assassination attempt and how he had been followed back to Bordeaux and compromised the agent, Maurice. He recounted how he had been imprisoned in Bordeaux Castle, but after over three years, he had managed to fashion a lock pick from a piece of chicken bone and escape.

'Well, that explains a lot. She's damn clever and cunning, Catherine de Medici. You were unlucky, Foscari, you almost pulled it off. I know you speak many languages, how's your English?'

'I have English friends who say I could pass for an Englishman.' Anthony replied.

'Good. We have an Englishman working for us, a man called Anthony Rolston. He feeds us information from England and we give him some plausible, but false information to pass back. I'd like you to befriend him, pass yourself off as an Englishman and let me know what you think.'

'What is it that you're concerned about?' asked Anthony, genuinely puzzled.

'I'd like to be sure that it's only the information we provide him with that gets back to England. I've had him followed, of course, but we don't have the resources to follow him all the time. If you could gain his confidence, it might save us a lot of time. There's twenty ducats in it for you.'

'I'll do it. Where will I find him?'

'He has a room in a tavern near here, El Toro Negro. Here's 10 ducats in advance for expenses.'

Anthony took a room in the El Toro Negro tavern. Then he went out and found a blacksmith's forge, where he sketched out his much-missed lock picks and had replacements made. Fondling them, he walked back to the tavern and had dinner. He studied his fellow diners, their mannerisms, the way they held their cutlery, until he thought he knew which one might be Rolston. He thought about his objectives. First objective: money. English, Spanish, preferably both. Second objective, gain Queen Elizabeth's pardon. Possible clash with first objective. He needed to gather intelligence on Spanish plans. Could Rolston help with that? If he, as an impartial Venetian spy, could give Don Juan confidence that Rolston was genuinely working for him, then Rolston might be able to infiltrate deeper into Don Juan's real plans. He could feed Rolston with whatever Bacon wanted him to feed him and turn the tables on Don Juan. Where was Rolston getting the intelligence on England that he was currently feeding to Don Juan? He waited until the man he thought was Rolston left the table and followed him. He saw him open his room and Anthony walked past to his own room, opened it and retired to bed.

The following morning, Anthony waited until he heard a door close and carefully opened his own door. He watched the man he thought was Rolston lock his door and go downstairs. Anthony followed. He watched him leave the tavern and then Anthony went back upstairs and picked the lock of Rolston's room. He searched under the mattress and had a look up the chimney. As he paced softly about the room; he felt a floorboard give slightly under his weight. He rolled back the rug and examined the floorboards. One was loose. He prised it up with a knife and found a metal box hidden beneath. He replaced the floorboard and rug, then left the room, locking the door behind him, and went back to his own room. It took only a minute to unlock the box, in which there was a pile of documents. He noticed that most of them were in Robert Clark's handwriting. He set about deciphering them.

He then waited until he heard footsteps in the corridor, and a door being unlocked. He stepped out of his room just in time to see Rolston entering his room. He went along the corridor and knocked on Rolston's door. The door opened.

'May I come in?' Anthony asked.

'What do you want?'

'I've come to give you this back,' Anthony said, handing Rolston the box. 'Now, may I come in?' Rolston stepped aside. 'Close the door, would you, I don't think we want to be overheard.'

'Who the hell are you?' asked Rolston.

'I will tell you who I am, but first let me tell you what

I know about you. Your name is Anthony Rolston. You're an English spy and you were working for Francis Walsingham until he died. You have been feeding false intelligence that Walsingham gave you to Don Juan. You have also been feeding false information from Don Juan back to Walsingham. I assume you have been paid by both parties. How am I doing so far?' Rolston slumped down on the bed.

'It's true. I was recruited by Walsingham because I was a cloth merchant travelling across Europe and spoke good Spanish. He wanted me to recruit agents within the Spanish government and feed back intelligence. I tried to recruit a secretary, but he wanted more money than I had. He threatened to expose me to Don Juan.'

'What did you do?'

'I got to Don Juan first, told him the whole story. He said he'd pay me to feed false information to Walsingham.'

'What did you do after Walsingham died?'

'I've been making it up.'

'You really are in trouble. Now I'll tell you who I am. Don Juan thinks my name is Antonio Foscari and that I'm a Venetian spy. Actually, my name is Sir Anthony Standen, and I was a spy working for Walsingham, too. I'm now working for Cecil.'

'Are you going to expose me, Sir Anthony?'

'No, I'm going to help you. Don Juan has asked me to befriend you and find out whether you're passing any information back to England that you shouldn't be.'

'I'd like to know how to get it.'

'Yes, we'll come to that. Here's my plan. I tell Don Juan that I'm sure you're genuine. I'll say that I've seen the messages you're sending back and check with him that they are the ones Don Juan is feeding you. I'll say that I've checked the intelligence you're feeding him, and that it matches what the Venetians have found. I may throw in that you're not skilled enough to be double crossing him.'

'That's true.'

'That's not your fault. I was rather inept to start with. You carry on as you are, except I will get real false information from London to feed you. As Don Juan becomes more confident in you, I want you to watch him. Watch where he keeps the documents you give him. I want to know the layout of the office and the layout of his secretary's office. Is it the same secretary, by the way, the one you tried to bribe?'

'No, it was another one. I couldn't even bribe the right secretary. So you're really going to help me?'

'Spy's honour. We're a team now.'

For the next few months, Rolston and Anthony met as little as possible. Anthony slept during the afternoons and slipped out in the early hours of the morning to watch Government House. The guardroom was just inside the main entrance. Two sentries patrolled the perimeter of the building. There was a tradesman's entrance on the side of the building, which they passed four times between the cathedral clock striking the hour. Each time they tried the door to check that it was secure. The first staff arrived just after the clock struck six. Most staff had arrived by seven. Don Juan and his secretary usually left the building by ten in the evening, occasionally an hour later.

'Sir Anthony, I think I have what you want. I was there when Don Juan came back from a war council meeting. His secretary was with him. The secretary gave Don Juan his notes to check, and Don Juan approved them. I saw them put in a file in a cupboard in the secretary's office, which has two large locks,' Rolston said, smiling.

'Excellent. You rest, I'm going out to do some shopping. I'll need some of your money. Ten ducats should be enough.'

'What for?'

'Consider it an investment in your future.'

Anthony went out into the city centre and found a watchmaker. He bought a plain pocket watch which the watchmaker said would keep excellent time. Then he went to a tailor and bought two thick black cloaks, into the linings of which he had large pockets sewn. He also bought four thick squares of wool. He went to a stationery shop and topped up his supply of paper, quills, sealing wax and ink. Finally, he went to a hardware store and bought a portable oil lamp, some oil, a long-handled spoon, plaster of paris, some string and some lead. Then he went back to the tavern.

That night, he and Rolston donned their cloaks and walked to a street corner opposite the tradesman's entrance of Government House.

'Wrap this wool around your boots and tie it with the string. It'll muffle the sound of our footsteps.' Anthony passed two squares and some string. He did the same himself. They watched the sentries check the lock, then continue on their patrol. Anthony looked at his pocket watch. 'Right, follow me.' They ran silently over to the door and within a minute, he had picked the door lock.

'How on earth did you do that?' Rolston asked.

'Not now, I'll show you one day.' They slipped inside, and Anthony locked the door behind them. The corridor was completely dark. Anthony took out the oil lamp from his cloak pocket, a piece of wick that he had soaked in oil and his steel and flint. 'Check along this wall and make sure the shutters are across the windows, will you.'

'Yes, the shutters are in place.' Anthony struck his flint with the steel and sparks lit the wick, which he used to light the oil lamp.

'Right, which way to the office with the file cupboard?'

'Follow me,' Rolston said.

When they got to the office, Anthony quickly picked the lock of the office door. He sent Rolston in first, to check that the window shutters were closed.

'All secure,' Rolston said, as Anthony entered with the lamp. This is the cupboard. As I said, they're big locks.'

'I like big locks. Small locks are a bit fiddly.' Anthony soon had the cupboard open. 'Right, I'll skim through the notes of the war council meetings and show you the pieces that I want copied. You make the copies. If we work as a team, we'll be through this pile in no time.'

'What do we do if somebody surprises us?'

'Kill them. Quietly.' It took them from eleven until five o'clock in the morning, but they had copied the key points from the last eight war council meetings. 'Right, that will do. Let's get all these back in the cupboard, exactly how we found it.' When they were ready, Anthony locked the cupboard again. They slipped out of the office, locked it behind them, and made their way back to the tradesman's entrance. Anthony looked at his watch. 'The sentries should be back any minute now.' They waited until they heard heavy footsteps outside and the door handle being tried. Anthony looked at his watch and after three minutes, unlocked the door. He opened it cautiously and looked out. 'All clear. You dash back to the corner while I lock the door.' Anthony locked the door, then ran over to the corner himself.

'Goodness, that was real spying,' whispered Rolston. They walked in silence back to the tavern. They both went to Anthony's room. 'What happens now?'

'I'll take this evening's haul back to my controller in Bordeaux. You stay here and carry on as normal.'

'Can't I come with you?'

'Not yet. If we both disappear, Don Juan may suspect something. I'll recommend you to my controller, and we'll get you out. Then I'll teach you how to pick locks.'

Anthony rode through the city gates of Bordeaux, looking anxiously up at the castle. He tied his horse up outside Bacon's house and knocked on the door. The housekeeper opened it.

'Is he in?'

'You've just caught him; he's packing to leave. Come in, sir. There's another gentleman with him already.' Anthony was led from the hallway into the parlour. Anthony Bacon was indeed packing a trunk, watched by a tall man, around his own height but younger, probably in his late twenties. Anthony Bacon looked up from his packing.

'Anthony, what a pleasant surprise. You probably haven't met Captain Allen. He works now for my uncle as a courier. It was Captain Allen who carried the dispatches, that Tom Lawson brought here, on to London. This is Sir Anthony Standen, captain.'

'I'm very honoured to meet you at last, Sir Anthony. You should have been able to see the sparkle in Walsingham's eyes when he read your intelligence,' Captain Allen said, reaching out to shake hands.

'And it's a pleasure to meet you too, captain. I know how dangerous and essential a role the courier's is too,'

Anthony replied, warmly shaking the outstretched hand.

'To what do I owe the pleasure?' Bacon asked. Anthony swivelled his eyes towards the housekeeper. 'That will be all. Thank you, Florence. Would you rustle us up some lunch please?' When she had gone into the kitchen, Bacon closed the door behind her.

'I assume I can speak freely in front of Captain Allen.' Bacon nodded. 'I have the key points from the last eight Council of War meetings. Philip is building another armada. The Irish have offered him Galway as a base. The Scots have been petitioning him to land in Scotland.' He handed the papers to Bacon.

'Great Scott, you're a marvel, Anthony. How did you get these?'

'With help from another Walsingham spy, Anthony Rolston. It's getting to be like the War of the Three Henrys. You, I and Rolston. I've left him behind in Madrid, but we should get him out, he's in danger now.'

'Yes, you're right. Something's cropped up and I'm heading back to London now, with Captain Allen. Let me see how the land lies with respect to the queen and whether you can return or not. Frankly with the intelligence you provided on the armada, and now this, I would have thought she'd welcome you with open arms. You stay here and I'll write to you when I have news. We'll also see if we can get this fellow Rolston back to London.'

CHAPTER ELEVEN

1593 - 1595, England

It was 11a.m. on the 12th of June 1593 when Anthony stepped ashore in Dover. He had been nineteen when he last left England for Paris in 1567. So much had happened in the intervening twenty-six years, yet he felt no nearer to proving his worth to his father, nor building a home fitting for Francesca. He found a coach bound for London, paid the coachman, and took his seat inside. His travelling companions were an elderly man with two chickens in a cage at his feet; a rather plump, middle-aged woman, fiddling with the rings on her fingers; and a finely dressed young man. He quickly tired of the conversation, which largely revolved around how bad the plague was this year. They stopped in Canterbury to change horses, stretch their legs and eat. The passing countryside eventually gave way to the sights, sounds and stench of London. Anthony took his bag from the coachman, who was handing luggage down from the roof, and made his way towards London Bridge. He had to step aside frequently as there were bodies rotting in the streets, victims of the plague, he assumed. He crossed the bridge and continued past the magnificent spire of St. Paul's Cathedral until he saw Smithfield Market to his right. He shuddered at the childhood memory of seeing the Islington Martyrs burnt at the stake. He hurried by, continuing along Holborn until he found Gray's Inn on his right. He asked at the porter's lodge for the rooms of Francis Bacon and the porter gave him directions. He knocked on the door and it was opened by Anthony Bacon.

'Ah, you've arrived safely. Come in. Francis, this is Sir Anthony Standen,' Anthony Bacon said, turning to his brother.

'Welcome, Sir Anthony. My brother has told me so much about you. How does it feel to be back in England after so many years?'

'I have dreamt of returning to my homeland for so long, but I hadn't expected bodies rotting in the streets. Have you been affected by the plague here?'

'Thankfully not yet, not in Gray's, although we know people who have,' Francis replied. 'Anthony, fetch Sir Anthony a chair. I'm going to call you Sir Anthony, to avoid confusion,' Francis said, turning to Standen.

'Anthony, that reminds me. Rolston, that spy in Madrid I told you about, who had worked for Walsingham. Did you speak to your uncle about him? He had no proper training in the craft, like me, to begin with, and so was not very effective. I think he's in real danger now. If we could get him back here for a few months, I could train him, and make him a very effective agent. In fact, I promised him I would.'

'I'll chase our uncle, Baron Burghley.'

'Please don't tell me he's another Anthony,' pleaded Francis Bacon.

'Actually I'm afraid he is, Anthony Rolston.'

'Oh, that does it. If we are to have three Anthonys under one roof, then you shall be Standen, he shall be Rolston, and my brother shall be Anthony. I can't have three people answering me when I ask a question. Is that fair?'

'Yes, fair enough,' replied Standen. 'I just want to honour my promise to Rolston.'

'Anthony, we had a message yesterday from our cousin Sir Robert Cecil, who is at court,' said Anthony Bacon. 'I'm afraid he says that Her Majesty cannot yet say what her pleasure is concerning you, and he advises that you stay here with us for the time being.'

'What about your uncle, the Lord Treasurer? Surely the notes of the Spanish war council count for something. You did send them to him?' Standen asked.

'Yes, of course, he's always full of promises. They're cheap. I also sent copies to the Earl of Essex, Robert Devereux, and I have this for you.' Anthony Bacon then placed a gold chain with a large gold medallion of the Earl of Essex on it around Standen's neck. 'You must meet him Anthony, Sir Anthony. He's magnificent. Handsome, charming, witty, brave, not at all like our uncle. Essex is expanding his own intelligence network. I'm working for him now, and I think you should too.'

A few weeks passed, the three of them enjoying each other's conversation and far too much food and wine. The plague was getting worse each day and eventually Francis suggested they should move to their brother Edward's second home at Twickenham Park. It was a very fine house, which had been built as a hunting lodge for Edward III. It was set in eighty-seven acres of parkland which led down to the Thames opposite Richmond, where the Earl of Essex was staying when not at court.

On 17th July the Earl of Essex visited. Anthony was at once captivated by his wit and charisma. He could see why he was the queen's favourite. For his part, Essex wanted to know every detail of Anthony's adventures.

'I really think Philip would be king now, if it weren't for you, Sir Anthony. You can rest assured that I will do everything in my power to plead your case with the queen. I fear, though, that Walsingham's death upset the balance at court. I jostle with the ageing Burghley, and his ambitious son — Sir Robert. You are, through no fault of your own, caught in the crossfire, as is Anthony.' Just as Essex finished speaking, a messenger arrived and handed him a letter. He read it and then continued. 'Our agent — Morrison in Scotland — sends word that the Scottish lords have signed a secret treaty with King Philip by which he will send 30,000 troops to Scotland. I must go to court and inform the queen.'

Just over a week later, news arrived that King Henry IV of France had renounced Protestantism and had been welcomed back into the Catholic faith. A day later, Michael Hicks, the Lord Treasurer's secretary, arrived to advise Anthony that the queen would see him at Windsor. Anthony wrote a note to Essex asking if he would meet him at Windsor so that he could be primed on how best to please the queen. The reply, when it arrived the next day, read:

It would be foolish of me to give you any direction. I know your sufficiency and my own weakness. Only this caution I make, that your affection for me breed not too much jealousy in other parties, or offence against you. I hope this first access will make so good an impression, as they, that shall labour for your good with the queen afterwards, shall find the mark easy.

I'm on my own then, he thought, as he boarded the Bacon's carriage and set off for Windsor.

On the way there, the road ran through East Molesey, and Anthony called to the carriage driver to stop. Anthony climbed down from the carriage. He felt his legs trembling at the prospect of seeing his father and mother again. He didn't have much to show yet for all the intervening years, but he had a long story to tell. He called up to the driver again.

'This is where I lived as a child. Would you wait just ten minutes while I see if my family is still here?'

'We have plenty of time, sir. The queen always keeps people waiting for days, if not weeks. As long as we get to Windsor some time today, nobody will be any the wiser.' Anthony opened the gate to his parents' house and knocked on the front door. A pretty woman that Anthony estimated to be in her late twenties opened the door. 'Good morning. I've been abroad for many years, but I used to live here. I wonder, are my parents still here?'

'Who are you?'

'I'm Anthony Standen, who are you?'

'Good lord! You're Edmund's long-lost elder brother. I'm Dennise, Edmund's wife. Please come in.'

Anthony turned to the carriage driver. 'I won't be long.' The driver waved his agreement, and Anthony crossed the threshold of his family home. He followed Dennise to the parlour. 'The furnishings are a little different, but not much has changed. Are Mother and Father in?'

'Please sit down, Anthony. Can I get you something to drink? Some wine perhaps, or a brandy?' Anthony looked at his father's favourite chair, then sat in the chair that guests had been offered when he was young.

'No thank you, Father doesn't approve of drinking, I'm surprised he has any in the house.'

'I can't think of the right way to tell you this, but I'm afraid your mother and father both died in 1571. Edmund said that your mother died first, heart failure he said it was. After that, your father just seemed to fade away. At first, he immersed himself in his work, but it wasn't enough.' She paused for a second. 'They didn't get to meet any of their grandchildren. Sadly, Anthony had only just started courting Jane by then, and I wasn't to meet Edmund for several years. Perhaps if there had been a grandchild, it would have given him something to live for.' Dennise spoke softly, carefully studying Anthony's face. She saw something ebb away from his eyes. He looked suddenly hollow.

'I think I will have that brandy now, if you don't mind,' Anthony whispered. Dennise went into the kitchen for a minute and returned with a goblet of brandy. She handed it to Anthony, who grasped it with both hands, which were trembling. He took a long gulp.

'I am so sorry to have to tell you this. I do know they talked about you a great deal, wondering where you were and what you were doing.'

'Did they? Did they really? It always seemed that I was a great disappointment, to Father especially. He wanted me to go into the law, but I didn't have any interest in it. I'm sure he thought I wouldn't make anything of myself, and I've spent the last quarter of a century trying to prove him wrong. For most of that time, he was probably right, but I have been of service to England, and I hope very soon to be knighted by the queen. I'm on my way to Windsor now. I was knighted by Mary Queen of Scots a long time ago, but nobody recognises that. And if I am knighted now, I can't tell them. What's it all been worth? What's the point?'

'I'm sure they're both looking proudly down on you now, from heaven. Oh, I wish Edmund was here. He talks about you all the time. He adores you, you know. Are you sure it was their approval you wanted, or was it love? Are you married?'

'No, I've led rather an itinerant life, but I hope to settle down one day, when I've made my fortune.'

'William will be home from school soon, he's your nephew.'

'I'm an uncle. William did you say?'

'Yes. He's just turned eight. Do you wish we'd named him after you?'

'No, not at all. Our middle brother is Anthony. I don't know what possessed our parents to baptise two of us with the same name. And our father's name was Edmund. It caused quite a bit of confusion, so our brother Anthony was known as Freddy, and your Edmund as Eddy. I'm beginning to think I have the commonest name in Christendom. Where is Edmund? Is he here?'

'No. We have been staying here whilst the queen was at Hampton court, but she went to Windsor. Edmund had to rush back to Chancery. He's the senior clerk of the Petty Bag you know.'

'Good heavens! From what I remember, that's a very important position.'

'Yes. He works very hard, and makes a lot of money. But I worry about him so. He's constantly dashing between Chancery and Westminster when he's not rushing around after the queen. He's been buying houses all over the place. He sees them as staging posts when he's travelling as well as investments. We have all the money we could possibly want, but he seems driven to make more.'

'How is Anthony?'

'He's very well. We see him often because we both have houses on Chancery Lane. He's something to do with the equity side of the law I think. You'll have to ask Edmund. I think it's something to do with the chancellor. His wife, Jane, is delightful, and they have children too.'

'Why I've been staying at Gray's Inn, just opposite Chancery Lane. We might have passed each other in the street. What are his children's names and how old are they?'

'Let me see, the eldest boy, Richard. He must be thirteen or fourteen now. Simon is a year younger, and Mary is ten.'

'I'm so glad that my brothers have overcome the family trait of giving virtually everyone the same name.'

'I think Jane and I may have had something to do with that,' Dennise said, smiling.

'Of course, I didn't mean… that is, I think Edmund is a very lucky man, Anthony too, by the sound of it.'

When William got home got home he wanted to hear all about his uncle's adventures. Anthony sat with them both in the kitchen for almost an hour telling his tale. His heart warmed with William's smile. When he started to feel an emptiness, and the first stab of jealousy, he decided to say his farewells, went back to the carriage, and started to worry about meeting the queen.

When he arrived at Windsor Castle, Anthony was asked to wait in the hall. There were dozens of people waiting, some talking excitedly, some pacing around, and others sitting quietly. Anthony paced back and forth like a pendulum, marking time. A short, hunchbacked man of about thirty came into the room.

'Anthony Standen.'

'Yes.' Anthony walked over to the hunchback. 'I'm Anthony Standen.'

'I'm Sir Robert Cecil. I will present you to Her Majesty. You should say nothing unless you are spoken to. Follow me.' Anthony followed him down a long corridor and into the throne room. There were a number of people milling about at the back of the room, including Francis Bacon. Anthony smiled at him and he smiled back. Anthony walked to one side of, and a pace behind Cecil towards the throne. The queen was wearing a dazzling dress with jewels of red, white, and blue glistening in the sunlight pouring through the high windows. Her hair was fiery red and her face pure white. Cecil stopped and made a deep bow. Anthony did the same. 'Your Highness, I present Anthony Standen.'

'Good morning, Standen. If you write a few pages detailing everything you have done since leaving my realm in 1565, I will consider it. No more than two pages, I think. That is all.' Cecil bowed, Anthony did the same. They backed away towards the door, continuing to bow every few steps. When they were in the corridor, Anthony turned to Cecil.

'Was that it? How long have I got to write my account?'

'At least a week, perhaps more. You should return to Twickenham and write it. When you have completed it, either send it or bring it to me.'

So Anthony returned to Twickenham. He had hoped that Anthony Bacon would help him compose his two-page summary of the last twenty-six years, but Bacon was suffering from gout and a kidney stone, probably caused by too much good food and wine. Anthony set about the task himself. Francis was still at court, hoping to be appointed to the vacant Attorney General post. The writing was constantly interrupted with beer, wine and lavish feasts, together with laughter and music, but the summary was completed after a few days, and Anthony took it to Windsor. Cecil delivered it to the queen, and Anthony was given a guest bedroom while he waited for a response. One day, whilst walking in the grounds, he saw a face he recognised, walking with an older man who seemed to be doing all the talking.

'It's Captain Allen, isn't it?' Anthony asked.

'Good heavens, Sir Anthony Standen.' They shook hands. 'Sir Roger, allow me to introduce Sir Anthony Standen. We both worked with Anthony Bacon on undercover work in Bordeaux. Real cloak and dagger stuff, not the grand battles you're used to. Sir Anthony, this is Sir Roger Williams.' Anthony shook Sir Roger's outstretched hand. Sir Roger had a very firm grip. 'Why don't you stroll together? I'm afraid I've just remembered an appointment. Do excuse me.' Captain Francis Allen bowed and strode back towards the castle.

'So you are a soldier, Sir Roger.'

'Scholar and soldier. I studied at Brasenose College, Oxford, before serving in the army of the Earl of Pembroke.'

'Have you seen many battles, Sir Roger?'

'Many battles? Haven't you read my book, A Brief Discourse of War, with Opinions on Martial Discipline?'

'No, I'm afraid not.'

'Then I shall have to tell you all about it.' Sir Roger didn't notice Anthony's eyes glazing over as he recounted all the battles he had fought in, the men he had killed, and the close escapes he'd had himself. He had reached his service in Flanders, fighting for William of Orange, when Anthony regained interest.

'Why, I too fought for William. I was a lieutenant in the Sea Beggars. I met him, you know, King William. He's a wonderful man, and so wise.'

'Was a wonderful man, I'm afraid. He was assassinated, you know, back in eighty-four. I caught the assassin, Balthasar Gérard, his name was. So you must tell me what it was like in the Sea Beggars, but I'm getting thirsty. Let's find a tavern in the town and continue this discussion there.'

Anthony and Roger became firm friends over the next weeks and months. Anthony asked Cecil, whenever they passed, if the queen had come to a decision yet. He was told she was very busy and that he would have to wait. One of the things Anthony liked about Sir Roger was his fearless wit. Whilst everyone else quivered in the queen's presence, Sir Roger joked with her. One day, he was walking with him when the queen passed. They both bowed to the queen, and she turned to Sir Roger and said, 'Williams, I pray thee be gone, your boots stink.' And Sir Roger replied.

'Pah, it's not my boots, it's my suit that stinks.'

Despite the pleasant company, Anthony was becoming increasingly frustrated at the passage of time and his powerlessness. He had, in the main, enjoyed action, planning his next move, striving to achieve his objective. This waiting game wasn't his forte at all.

'Sir Roger, who is the greatest general you have served?'

'That's easy, Essex.'

'He certainly commands devotion. Anthony and Francis adore him, and he has been very kind to me. He's intelligent, well educated and witty. He's handsome too. But what is it that makes you all so devoted?'

'Well, speaking as a soldier, he leads from the front. He's not one of these generals who leads from an office fifty miles behind the front line. He knows what he wants, and he knows how to get it, and he tells us how we're going to win. You must know yourself how terrifying it is to enter battle, but if you enter the battle with the certainty that you will be victorious, you can do it. It's as simple as that. I'd certainly lay my life down for him, and I dare say you would too, when you've been in action with him.'

Anthony spent the Christmas of 1593 at Barn Elms, Essex's house across the river in Richmond, with Essex, Sir Roger and Anthony. Francis Bacon remained at court, still lobbying for the attorney general post. They were joined there by Antonio Perez. He was quite a catch. He had been secretary to King Philip, but had defected.

'Why did you defect?' Essex asked.

'It is hard to deliver bad news. I became aware that the king's half-brother, Don Juan, was being encouraged by his secretary, Juan de Escobedo, to plot against the king. I made the king aware of this, and he instructed me to arrange the death of Escobedo. Don Juan, the king's half-brother, died of natural causes a few months later. The king blamed me, and I had to flee.'

'I almost met Don Juan once,' Anthony said. 'No, perhaps I'll tell you another time.' Anthony's gaze drifted to a distant past as he wondered what had become of Barbara and her children.

Essex had to return to court after Christmas and the two Anthonys were given the task of thoroughly debriefing Perez and documenting every detail. Essex had said that every detail should be recorded. But there was one small detail that emerged, which could have no intelligence value. Perez had met a Jewish Portuguese physician, Rodrigo Lopez, who had told him that he had once treated Essex for venereal disease. Doctor Lopez was now the queen's physician.

'Do you think we should tell him, Anthony?' Standen asked.

'It is hard to give bad news. But at the same time, Essex is the queen's favourite, and if this doctor is loose with his tongue, I think he should know. I'll encipher a message and send it to him.'

When Essex returned a month later, he was bubbling with excitement.

'I have foiled a plot to assassinate the queen. I have extracted two confessions from couriers who had carried messages between Don Antonio, the Portuguese pretender, and King Philip. There was a plot to poison the queen, and it was Doctor Lopez who was to do it. I have documentary evidence and Burghley is convinced, even if the queen seems sceptical. He is to be tried, with his fellow conspirators, and I will head the commission.'

'Has he confessed?' Anthony Bacon asked.

'He confesses, then retracts it. When I was with Burghley, he asked me to tell you that he agrees you should bring that fellow, Rolston, I think it was, here. Does that make sense?'

'Yes, it does,' Standen murmured.

It wasn't long before Essex returned to court.

'Do you think he's really guilty, this Doctor Lopez?' Standen asked Anthony.

'He might be, but he's had ample time to kill her if he wanted to. Then on the other hand, Essex has confessions.'

'Confessions extracted under torture, I dare say. Should we have told him? Don't you think he may have gone looking for evidence to shut the doctor up, discredit him.'

'Perhaps, Sir Anthony. But perhaps the doctor really was going to poison the queen. How could we know?'

News of the trial arrived every week. Doctor Lopez, Ferreira da Gama and Manuel Luis Tinoco were found guilty. The prosecutor, Sir Edward Coke, denounced the doctor as "a perjured, murdering villain and a Jewish doctor worse than Judas himself, not a new Christian, but a very Jew." Standen wondered if he had passed Doctor Lopez when he was at Windsor. It took another three months for the queen to sign the death warrants. Anthony had no mental image of Doctor Lopez. He imagined his Jewish friend Joseph, who had taught him Arabic in Constantinople, swinging from a rope.

Anthony was relieved when Rolston arrived. He had some new lock picks made by a local blacksmith, removed the lock from an old store room that wasn't being used, and spent the following four months teaching Rolston everything he had learnt about ciphers, picking locks, following and being followed, and combat. He was very glad to be doing something practical again.

It was a crisp, bright day in January 1596 when Anthony was summoned back to Windsor. He was taken directly to the throne room by Sir Robert Cecil. The queen told Anthony to kneel, and Sir Robert handed her a sword.

'I dub thee knight,' she said, laying the tip of the sword on each of his shoulders in turn, 'arise, Sir Anthony.'

Anthony was somewhat stunned. The next few minutes were a daze. When he was outside the throne room, he turned to Sir Robert.

'Did she say anything about a reward for my services? Is there to be a pension?'

'You have been granted a pension of £100 per annum, back dated to 1588.'

'Is that all? You mean I risked my neck to get every detail of the armada, and detailed notes of the Spanish Council of War, for less than forty shillings a week.'

'That's quite a lot of money.'

'It won't buy me a great country house with parkland though, will it?'

'I think you have ideas above your station, Sir Anthony, good day to you.' Sir Robert walked away.

Essex helped Anthony plead with the Lord Treasurer for a reward more befitting the very great service that Sir Anthony had done for his queen and country, but it was increasingly obvious that they were flogging a dead horse.

'Look, Sir Anthony, join me on my voyage to Cadiz,' Essex suggested. 'I have assembled a great fleet. We are going to catch the Spanish treasure ships when they arrive in Cadiz. I'm sure that your fluency in Spanish, and your cipher-breaking skill, will be a great asset to the expedition. Your share of the loot will vastly exceed your wildest dreams. It's no use wasting more of your time here.'

'Yes my lord, you're right, but I do have some very wild dreams.'

CHAPTER TWELVE

1596 - 1597, Cadiz & Azores

On the 3rd of June 1596, Anthony, Essex and Sir Roger boarded the Due Repulse in Plymouth. They were welcomed aboard by the ship's captain, William Monson.

'She is a very fine ship, captain. She looks new,' Essex remarked.

'Thank you, my lord. They launched her on the first of March this year, in Deptford. We have barely completed bringing her into commission, but all 622 tons of her, and her forty-eight guns are ready to chastise the queen's enemies now. Let me show you to your cabins. We will sail on the ebb tide this evening.'

They dined in the wardroom and later joined Captain Monson on the quarterdeck as the cutters hauled the great ship off the quayside into clear water. At the captain's command, the men in the cutters released the tow ropes, came alongside and shipped their oars. Most of them then scrambled up the netting on the ship's side, whilst those remaining in the cutters attached halyards, lowered to them from the ship, and were winched up and hauled on deck. The sails were unfurled and Due Repulse steadily gained speed and slipped out of Plymouth Harbour.

'What a sight, captain,' Anthony said. 'There must be a hundred ships at least.'

'One hundred and twenty combined English and Dutch ships,' replied Captain Monson. 'There's Admiral Howard's flagship, the Ark Royal,' he said, pointing. 'And over there is the Merhonneur, Sir Walter Raleigh's ship.'

When they were out of sight of land, they retired to their cabins. It took ten days for them to reach Cape Finisterre, then as they turned and headed south down the coast of Portugal, the west winds came on the beam and their speed increased. They reached Cape St. Vincent on the 18th June, just 140 nautical miles from Cadiz, but the winds slackened and it was not until Sunday 30th June that they had Cadiz in sight. At five o'clock in the morning, the crash of guns awoke Anthony. He got up, dressed, and rushed onto the quarterdeck. They were under fire from shore artillery, and were returning fire where possible. The Spanish fleet was bearing down towards them and Due Repulse was third in the English line. Essex was already on deck, talking with Captain Monson.

'Why is the ship ahead lowering a boat, captain?'

'I have no idea, my lord. The ship lowering the boat is the Crane, which has the marshal of the army, Sir Francis Vere, aboard. The ship ahead of his is Merhonneur. They're rowing like blazes now, dragging a line behind them. Good god, they're attaching themselves to Merhonneur. I don't think Raleigh has noticed. Look, they're hauling themselves forward trying to overtake Merhonneur. Vere seems very keen to be the first ashore. Ah, Raleigh has noticed now. He's cutting the line.'

'Captain, they've both slowed. Can we overtake?' asked Essex.

'With pleasure, my lord.'

With Crane and Merhonneur exchanging hostile words at each other, Due Repulse sailed past both of them, surging through the surf as the wind freshened. She sailed between the lines of Spanish galleons, firing broadsides to port and starboard. The English rate of fire was considerably faster than that of the Spaniards, and as other English and Dutch vessels joined her, they inflicted massive damage on the Spanish fleet. They watched as the bulk of the Spanish fleet still ahead of them turned and sailed back into Cadiz Bay. As they surged on towards Cadiz, Captain Monson peered towards the harbour.

'They're burning their own ships. They don't want us to get them.'

'I hope it's not the treasure ships they're sending to the bottom,' Essex exclaimed. 'Anyway, we're getting close now. I'll get my forces ready. How close can you get to the headland there, and put us ashore in the boats?' Essex asked, pointing at the headland.

'Close enough, my lord, and we'll give you covering fire as you go ashore.'

'Come on, Sir Anthony, Sir Roger. It's time to arm ourselves.'

Anthony went back to his cabin. He loaded and lit the matches on his matchlock pistols, put on his sword belt and tucked the pistols in the belt, then he went back on deck. They were now dropping anchor just off the city of Cadiz. The boats were being readied to lower and Essex was directing the men of his regiment into the boats. Then Essex, Sir Roger and Anthony got aboard and they were soon being rowed towards the land. The regular thump of the English and Dutch fleets' guns mainly drowned out the occasional zing of musket balls passing close by. They were soon wading the last few yards ashore, and Anthony pulled out his pistols and blew on the matches to keep them glowing. They ran to the city walls, where the Spanish defenders were having difficulty firing down at them.

'Be quick with the ladders, men,' shouted Essex. The first ladder arrived and was placed against the wall. It only reached about half-way up, but the wall above appeared to be quite ragged from the cannon ball impacts it had taken, and was continuing to take. 'Right, I'm going up,' Essex shouted above the clamour of gun and cannon fire. He started climbing the ladder. He was already off the top of the ladder and searching for foot and handholds on the remaining section of the wall. As more and more ladders appeared, everyone followed his example. When Anthony reached the top of the wall, Essex was clashing swords with Spanish soldiers and beating them back along the battlements. Anthony discharged one of his pistols into a Spaniard who was racing towards Essex from behind, and he crumpled as Anthony's ball struck home. More and more English and Dutch troops joined them, and the Spanish were soon in full retreat. By five o'clock, after three hours of heavy fighting, the city had been taken. Essex gathered his troops around him in the main square.

'Congratulations, men, you have won a glorious victory, I thank you. Shortly, we shall search the city and the remaining Spanish ships for treasure. You are to bring anything valuable back here where we will distribute it according to custom. The citizens of Cadiz are to be treated with respect and are not to be harmed, particularly the women and children. If any of you disobey this rule, I will have them shot. Have I made myself clear?'

'Yes, my lord.' the crowd murmured.

Anthony had been helping Essex, Admiral Howard, Raleigh, Vere and the Dutch commanders interrogate the Spanish senior officers. It appeared that reinforcements were on the way. They agreed that the citizens could leave the city in exchange for a ransom of 120,000 ducats and the release of English and Dutch prisoners. They would hold the city councillors as hostage until the ransom was paid.

'We should garrison the city as a base for further Anglo-Dutch operations. From here, we can strike against returning treasure ships,' argued Essex.

'I agree,' added Vere. The Dutch commanders all added their agreement.

'You have just heard that reinforcements are expected. We have secured a great victory already. It would be sheer folly to risk it all against an unknown force which approaches, even as we speak. And there is, of course, the fact that it would be expressly against the queen's orders. Have you forgotten that?' Admiral Howard retorted.

'As you know, admiral, sometimes the commander in the field has to act on their initiative,' Essex replied. The argument raged on, but the tide swung against Essex. Reluctantly, he agreed that they would burn the city once the ransom was paid, and then sail home with their treasure.

On the 14th of July, news arrived that Spanish reinforcements were within a few days of reaching the city. No ransom had been forthcoming, so the prisoners, together with all the treasure, were loaded onto the ships, and they set the city ablaze. The following day, they set sail for England.

When they arrived back in Portsmouth in August 1596, they divided the spoils. Anthony's share was, if not enough to buy a grand country house set in a hundred acres of parkland, enough to go a good way towards it. He travelled with Essex to Windsor, where they presented the queen with their report of the raid and the lion's share of the spoils. Anthony judged that this was a good time to collect his back pay from 1588, and the queen agreed that he should collect it from the lord chancellor.

He and Essex had just left the throne room when they met Sir Robert Cecil and Sir Walter Raleigh about to enter.

'I hear congratulations are in order, Sir Robert. You are finally Principal Secretary of State,' Essex said, not quite between clenched teeth.

'Thank you, my lord. It is gratifying to be recognised for my labours.'

'And what, may I ask, is your business with Her Majesty, Sir Walter?' Essex asked.

'Simply to render my account of the campaign, my lord,' Sir Walter replied.

'Of that, there is no need, we have just this minute given full and frank account,' Essex replied.

'Come, Sir Walter, the queen does not like to be kept waiting. We bid you good day, my lord, Sir Anthony,' Sir Robert said, smiling as he led Raleigh into the throne room.

'Sir Anthony, you see to your business with the lord chancellor. I will see you back at Barn Elms. Wait for me there, would you?'

'Of course, my lord.'

When he had obtained his money from the lord chancellor, he went first to a gunsmith and purchased a pair of wheellock pistols. He bought a horse next, which he named Lightning. Then he went to Hatton Garden and converted all of his wealth into diamonds. From there, he rode to East Molesey. This time, his brother Edmund was in. He discovered that he now had another nephew, Thomas, who was two. He played with his nephews until bedtime, then he sat up late drinking and reminiscing with Edmund. After everyone was fast asleep, Anthony got up, went outside to the toolshed, and selected a shovel. He checked that nobody was stirring in the house and went down to the large oak tree in the garden. He dug a deep hole in the ground beneath the tree, two paces from the trunk in the direction of the house. There he buried his purse with the diamonds, tamping down the soil, and scattering leaves to disguise his hiding place.

Anthony was walking in the grounds of Barn Elms when Essex arrived.

'Sir Anthony, I'm going to need your help. Raleigh has given the queen an entirely fictitious account of the raid. He has exaggerated his own part and played mine down. But the worst of it is his claim that the land forces took the lion's share of the loot, and kept it to ourselves. You know the truth of the matter; I shall write a pamphlet setting out the true account. You can help where my memory fails.'

'Surely the queen believes you rather than that knave, my lord?'

'Unfortunately, where money is concerned, the queen is quick to doubt that she has received her fair share. She is to set up a commission to investigate. Come, we must get writing.'

Over the coming days, they put together a full and detailed account of the raid, and Essex had it published. The queen was furious and had the remaining copies seized. She banned Essex from writing any more accounts of the raid.

'What shall we do now, my lord?' Anthony asked.

'We are banned from writing, but I have asked the Archbishop of Canterbury to hold a day of public thanksgiving on the 8th of August, celebrating the success of the raid and making the people clearly aware of my part. I am also going to have a map of Cadiz made, with illustrations of my scaling of the wall and other key events.'

'It's inventive, my lord, of course, but won't the queen see that as flouting her rule?' Anthony suggested.

'Raleigh has now published his own account, and she hasn't banned that. What else can I do?'

'I don't know, my lord.'

'Oh, that is coming along magnificently, Signor Boazio. Could we make the city walls just a little higher?' Anthony asked.

'You can call me Baptista, you know, if I may call you Anthony.'

'Yes, that's very good. How can we make it clearer that it is our lord Essex scaling the wall? We can't write it. Using his coat of arms is akin to writing, but could you reference his coat of arms somehow? Oh yes, I see, that's perfect.' Essex entered the room. 'My lord, the map is nearly finished. What do you think?'

'Yes, it's very good. Anthony, there is marvellous news from court. The Spanish treasure fleet has returned to Cadiz, vindicating my argument for holding the city and delaying our return. The queen is incensed with the leading seamen, and Raleigh in particular. How do you fancy another voyage? I'm planning an expedition to sail to Ferrol, and perhaps the Azores to intercept the next treasure fleet.'

'I suppose you can never have too much treasure, my lord,' Anthony replied, smiling. With a share of treasure like the last one, that will finally be enough to build a grand house for Francesca, he thought.

They sailed from Plymouth at the beginning of July 1597. Essex had been given command of five thousand men and seventeen of the queen's ships. Anthony and Essex were aboard the Merhonneur, and Raleigh was on Warspite. The queen's orders were to find and destroy the Spanish fleet, and only then to intercept the treasure ships. As they crossed the Bay of Biscay, severe gales battered and scattered the fleet. They reassembled off Lisbon, but had lost too many ships and men in the gales to mount an attack against the Spanish fleet.

Anthony listened to the commanders debating the next move. They considered blockading the Portuguese coast, but eventually decided to head for the Azores and try to intercept the treasure ships there. The ships had been seriously damaged in the gales, and the voyage south was difficult and slow. By the time they reached the Azores, there had been much sickness and death amongst the crews. They took on fresh water and provisions, but there was no news of the treasure ships, so with reluctance, it was agreed that they should return home. As they approached the Isles of Scilly, they were hit by a storm, and the fleet was once again scattered. When the Merhonneur eventually reached Falmouth, they were told that an armada of a hundred and thirty-six ships had been launched against England. Fortunately, the armada had been decimated by the same storm that the Merhonneur had just survived. Many Spanish ships had been wrecked on the Cornish coast, some had taken refuge in Falmouth and been captured.

'I had better go to court. I think I have some explaining to do,' Essex said.

'Shall I come with you, my lord?' asked Anthony.

'Thank you, Anthony, but no. There is no good to be done by your good honour suffering alongside mine. Go back to Barn Elms, or Twickenham as you see fit. I hope I shall see you again.'

A tear ran down Anthony's cheek as he saw his good friend and master walk off, head downcast.

CHAPTER THIRTEEN

1597 - 1604, Ireland

Anthony stayed at Twickenham with Francis and Anthony Bacon throughout the winter of 1597. Francis had been elected as a Member of Parliament for Ipswich and was busy drafting speeches. Essex visited occasionally from Barn Elms. The queen still held Essex responsible for failing to stop the third armada, and he was unwelcome at court.

'What are the speeches about, Francis?' his brother asked.

'The first is against enclosures, the theft of common land from the people, but the second is in favour of the bill of subsidy. That provides for a tax on wealth to swell the queen's coffers. I shall use this speech to side for the crown, but warn of the threat of invasion and the ulcer of Ireland. I shall heap praise on Essex for the success of the Cadiz raid, and point out that the severe weather, rather than any fault on Essex's part, robbed the expedition to Ferrol and the Azores of success.'

'Well said, brother.'

When Francis returned a few weeks later from parliament, he reported that the subsidy bill had been passed and the queen had been delighted. She had even invited Essex back to court again. Throughout 1598, a tussle took place between Essex and Robert Cecil over who should take over command of the English army in Ireland. Essex put forward candidates from Cecil's allies and Cecil put forward friends of Essex. Each wished to weaken the other's voice in court. In the summer, Essex came to visit the Bacons at Twickenham.

'My lord, we did not expect you. You look troubled,' said Anthony Bacon.

'My temper has overcome me. I fear that in a heated exchange in council, I turned my back on the queen and she slapped me. I reached for my sword and it was only the intervention of the Lord Admiral that restrained me. I am banished from court again.' For a long interlude, everyone was silent.

'I shall fetch some wine,' said Anthony Bacon. 'It will calm our nerves.'

'My lord, something will turn up. I have found that when all hope is lost, something will turn up. Do you remember my story of when I was imprisoned in Bordeaux Castle? I had lost all hope. My lock picks had been taken, yet one day a guard dropped some pamphlets. I was able to secure some sheets and send a message to Anthony on a paper dart, thrown from the window.'

'Thank you, Sir Anthony. I hope you are right, but I know not what might turn up.'

In August William Cecil died aged seventy-seven. Ten days later, the English army in Ireland suffered a massive defeat at the Battle of Yellow Ford. Essex was recalled to court. Robert Cecil and Essex continued their verbal jousting until, when all other candidates to lead the English army had been exhausted, Cecil proposed Essex. Essex, against his better judgement, accepted. He visited Twickenham once more.

'I have at least secured the largest army ever sent to Ireland. Sixteen thousand troops, thirteen hundred horse, and two thousand more troops every three months. Will you come with me, Sir Anthony? You said something would turn up, and it has. I would welcome your company and your good council. I know I can trust you to watch my back, just as you did on the battlements in

Cadiz. Say you will.'

'My lord, it will be an honour,' Anthony said hesitantly. 'I hope we shall soon defeat the rebels.'

Essex arrived in Dublin on Sunday, the 15th of April, 1599. He met with the council of Dublin to discuss strategy. The rebel leader was Hugh O'Neill, Earl of Tyrone. His confederates were Hugh O'Donnell and Edmund Fitzgibbon, known as the white knight. The council suggested attacking to the east of Dublin. Essex agreed to reinforce the garrison to the east, but decided that he would lead an army south. Their first significant encounter with the rebels was at the Cashel pass. It was wooded and boggy. From the cover of the trees, the soldiers were an easy target. Essex encouraged his army to get through the pass as quickly as possible, but lost around a third of his army in the ambush. The remaining army continued south to Kilkenny, where they received a warm welcome.

Essex took Cahir Castle after two days of an artillery barrage breached the wall. He then marched west to Limerick, where he took on numerous baggage porters to help carry supplies. Unfortunately, they turned out to be slow, and a hinderance. Essex marched his men all around Southern Ireland, constantly trying to draw the rebels into battle, but without success. The rebels just picked away at stragglers, bit by bit, weakening Essex's army. After eight weeks, he returned to Dublin.

'Anthony, this is hopeless. I asked you to watch my back, and you have loyally followed me. But now I think I need to let you off the leash and use your greatest talents.'

'What do you mean, my lord?'

'I need you to go undercover, join Hugh O'Neill's

army.'

'I see. How can I do that? My languages don't stretch to Gaelic.'

'I'm sure you'll think of something. Pretend to be a Catholic perhaps, or a deserter, a Spanish emissary possibly. Whatever you decide, I need intelligence on his strength, his hiding places, and his plans. You could try getting close to Mabel, Countess of Kildare. She was a courtier of Queen Mary and was known to keep priests in her household during Elizabeth's reign. She married Fitzgerald, Earl of Kildare, and came here. Approach her as a Catholic and she may tell you how to find O'Neill.'

'Where do I find her, my lord?'

'Kilkea Castle, a day's ride southwest from here.'

Anthony judged Mabel to be in her early sixties, but in good health.

'So what can I do for you, Sir Anthony?'

'My lady, I worked abroad as an agent for Mary Queen of Scots. It was she who knighted me. When she was executed, I went to work for Spain. I was with their third armada, but we were shipwrecked. I barely survived. I struck my head on a rock and lost all memory of who I was. Some good Catholic Irishmen pulled me from the water and looked after me. Only in the last month has my memory come back to me. I want to help the Catholic cause, and they told me that you might be able to advise how I could do that.'

'How do I know you are who you say you are?' Mabel asked. Anthony talked for the best part of an hour, giving details of Mary's court in Scotland, the Spanish nobles he knew, his time in Florence and Rome, and details of the armada.

'Well, your story sounds authentic. I may be able to

introduce you to someone. Quite what he will do with you, I cannot judge.'

'Thank you, my lady.'

'Of course it may be some time before he is available to see you. Until then you can stay here.'

It was the middle of the night in mid-August when three armed men arrived at the castle to collect Anthony. They tied his hands behind his back and blindfolded him. Then they bundled him into a cart and drove off. Anthony was bashed around as the cart rocked on the deeply rutted roads. He estimated they'd travelled around ten miles, but in which direction he had no idea. When they stopped, he was helped down from the cart. He was guided to a door, which was opened, and led inside. The door was closed behind him, and then his hands were untied and his blindfold removed.

'I'm sorry about the rough treatment, but we have to be careful. Please take a seat. Would you like some of our good Irish whisky?'

'Yes, please. May I ask who you are?' Anthony enquired, as he studied the man in front of him. He was tall, had red hair and beard, and was probably close to Anthony's age, late forties.

'I'm Hugh O'Neill, Earl of Tyrone. I understand you'd like to join us. Now why would that be?' Anthony told him the story he had told Mabel, finishing with the shipwreck. 'Well that's all very well, but you're English aren't you.'

'Yes, but I'm a Catholic first and foremost. The treatment of us by my countrymen abhors me, whether it's in England or Ireland.'

'I'm not fighting the English because I'm Catholic, I'm fighting them because I'm Irish. You're English

246

whether you like it or not, it's where you were born. I don't need you. I know the men who fight for me. I know their fathers, and in some cases their grandfathers. I know my allies too, if not their men.'

'I suppose your men love you.'

'Some do, but plenty hate me as well. If we weren't fighting the English, we'd be fighting each other in the old clan rivalries. I hear Essex's men love him, that great crowds lined the streets of London to cheer him on his way when he came here. Well, they'll not be cheering when he goes home, if he goes home. But my men would continue fighting without me, because they're fighting for their land. What is it to be English? Romans, Germans, Vikings and the French have conquered you. You've become well acquainted with being conquered. We've only been conquered by yourselves, and we're taking a while to get used to it.'

'I can help you. I know the Spanish. I can liaise with them for you.'

'We already have all the help we need from the Spanish. But you've got balls, I'll give you that. I'm actually getting to like you a little. Here, have some more whisky. But I don't need you in my army.'

'What are you going to do with me?' Anthony asked.

'I've gone to great trouble to ensure you don't know where we are. We'll be moving on soon, in any case. As I say, I quite like you, so you'll be taken back to Kilkea Castle, the same way you were brought here. I suggest you stay there. If a hair on Mabel's head is harmed, I'll track you down, you can be sure of that.'

'So how did you get on, Sir Anthony?' Mabel enquired.

'Well, we did get on, at least. That is to say, I liked Hugh very much, despite the rough treatment I had. And he seemed to like me. But he doesn't want me in his army.'

'I thought he might say that. So what will you do now?'

'He suggested that I sit it out here, if that's all right with you?'

'It will be nice to have someone new to talk to. Are you married Sir Anthony?'

'No. I'd like to be, but what with working for Queen Mary, and then the Spanish, and trying to make my fortune, I haven't got round to it.'

'You haven't met the right girl, that's what it is.'

'No, you're wrong there,' Anthony said sadly. 'I did, but work got in the way again, and I was still trying to make my fortune. And now I fear I've left it too late.'

'Is she a Spanish girl?'

'No, Italian. Her name's Francesca. But it's been sixteen years since I saw her.'

'That is a long time to keep a girl waiting. Shame on you.'

'I take it you were married.'

'I was eighteen when I married Gerald. We met at a masked ball and it was love at first sight.'

'At first sight, seems an odd phrase for a masked ball.'

'I can see we're going to get along famously; you have a sharp wit, Sir Anthony. Can we drop the sirs and countesses?'

'Of course, Mabel. I'm sorry, I take it Gerald is no longer with us?'

'No, he died fourteen years ago, imprisoned in the Tower of London. Queen Elizabeth liked him, but he had enemies too. They used to call him the Wizard Earl because of his interest in alchemy. He had a laboratory in the west tower. I haven't been in there since he died.'

'I learnt quite a bit about alchemy, at the same time that I met Francesca. I was working for the Grand Duke of Tuscany. He was a keen alchemist. I translated some Arabic books for him. Did you have children?'

'Three boys and two girls.'

Anthony enjoyed Mabel's company and exploring the castle and grounds. He had really liked Hugh O'Neill, and didn't really want to fight him any more. He did want to help Essex, but wasn't at all sure the fight was a good fight. And there certainly wasn't any treasure to be had. On Tuesday 25th September, Mabel told him that Essex had sailed for England the previous day. Anthony was still in Kilkea Castle in February when news arrived of Essex's house arrest. He was still there when he heard Essex was being tried for treason and in February 1601, when he heard that Essex had been beheaded. Anthony was once more without a master and wondered how his close association with Essex would be considered by Queen Elizabeth. He was still in Kilkea Castle at the end of March 1603 when news arrived that Queen Elizabeth had died and that James was King. He packed his bag, saddled his horse, thanked Mabel for her kindness and generosity, and rode like the wind to Dublin.

CHAPTER FOURTEEN

1603, England

Anthony waited in the hall of Whitehall Palace until he saw the familiar short, hunchback figure of Sir Robert Cecil limping towards him.

'Sir Anthony, it's so good to see you again. How was Ireland?'

'Wet, it hardly ever stops raining, Sir Robert. Is King James ready to receive me yet?'

'We should give him a little more time; he is reading the dossier on you that I prepared for him. It is quite a long dossier.'

'Good. I hope you have missed nothing out.'

'Nothing at all, Sir Anthony. I have your pension here, for the period you were in Ireland. It is a tidy sum.' Sir Robert handed Anthony a purse.

'Thank you, Sir Robert. I wonder if the king would consider the back pay his father owed me from when I was in his service. That would amount to around two hundred pounds.'

'Shall we see if he has finished reading the dossier? You can ask him yourself.' Anthony followed Sir Robert to the throne room. 'Wait here a moment.' Sir Robert went in and moments later beckoned Anthony to enter. Anthony went in and bowed before the king and queen. He noted how tall King James was, and thought that he was definitely Darnley's son. The rumours concerning David Rizzio, Mary's secretary, were obviously unfounded. Rizzio was very short. Queen Anne of Denmark was strikingly beautiful, probably in her late twenties, Anthony thought.

'Your Majesty, Your Majesty,' Anthony said, bowing again to each.

'Sir Anthony, I have read this account of your work. You have had quite an adventurous life.'

'Indeed, Your Majesty. Does it include the fact that I saved your mother's life when she was carrying you? That was when her secretary was murdered. I was knighted by her for that.'

'No, I don't remember reading that. Sir Robert, would you verify that and add it to the account, if true,' King James ordered.

'I trust, Your Majesty, that it does include the intelligence I supplied concerning the armada of 1588?' Anthony asked.

'Yes, that is included. You did England a very great service in that respect.' The king stifled a yawn.

'I wonder, Your Majesty, if it pleases you, there is a small matter of some back pay I am owed, for the time I was in the service of your late father in Scotland. My service was interrupted, as you will know, and I am still owed around two hundred pounds.'

'Perhaps. I have a mission for you. Your facility in languages may be of service to me. I need an envoy to visit all the crown princes of Europe carrying news of my ascension. Sir Robert will give you letters of introduction and gifts, portraits of us. We will cover your expenses together with a handsome salary.'

'Your Majesty, it will be a very great honour.' Anthony bowed again, and Sir Robert tugged at his sleeve to draw him away.

They went to Sir Robert's office.

'That box in the corner has everything you need. Portraits of the king and queen with the princes and princesses, as gifts; letters of introduction; a script of the news you are to convey, and an itinerary, which has been carefully calculated to get you around all the royal houses in the shortest possible time. You will finish with a visit to the pope and then return here. There is a purse which will cover your expenses, although I expect you will be entertained quite adequately en route. There is a coach and driver waiting to take you to Dover. The coach and driver will be put aboard one of His Majesty's ships, which will convey you to Calais. The coach and driver will then be at your disposal for the rest of your mission. Any questions?'

'You won't forget the back pay from my time in Scotland, will you, Sir Robert?'

'I'll have it looked into. Good day, Sir Anthony.'

'Oh, there is one other thing, Sir Robert. If I am provided with a coach, will you have someone look after my horse? He was taken to the stable when I arrived, a big, black stallion, his name's Lightning.' Anthony picked up the box and left.

He carried his box out to the courtyard, where there was a coach and coachman waiting, so he walked across to them. As he approached, he thought he recognised the driver. The driver climbed down and opened the carriage door for him, smiling.

'Walter, is that you, my old shipmate?'

'Indeed it is, Anthony, sorry, Sir Anthony. It's very good to see you again, sir.'

'Forget the sir. How are you, Walter? It must be over thirty years. My god, where do the years go?' They shook hands and slapped each other on the back. 'What a coincidence, to see you here now, and you're my driver.'

'Well, it is a bit of a coincidence, but not totally. When I came back to England, I met a girl and we have a small house and a patch of land. We've four boys and two girls now, and I needed to make a bit more money. A chap I know recommended me to the palace as a coach driver. I've been driving the royal family and their guests around for three years now, and when this job came up, I said, I know an Anthony Standen, and here I am Anthony. Would you like to get in?'

'Not a bit. I shall sit up on top with you. We can catch up as you drive.' Anthony climbed up and Walter placed the box in the carriage, climbed up and sat beside Anthony. He took the reins, and they drove off on the road to Dover. Walter wanted to know about Anthony's adventures, and Anthony was happy to recount them.

'So do you have any children, Anthony?'

'No. I wanted children.'

'Didn't you meet the right girl?'

'I did.'

'So why didn't you settle down?'

'I don't know. There was the job, and I was trying to make a fortune. But every time I got close to making one, I kept losing it.'

'I'm driving you all over Europe on the king's business to meet kings and princes. Don't tell me you have no money now?'

'You're right, I have a reasonable fortune now.'

'So what about that girl then? Where is she?'

'I can't be sure. She may still be in Florence. It was, let me see, getting on for sixteen years ago. She's probably married by now. She could even be dead. Who knows?'

'Anthony, what earthly point is there in having a fortune if you don't have a wife to spend it for you?'

'Walter, you're probably the second wisest man I've ever met. Possibly the wisest.'

'Really, who am I competing against?'
'William of Orange.'

CHAPTER FIFTEEN

1603 - 1604, France, Venice & Florence

They had driven throughout a long, hot summer and autumn across the parched landscape of Europe.

'Well, just Rome next and then we can go home, that's right isn't it, Anthony?'

'Yes, Walter. I'm rather looking forward to Rome, at least, and meeting the pope.'

'How have all the other meetings gone, Anthony?'

'To be honest, Walter, my heart hasn't been in it. It's your fault. I haven't been able to stop thinking about Francesca. She was the girl in Florence. And they're all such hypocrites. They're Protestant when it's fashionable to be Protestant, and Catholic when that's in favour. Nobody seems able to live and let live. I've tried to tell them about William of Orange and how he didn't see that it was the role of a king to tell his subjects what their faith must be, but I don't think it went down well. They seemed to think I was getting above my station.'

'Are you going to give the pope a good talking to Anthony? About the Spanish Inquisition and all that?'

'We shall see. I'll certainly be interested in what he thinks.'

Much needed rain was falling on an unusually bitter day in early November 1603. Anthony entered the guardroom and presented his letter of introduction to Cardinal Aldobrandini. He was told to take a seat while one guard went off with his letter. Anthony warmed his hands in front of the fire. He was just getting warm when the guard returned and took him to meet Pope Clement the Eighth. He told the pope about the ascension of King James and gave the pope the king's greetings and the portraits of the king and queen and their children.

'Queen Anne of Denmark is a Catholic, of course,' the pope stated.

'Yes, Your Holiness, but I believe she has had to swear to forego the Catholic rites for the purpose of her marriage to the king. She is outwardly a Protestant.'

'And what about you, Sir Anthony, are you outwardly a Protestant too?'

'I have had to be, since I was a child, Your Holiness. It is not too hard. When I was a child, I saw Protestants burnt at the stake. They cried out to Christ to forgive those who burnt them. All I wish for is that rulers would permit their subjects to follow the faith that they chose, so long as it doesn't affect anyone else.'

'Wouldn't it be better if one faith united all of humanity?'

'It would be, if it prevented war. But it never has, has it, Your Holiness? It seems to me that there is very little difference between the faiths. I spent some time in Constantinople and learnt a little about Islam. I really don't know what we have been fighting over, or why the Jews have been persecuted, when Christ himself was a Jew. The inquisition has tortured and burnt many good men in the name of the Catholic Church. Is it not so, Your Holiness?'

'I am supposed to be the representative of God on earth, yet although I have considerable power, I am often quite powerless. Pope Innocent the second banned crossbows as a weapon too dreadful to be used. Pope Julius the third banned the wheellock mechanism for guns. Yet these weapons are used in ever greater numbers.

Often all I can do is try to influence. God lives within each one of us, but so does Satan.'

'The only thing I miss about Catholicism is the confession, Your Holiness. I beg your forgiveness, if I talk too frankly.'

'It is refreshing to be spoken to frankly, my son. Would you like me to hear your confession?'

'Your Holiness, do you mean that?'

'I wouldn't say it otherwise.' And so Anthony made his confession to Pope Clement. 'You have lived a very interesting life, Anthony. Of course, the sanctity of the confession is absolute, but you should be careful. If you had made your confession to Pope Sixtus, you might have found yourself burnt at the stake. I try to mediate between the warring nations: the wars of religion grieve me deeply. I don't share your respect for the Ottomans, but I have never been there. You can trust my nephew, Cardinal Aldobrandini, but I would otherwise suggest that you keep your work for the Protestants to yourself. On a lighter note, it is funny about the cipher breaking. In 1593, King Philip the second appealed to me to put a man, Francois Viete, on trial for witchcraft. It was because he had published the contents of certain letters that Philip had written. Because the letters had been in cipher, Philip honestly believed that Viete must have used witchcraft. Of course, everyone had been reading the Spanish ciphers. They were so easy to break. Viete was a mathematician, a brilliant man. He invented something quite new called algebra in which they substitute letters for numbers in equations. It is a powerful technique which may be put to the greater good of mankind. On the other hand, it may be used to develop new and more powerful weapons.'

'I know of algebra, Your Holiness. The Persians used

it. I have read about it in Arabic texts.'

'You are indeed a very interesting fellow, Sir Anthony. There is a man that Cardinal Bellarmine has told me about, at the University of Padua. He is a brilliant scientist and astronomer called Galileo. I am told that he is working on a theory that the sun does not move around the earth, but that the earth moves around the sun.'

'Nonsense, Your Holiness, surely? Everyone can see the sun rise in the morning, cross the sky and set in the evening.'

'I think so, and the idea conflicts with the scriptures. We are keeping a close eye on him, and some day we may have to act. If people lose their faith in a small part of the scriptures, who knows where it might end? Now this girl in Florence, Francesca wasn't it? If you bring her to Rome, I will marry you myself, if she is not, as you fear, already married of course.'

'Would you really, Your Holiness? That would be such an honour.'

'As I said, I wouldn't say it if I didn't mean it. You could settle down here and raise the family you want. There are several villas that the church owns. We could sell you one. There is one thing I would like you to do first, though, if you are happy to do so. The executions of Catholics in England pain me. Those who wish to be Protestant, should be allowed to be. But those who wish to be Catholic should also be free to observe their faith, as you have already said. I would like you to take a gift from me to Queen Anne. I would like to see if she could influence the king to be more lenient in his treatment of Catholics. Would you do that?'

'It carries great danger, Your Holiness. The message would need great subtlety, but yes, I would do it.'

'I agree, it must be carefully thought through. Would

you discuss the details with Cardinal Aldobrandini? There are also two Englishmen here who may be able to help. He will introduce you. Go in peace, my son.'

Anthony was directed to the cardinal's study. He knocked on the door and was told to enter. 'Cardinal Aldobrandini, his holiness asked me to discuss with you the details of a mission I am to carry out for him,' Anthony said.

'Yes, please take a seat. Would you like some wine?'

'Yes please, Your Eminence. I am quite thirsty,' Anthony replied. Cardinal Aldobrandini got up from his chair and went to a room next door for a moment, then he came back. He was a tall, quite handsome man in his early thirties. Moments later, a servant arrived with two silver goblets and a flagon of wine. He poured wine for them both, then left. The cardinal reached into his desk drawer and took out a gold casket encrusted with diamonds, rubies, and sapphires. He placed it on his desk.

'It's beautiful, isn't it? It's worth a king's ransom.' He turned the key and opened the casket. Inside there was a letter, which he took out. 'This is a letter that his holiness has written to Queen Anne. It has been translated into Danish, the language of the queen's homeland, as a precaution. It is unlikely that King James speaks Danish. It asks her to persuade the king to exercise some tolerance towards the Catholics in his realm. If she can do this, then it asks her to write a thank you note for the gift to his holiness. Using three particular specified words in the letter will be a sign that she has done this. On receipt of this note, his holiness will make you a cardinal. I suggest you give the queen the casket, but find a way of slipping the key to her, warning her, if you can, not to unlock it immediately. There, what do you say to that?'

'A cardinal, I'm, well, I'm speechless. But I don't

think I have the holiness to be a cardinal. The gold from a cardinal's vestments would suffice.'

'We shall see what we can do. As to being speechless, I know a fellow who will do all the talking for you. He's a fellow countryman of yours, studying for the priesthood. Edmund Thornhill is his name, he's a clever fellow.' Cardinal Aldobrandini drained his goblet of wine, got up and led Anthony out of his office and down a corridor to a small office where a short man in a black habit was writing at a desk.

'Edmund, this is Sir Anthony Standen. I'll leave you two to become acquainted,' Aldobrandini said as he left.

'Sir Anthony, I'm delighted to meet you. Please sit down. I'm sorry it's a bit cramped in here. I have heard that you were knighted by Mary Queen of Scots. I'd be fascinated to hear about her. There are so many views about Mary that to meet someone who actually knew her, well it's an opportunity I can't miss.'

'Yes I was. I served as master of horse to Lord Darnley, her husband.' Anthony told Edmund at some length the whole story of how he had saved her life when she was carrying the unborn King James, and how she had then knighted him. 'Of course, many people didn't recognise my knighthood, but years later I was knighted by Queen Elizabeth.'

'How wonderful to be knighted twice. What did you do to impress Queen Elizabeth?'

'Well, it's a long story, but I managed to gather… well, no, we digress. Cardinal Aldobrandini said that you had something to talk about. What is it?'

'I see you have the casket. My argument, for what it's worth, is that when Queen Ann is aware of the pope's wishes, she may wish to have close confidants around her, ladies of similar persuasion, the Countess of Arundell perhaps. There should also be some incentive for the king to be tolerant. I am trying to persuade the cardinal that we might make it known that in return for toleration, his holiness would undertake to excommunicate any Catholic found conspiring against the king.'

'Your argument makes excellent sense, Edmund. I have always found the carrot more effective than the stick.'

'Yes, according to my reckoning, there are at least five hundred Catholic priests in England and innumerable Catholics of all ranks in English society. There is no shortage of Catholics in Scotland and Ireland either. Without a leader, if they see the king defending the heretics and persecuting Catholics, they may find a leader themselves. But if the king permitted a few cardinals to head the Catholic Church in England, Scotland and Ireland, and if these were men he could trust to quell any conspiracy against his throne, then surely that would be good for everyone.'

'I agree. So is this the agreed policy of the pope?' Anthony asked.

'Almost I think. The problem is that he has to listen to all the cardinals. There is one other Englishman here, of significant influence. He's a radical Jesuit. He has been working to overwhelm England with Jesuits, and considers any toleration of heretics a sin. In my opinion, if Father Persons had stuck to tending to people's souls rather than politics, England would have converted to Catholicism by now,' Edmund whispered.

'Persons you say. Robert Persons?'

'Yes, have you heard of him?'

'I met him the last time I was in Rome. That would have been November 1587,' Anthony said, stroking his beard.

'Would you like to meet him again? He's just next door.'

'Yes, I suppose it would be best to reacquaint myself with him.'

'Robert, this is Sir Anthony Standen,' Edmund said.

'Sir Anthony, we've met. I remember you well. I was going to enrol you in the English College, but you didn't turn up.'

'No, I was delayed. A ruffian attacked me.'

'There were many ruffians in Rome that year. A good friend of mine was attacked the same night, near the college. Perhaps it was the same man.' Persons said. 'Would you leave us please Edmund, we have much to catch up on.' Edmund left and closed the door.

'I trust your friend recovered?' Anthony asked.

'Unfortunately not. He had a weak heart.'

'I'm sorry to hear that,' Anthony replied. 'What is your role in the mission with which his holiness has entrusted me?'

'I have worked long and hard to prepare Jesuits for the ministry in England. A full conversion of England to Catholicism is almost within our grasp. I can feel it. In France, there have been gains and setbacks. I continue to urge his holiness to be forceful with the heretics. I extol one strategy, and Edmund urges another. Cardinal Aldobrandini puts all the arguments to his holiness, and he decides.'

'I see. Well, I must be getting along. It's been good to meet you again. I'm sorry to hear about your friend, I've forgotten his name.'

'Charles Neville.'

'That's right.'

Anthony closed the door behind him. As he walked back along the corridor towards the cardinal's office, Edmund opened the door of his office as he passed.

'Sir Anthony, where will you be staying on your way back to London? In case there are any changes to instructions.'

'I'll probably stop a while in Florence, and then in Paris. I'll visit the Thurn and Taxis offices before I leave, to see if there is any mail for me.'

'Excellent. Good luck, Sir Anthony, I wish I was coming with you.'

'Thank you, Edmund.'

In his office, Robert Persons was thinking about the conversation he had overheard from Edmund's room. What was it that Standen did to earn Queen Elizabeth's favour, and why did he stop himself from revealing it? Charles will be very interested to know that Standen is here, he thought.

'There's Florence ahead, Anthony. Where exactly does Francesca live?' Walter asked.

'I'm not sure I should visit Francesca Walter. Let's just go to the Thurn and Taxis office and see if I have any mail. We can find a tavern for the night and get on the road again tomorrow.'

'Are you completely mad, Anthony? You're obviously in love with the girl. It doesn't take a genius to see that.'

'It's such a simple word, isn't it, love? Do you know that the Greeks had seven words for love? Let me see if I can remember them all. Storge is unconditional familial love. I don't think father was very good at showing that. Mother was better. If I'm honest with myself, I'm also chasing philautia.'

'What kind of love is that?' Walter asked curiously.

'Self-love, or self-esteem. I do crave status and fame. I've had my moments of eros too, that's romantic passionate love. Thinking about Barbara, I've encountered ludus too. That's playful, flirtatious love.' Anthony paused.

'Barbara sounds interesting. Who's she?'

'It would take longer to tell than the time it took in reality. She's stunningly beautiful, a little older than me. I had only a few days before I discovered that she was the mother of Don Juan of Austria, who had been taken away from her at birth, when Don Juan started banging on her front door. It was rather bad timing.'

'Oh, you don't mean…'

'Yes, I do. Then there's philia, that's great friendship. That's the love that we have, shipmate love. Do you know which seems to me to be the rarest of the Greek loves?'

'No.'

'Agápe. That is empathetic, universal love, a love of God, of nature and of humanity itself. So many people claim to love God, but are quick to burn people who worship God in a slightly different way. It's a crazy world. We've both seen such cruelty, and far too much death.'

'You're right about that. I've been counting, and I think that's six. What is the seventh word for love?'

'Pragma, that is committed, long-term love and understanding, the love rooted in romance and companionship.'

'So which is it with this Francesca girl then?'

'She's not a girl anymore, Walter. She'll be thirty-three by now. I'm sure she'll be married, with children. I shouldn't interfere.'

'If she is, she is. But surely if there's even a chance,

then you should find out.'

'You're right, Walter. It's just that I'm scared. I don't think I could bear it if she were married, and even that would be better than if she had died.'

'Well, you're going to find out. I'm going to make you. If she is dead or married, you can move on, find someone else. All the time you've got her in your dreams, you're stuck. Hang on, look at those flowers. I'll stop a minute and you jump down and pick some.' When Anthony climbed back up holding a bunch of wild flowers, Walter set off again. 'Now where is her house?'

Anthony gave Walter directions to Francesca's mother's house. His mind was spinning as they drove through the familiar streets. He would be an embarrassment, a long-distant, faded memory. They should just drive on to Paris and then to England, his homeland, and then they turned onto Francesca's street.

'This is it, Walter, stop here.'

'Good luck, Anthony. I'll wait here.'

With his stomach churning and his palms sweating, Anthony knocked on Francesca's mother's door. He heard footsteps and then the door opened.

'Anthony, I knew you would come back. Oh, my darling, hold me, tell me it's true. I'm not dreaming, am I?' Anthony dropped the flowers he had picked from the roadside and hugged Francesca, squeezing her, feeling her warmth against him, her heart pounding with his, feeling her tears on his cheek.

'I'll go to the tavern we just passed. Come and find me when you're ready. Take your time!' Walter shouted down from the coach as he drove off.

'No, my darling, it's not a dream.' They hugged and cried. Then Anthony noticed a young man sauntering towards them from the kitchen, carrying some chopped firewood. 'Who is the young man? He reminds me of my younger brother, Edmund, when he was that age.'

'That shouldn't surprise you, Anthony, my love. Antonio, come and meet your father. I told you he would come one day.'

'I have a son. My god, I have a son.' The lad dropped the firewood, turned and walked back towards the kitchen. 'Doesn't he want to meet his father?' Anthony asked Francesca.

'They're almost sixteen. You've been away a long time. He's grown up with three women. He's had to be the man of the house. He's also had to grow up being called a bastard and beaten by the other boys. It hasn't been easy for them or me. I have my friends, but many people spit at me and call me a whore. I always told them you'd come back one day, but I don't think they believed me. I'm not sure I believed myself. They will take time.'

'My god, I didn't think, I'm so sorry. You said they?'

'We have twins. You have a daughter too, Maria. She works at the mill. She'll be home soon.'

'Is your mother still here?'

'No, I'm afraid Mother died last year. She was a great help when the children were young. I've been working as a seamstress to make some money. We eat, but the children only had a basic education. They're good children, you'll get to know them. It will take time, you'll have to be patient.'

'I have some money now. We will buy a big house, and I have much I can teach them. I assume Antonio de Medici is the Grand Duke now?'

'No, Ferdinando, his uncle is the Grand Duke. Didn't you know? I've heard he's in Venice on business at the moment though.'

'No, I didn't know. That is awkward. My darling, we will marry. Pope Clement said he would marry us himself, and we will buy a big house. Antonio and Maria will go to school properly, but I'm afraid it can't be here, not in Tuscany. Ferdinando poisoned Bianca, and he probably poisoned his brother too. He knows I know he did it, and it isn't safe for me here. It won't be safe for you either. I am on a mission for the pope and have to return to England. Will you and the children come with me?'

Francesca was silent for a while, just hugging Anthony and crying.

'Oh my darling, what would I do in England? I don't speak English. I wouldn't have any friends. Can't we stay in Italy? You speak Italian as well as I do. Won't you stay with us?'

'Of course I will. We can go to Rome? Have you been there? It's a wonderful city. We will buy a big house there. Here, take this.' Anthony pulled out his purse. He took out enough gold for his journey and handed the purse to Francesca. 'Keep this somewhere safe. I have much, much more buried in my brother's garden. I have to complete my mission for Pope Clement first, then I'll dig up my treasure and return here. And then we will all go to Rome.'

'You don't have to leave now, do you? Not now, not so soon.'

'No, not right now. I shall have to leave within a few days, but I'll be back in a couple of months, I promise. Now I want to get to know our children, and we have some catching up to do too.'

For the next few days, Anthony and Francesca made up for lost time. Anthony tried at every opportunity to get to know his children. Francesca had a long discussion alone with Maria, and Anthony felt that Maria warmed to him a little afterward. Antonio, however, left the room whenever Anthony entered it.

'Anthony, I told you it would take time,' Francesca said. 'I think Maria can see how much I love you, and perhaps that's enough for her. But Antonio is different. He's a man. They have trouble with emotions.'

'Of course you're right, my love. I need more time. I must see Walter and tell him we need to stay another week or so. I don't want to leave before my son and I can at least share the same room.'

Anthony set off for the tavern to find Walter. He found him in the bar having lunch.

'Walter, we need to stay in Florence a little longer.'

'Well, was I right or was I right?' Walter asked.

'You were absolutely right. Also, I have a son and a daughter too, twins that I never knew I had. They're almost sixteen. I've missed out on so much, trying to make my fortune. The problem is that my son, Antonio, won't talk to me. He won't even stay in the room when I enter. Francesca says it will take time.'

'Well, time's not a problem for me. You can take as much time as you like. I suppose it's been rough for them, growing up without a father. They'll have been the local bastards. That's no fun, no fun at all.'

'That's part of it, certainly. Antonio gets beaten up by the local lads a lot, I understand.'

'Are you sure he's your son? I've never seen a better fighter than you. You saved my life more than once. No offence, I'm sure he is your son,' Walter added quickly as he saw Anthony's brow crease.

'Walter, that's it. You're a genius. I'm not a natural fighter, I was taught. I've got to go. Give me a couple of weeks. Here's some more money.' Anthony fished a few ducats from his purse and pressed them into Walter's hand. Then he rushed back to Francesca's house.

As Anthony entered the house, Antonio tried to squeeze past him to leave, but Anthony grabbed him and pulled him back in.

'Sit down for five minutes, please. I know I haven't been a father to you, but I didn't know I was a father. I've been too busy trying to make a fortune. At first it was because I had disappointed my own father, and I wanted to prove to him that I was worth his love. When I met your mother, I wanted to make a fortune, so that I could build us a big house and we could start a family. I didn't know we had already started a family. I didn't know you were coming.' Maria and Antonio were both silent, but they were watching him and listening. 'I was obsessed with making that fortune. Every time I came close to having enough, it was taken from me. I now have a fortune, but I've lost something much more valuable. I've lost time with you. I can't put that right. I'm sorry. But there is something practical I can do. You've both suffered at the hands of others, through no fault of your own. I can teach you how to fight back and win. The next time a bully hurts you, you can throw them on their back and have them squealing for mercy. Would you like that?' He looked at them in turn, barely daring to hope. He'd used all his ammunition.

'I would Father,' Maria said. 'Come on, Antonio, it wouldn't do any harm to try, would it?'

'All right, I suppose not,' Antonio said, gazing at his feet.

'Right, let's go to the park.'

They found a quiet corner of the park, and Anthony

began with wrestling. They worked until dusk and by that time they had mastered how to fall without hurting themselves and several types of throw. Anthony was delighted that they wanted to continue their lessons. Over the next few days, they learnt how to hold their opponents down, then arm locks, knee and ankle locks and strangleholds.

'You're both doing really well. I will have to go back to London soon, but then I will return with my fortune and build us a large house. You can keep practising on each other until then.'

'What if the bully has a sword?' Antonio asked.

'Well tomorrow I'll teach you how to take it from him.'

'What if there are two of them, and they both have swords?' Antonio replied.

'Very well, we will have a different lesson tomorrow,' Anthony said thoughtfully. When they got back to the house, Maria and Antonio went to bed exhausted.

'Francesca, you said the Grand Duke is in Venice. Do you know if Vinta is his secretary?' Anthony asked.

'Yes, I've heard that name. I think he is.'

The following day, Anthony took a calculated risk. He led Antonio and Maria along a quiet side street above which the Palazzo Vecchio towered. He found the side door to the palace that he was looking for. He pulled his lock picks out of his purse, looked up and down the street, and tried the door handle. As he expected, it was locked.

'What are you doing?' Maria asked.

'Shh. Watch!' Anthony inserted the picks into the lock and in less than a minute, he opened the door. He stepped inside and was relieved to find the corridor deserted.

'Good god, how did you do that?' Antonio asked.

'Keep quiet and come in. We'll practise some fencing in the armoury. Lock picking will have to wait until I get back from London.'

'What if somebody finds us?' Maria asked.

'I'll ask them to take us to the duke's secretary — Vinta. He's an old friend. Actually, I know quite a few of the staff here. I was working here when I met your mother. The armoury is some distance from the main activity of the palace and rarely visited.' Anthony gave his children a small tour of the palace that he knew so well, ending in the armoury. He let himself in again with his lock picks and relocked the door behind them. For the rest of the day, he taught them the principles of fencing and then the best way to disarm a swordsman. 'As with wrestling, it's all about balance. You have to use their momentum to your own advantage.' Anthony found a blunt sword in a rack on the wall and took it down. By the end of the lesson, he had Maria deftly throwing Antonio onto his back as he lunged, and applying an armlock to his sword arm. Antonio winced and dropped the sword, which she swiftly took up and applied the blunt point to his throat. 'Very good Maria. Now Antonio, do you want to have a go?'

'Yes I do, Father.'

Anthony smiled. When they got home that evening, Maria and Antonio were fighting each other to tell their mother about their day. His risk had paid off.

A week later, Anthony hugged Maria and Antonio and embraced Francesca.

'Anthony, I can't bear losing you again. You are coming back, promise me.'

'Francesca, believe me, I will come back. Nothing

can keep me away now. I have a son and a daughter and I have you. I will complete this mission, dig up my fortune and then I will be back. I have missed too much already, and I don't want to miss any more.' They took one last, long, lingering kiss, and then Anthony walked down the road towards the tavern. He turned to look back several times, and they were still waving. When he got to the tavern, he found Walter finishing his breakfast.

'Walter, I owe you a great debt. Your idea worked a treat.'

'What idea?' Walter asked, puzzled.

'Never mind. When you've finished your breakfast, can you hitch up the horses? I'll go and settle your bill.' Twenty minutes later they were driving through Florence city centre.

'Walter, I just need to stop at the Thurn and Taxis office to see if I've had any letters. It's at the next corner.' Walter stopped the carriage and Anthony jumped down and went into the office. He enquired at the counter and was handed a packet. He opened it and found there was a covering letter from Edmund and another letter from Persons. He read the second letter.

22nd September 1603, Rome

Dear Sir Anthony,

I have the agreement of his holiness the pope that the Bishop of Evreux should become the papal nuncio in Paris. On your return journey could you inform the French king of this when you deliver the caskets. We are anxious that the king's leanings towards Calvinism be arrested. We are even more anxious for the success of your primary mission, that Queen Anne should encourage King James to return to the true faith.

Your friend, Robert Persons

He asked the man behind the counter for some paper and a pen, and wrote his reply.

7th October 1603, Florence

Dear Robert,

Concerning the matter of King Henry of France, I do not think that the Bishop of Evreux will achieve very much. From what I have perceived, the politics of state, and the ebb and flow of conspiracy and suspicion add up to a far greater heresy than Calvin may have been responsible for.

At least King Henry is content that most people may have a priest in their house. The queen, I know is very assiduous at sermons. I know not what will become of the tokens I shall deliver to her, for you know the laws and the dangers they threaten. I shall make the sign of the cross to her when I deliver them to her, and hope for the best.

Concerning the matter of King James and Queen Anne. I hope that the king, although a stiff Protestant, will not be too bloody with Catholics. Although the queen suppressed her Catholic faith because of her marriage, no doubt some embers still burn. She is still young and given to youthful pastimes and youthful thoughts. If the Countess of Arundell and some others are long in her company, we can only hope that good will come of it. But I will do absolutely nothing to support the Jesuit mission in England. I shall complete this mission for the pope as promised, no more can I do. It is in the hands of the king and queen.

Yours sincerely,
Sir Anthony Standen

He folded it and used the wax and standard Thurn and Taxis office seal to close the letter. He addressed it to Robert Persons and paid the man behind the counter the postage. Then he left the building and climbed back onto the carriage.

'Sorry for the delay, Walter. Let's get going to Paris. I want to complete this mission as quickly as possible and get back here to marry Francesca.'

Charles Neville knocked on his friend's door and went in. Robert was out. Charles wondered where he might be and had a look on his desk for any clues. There was a letter that bore the signature of the man who had blighted his life. He read it and smiled. Then he folded it and tucked it inside his doublet.

They arrived in Paris a few days before Christmas 1603. Anthony directed Walter to the Louvre Palace. He showed his letter of introduction to the guards and they were allowed to drive into the courtyard.

'So what are the French king and queen like, Anthony?' Walter asked.

'I only met them briefly when we were on our way south, carrying news of the ascension of King James and handing out those portraits. Henry seemed nice enough, certainly a lot more amiable than the previous Henry. Queen Marie I knew from when she was three until she was twelve. Although she was Maria then, she's changed to the French version, which is quite understandable. Her father was Grand Duke Francesco of Tuscany, I was there the day the current Grand Duke Francesco's brother poisoned Bianca, Queen Marie's stepmother. He may have had a hand in killing her father too. She was a pleasant girl, very interested in the arts.'

'Well, it looks like they're doing a lot of building work,' Walter said as he stopped the coach outside the main entrance. Anthony reached into his box and pulled out a gold casket. 'Strewth, that must be worth a fortune.'

'You should see the one I'm carrying back for Queen Anne, they're gifts from the pope. That's a good point, don't take your eyes off this box, not for a moment. Are you armed?'

'There's a matchlock musket in the back, but you can't keep blowing on the damn thing and drive as well.'

'Take this.' Anthony pulled one of his wheellock pistols from his belt and passed it to Walter. 'You cock it like this, and there's no match to worry about. It's already loaded. You should be safe in the palace grounds, but don't leave that box.'

'Don't worry, I won't,' Walter said as Anthony climbed down.

'I won't be long.'

Walter was stretching his legs around the courtyard, but keeping close to the carriage, when Anthony returned.

'How did it go?' Walter asked.

'Well I've delivered the casket and passed on the pope's good wishes. I feel sorry for Marie though. Her French isn't very good, and she hates it that the king spends so much time with his mistresses. They seem to argue all the time.'

'Still looking forward to getting married Anthony?'

'I only need Francesca. Let's get going. The sooner we get to London, the sooner I get back to her.'

CHAPTER SIXTEEN

1604, England

It was Friday, the 6th of January 1604, when they arrived in Westminster. Walter drove the coach into the Whitehall Palace courtyard and stopped by the palace entrance.

'Well, I suppose this is goodbye, old friend,' Anthony said. 'I'll just complete my mission and recover my fortune, and then I'll ride as fast as I can for Florence. If you ever fancy some winter sunshine, look us up in Rome.'

'Good luck Anthony. It's been really wonderful seeing you again.' They gave each other a hug, and Anthony climbed down. 'You'd better have this back,' Walter said, handing the wheellock down to Anthony.

'Yes, thanks again.' Anthony took his box and went through the palace door. A steward asked him to leave his pistols in the guardroom and then escorted him to the throne room.

'Your Majesty, Your Majesty,' Anthony said, bowing to the king and queen in turn.

'Sir Anthony, I trust your mission went well?' the king enquired, raising an eyebrow.

'Very well, Your Majesty. I have a gift from the pope for the queen. May I present it?' The king nodded, and Anthony gave the box to Queen Anne. He pressed the key into her palm as he passed her the box.

'Look, James, isn't it magnificent?' the queen said, smiling. At that moment, the door opened and Sir Robert Cecil entered with two armed guards.

'Your Majesty,' he said, bowing, 'I have here letters

outlining a plot to coerce the queen into influencing you towards Catholicism.' He passed a letter to the king. King James read it, his countenance growing sterner.

'What does the letter say, James?' Queen Anne asked.

'Well, it says that you suppressed your Catholic faith to marry me, but that the embers of your Catholicism still burn. It also says that you are young and given to youthful pastimes and thoughts,' King James replied.

'What impertinence!' Queen Anne exclaimed.

'What is in the box, Anne?' King James asked. The queen opened the box and passed it to James. He read the pope's message and passed it to Sir Robert. 'Have this translated, Sir Robert. I suspect it's in Danish.' Then he turned to Anthony. 'Do you deny you wrote this letter to Robert Persons?' he asked, showing Anthony the letter. An icy hand gripped his heart and squeezed hard. How could this be? Persons must have sent the letter to Cecil, but why? What had he to gain from it?

'It's in your hand, Standen. You cannot deny it.' Sir Robert Cecil smirked.

'I do not deny it, Your Majesty. I am guilty and deserve to die.'

'Take him to the tower.' the king commanded.

'And search him thoroughly. He is very resourceful,' Cecil added. With that, the guards marched Anthony off. They put him into a boat and rowed down the Thames to the Tower of London. They entered the tower via Traitor's gate. He was taken to the dungeons, strip searched, and his lock picks were taken. He was then pushed into a cell and the door was locked behind him.

Anthony still couldn't understand why Persons would have betrayed him. How could he have profited from it? It doesn't make any sense. Perhaps someone found the letter in Persons' room, who would profit from it in some way. Perhaps Cecil has a spy in the pope's inner circle. What was the point in speculating? He was there now. He'd be tried for treason and executed. That's all there is to it. At least he met his children, his only wish that he'd spent more time with them. No, he also wished Francesca had his fortune. He wondered if it would ever be found? Perhaps Edmund, or one of his children, would one day dig by the oak tree and find his purse full of diamonds. What would they think, and how would they spend the money? Oh, this was too hard. He couldn't bear it. He wondered how long it would be before he had his trial.

Some time in his second week in the dungeon, he had a visitor. He was a frail-looking elderly man.

'Sir Anthony, I am Sir Richard Berkely, Constable of the Tower. I am sorry that we have to keep you in this cell. I wouldn't normally treat a knight of the realm in this way, but it is the order of Sir Robert Cecil. Apparently, with just a piece of bent wire you could escape: maximum security is ordered. I will do what I can to ensure you get some decent meals brought down, and some excellent wine.'

'That's very kind of you, Sir Richard. Do you know when my trial is scheduled for?'

'No, I haven't heard a thing. It can take years sometimes. I understand you knew the Earl of Essex. He was in my custody before his trial, such a shame, he was a good man in most ways, just a little too ambitious and hot headed.'

'Yes, I was happy to serve him. Cadiz was a good time, Ireland not so good. I think he lost his way there. I fear ambition is the downfall of many men. It's been mine. I would have been happy as a pauper, married to the woman I love, but I didn't know it. Now I'll die, and she'll never know what happened. Sir Richard, do you know how I am likely to be executed?'

'I think, as a knight of the realm, you can hope for beheading. It depends on the judge. It could easily be hanging, drawing and quartering, though.'

'Not burning at the stake, then?' Anthony asked hopefully.

'That is still popular with some of the older judges, but timber is a precious building material for ships and houses. You can use a scaffold over and over, but not the stakes. I should try to prepare yourself for any eventuality, if I were you.'

'How do you prepare yourself, Sir Richard?'

'Praying, just praying. I'm sorry, I'd like to help you, but I can't. I'll do what I can about the food.'

A few months later Anthony was told by one of the gaolers that Sir Richard had died, and Sir William Wade was the constable now. The summer came and went, the leaves turned brown and fell. He didn't see this from his dungeon cell, he imagined it. When his gaolers brought him food and wine, they chatted a little. They told him what date it was, what the weather was like, and how their children were growing. He tried to picture Antonio and Maria, how they must be growing. He thought about what he could have taught them if he'd lived: languages, mathematics, more wrestling, picking locks. He could have taught them a little about alchemy and medicine. He started to think about his execution. In wrestling, when Harrison put me in a strangle hold, and the blood supply was cut off to my brain, it was only a few seconds before I lost consciousness. So if I'm beheaded, as long as I've paid the executioner well, I might see the inside of the basket for a few seconds before I pass out. I'll probably know that my head and body are detached, but only briefly. If I'm hung, drawn and quartered, I'll pass out as I'm choked. Then they'll let me down and I'll come to and see them slitting my belly and pulling my intestines out. I hope they'll quickly get on with chopping off my arms and legs so that I bleed out fast. I don't need to think about burning. I've seen it, heard it and smelt it. I hope Sir Richard was right about timber being in short supply. Dear God, please let it be beheading. I beseech thee, God, let it be beheading. Thank the lord that I made a full confession, and haven't had the opportunity to sin since. I confessed to the pope himself. Surely that must count for something.

It was starting to get much warmer. The food was becoming more varied, with fruits and fresh vegetables. Anthony asked the gaoler who collected his empty plate what day it was. It was Monday, the 1st of July 1605. He would always remember that day. It was the day that Sir William Wade came to his cell.

'Is it my trial? It's taken them long enough. I'm as ready as I'll ever be. Do you know who the judge is? Is he a young man?'

'No, it's not that. You are to be released, Sir Anthony.' Anthony dropped to his knees, and his hand searched his neck for his long-lost St. Christopher.

'Dear God, thank you for hearing my prayers. Thank you Lord, thank you, Mary, thank you, Jesus, thank you, St. Christopher, wherever you are. How could I have doubted you? Is it really true Sir William, you're not making fun of me are you? How can it be?'

'Well, I don't know much, but apparently Queen Anne had a change of heart on a carriage ride back from Hampton Court. She has persuaded King James to pardon you. You are to leave England, and can travel in the allied countries, France, Germany, the Netherlands, just not the Italian states or Spain.'

'Hampton Court, you say, they would have passed through East Molesey, where I was born. Perhaps it was that. No, the queen wouldn't have known that. I wonder if Walter was driving the coach. Could he have had anything to do with it? Maybe he had an opportunity to say something as he helped her down from the carriage. Surely, yes, that must be it. Oh God bless you, Walter, if it was you. God bless you anyway.'

'I don't know, come on get up, Sir Anthony, I haven't got all day.'

Anthony had to cover his eyes when he came up the stairs as sunlight poured through a window and blinded him. Sir Walter returned his pistols and purse to him, and handed him a passport with the travel restrictions spelt out. Although his legs trembled under him from lack of exercise, he walked as quickly as he could through the tower gateway. He thought about returning to Whitehall Palace and reclaiming his horse, but decided against it. At least the English gaolers are reasonably honest. I have enough money to buy a horse and get to East Molesey. I'm not going anywhere near the palace, he thought. He found a stable and enquired about horses for sale.

'This is the fastest horse we have, sir, a three-year-old mare. You can have her for twenty pounds.'

'Does that include a saddle?'

'Yes, I have a saddle I can throw in.'

'Does she have a name?' Anthony asked.

'We call her Beauty, but you can call her what you like, as long as you pay for her.'

'Here we are,' said Anthony, counting out twenty pounds. 'You're going to be Lightning from now on.'

Once clear of London, Anthony urged Lightning into

a gallop. They stopped at a tavern for lunch and reached East Molesey in the early afternoon.

'Anthony, is that you?' Edmund asked.

'Yes, you will not believe how glad I am to see you.'

'Come in, Anthony. You are welcome. We will boil some water and put the bath tub by the fire. I hope you don't mind me saying, but you stink dreadfully. I have some clean clothes that will fit you. Where have you been?'

'I have been in the dungeons of the Tower of London for eighteen months. The bathing and toilet facilities are quite basic. The bath and clothes will be very welcome.'

When he was clean and changed, he sat down to dinner with Edmund, his wife, Dennise, and his nephews, William who was now twenty and Thomas who was nine. They all wanted to hear his story and for the sake of Thomas, there was quite a lot he had to leave out. Anthony heard that William was also pursuing a legal career.

'That's a very sensible ambition. I'm sure your father and uncle are giving you all the help you need. There's not much I can do, but I will write you a letter for Francis Bacon. He was a friend of mine and a great lawyer and Member of Parliament. If he's still alive, he may be able to advise you, and help you, as well.' Anthony said. 'I wish I had become a lawyer.'

'Sir Francis is very much alive, Anthony. He is tipped to become Attorney General when the post next becomes vacant. How did you come to know him, Anthony?' Edmund asked.

'I have met many people on my travels. I can tell you about the Earl of Essex, William of Orange and Pope Clement, amongst many others. Do you have another flagon of this excellent wine, Edmund?'

'Yes, of course, I'll get one.' Edmund soon returned with more wine and topped up the goblets. When Edmund sat down, Dennise whispered in his ear. Anthony noticed Edmund frown. 'Are you sure, dear?'

'Yes, I'm sure he should know,' Dennise whispered back.

'Very well. Anthony, after you visited the last time, Dennise reminded me that you had told her that you thought you were a disappointment to father. That was the time you visited, and I was in London. I told her about a time when I heard father and mother talking, and I crept downstairs to listen. Dennise thinks I ought to tell you about it.'

'Yes, come along, Edmund dear, get to the point.'

'All right, Dennise, I'm getting there. It was after you had gone to Scotland. Father was, I think, feeling rather low and missing you terribly. He was talking about a time when he had taken you to Gray's Inn. He had meetings, and he had given you a few halfpennies and you had gone off to Smithfield Market. Unfortunately, you came across the burning of some Protestants.'

'The Islington Martyrs, that's right. Sometimes I can still smell their flesh burning and hear their screams.'

'Mother said that you were too young and shouldn't have been taken to London. Father said you had pestered him to be taken to work with him. He blamed himself. You had wanted to see what being a lawyer was like, and instead of sitting in on a meeting about land law, you heard an execution warrant read and watched men and women burnt at the stake.'

'One of them begged Jesus to forgive us. They were good people.'

'Father thought it turned you against the law. He thought that he had become a disappointment to you.

However much he encouraged you, you didn't seem to want anything to do with the law, his profession.'

'Father thought I was disappointed in him? I adored him. It's true that was a shocking experience, and I do question law makers who can burn people for no crime other than their beliefs, but I never blamed father for that. I was simply much better at languages than anything else. So all this time I thought I was a disappointment to father, and he thought I was disappointed in him. I wish you'd told me about this before, Edmund.'

'I was just so pleased to see you it slipped my mind. Dennise assumed I would tell you after she and the children went to bed. But I got carried away with your stories and the wine. In the morning, you'd left by the time I remembered. Dennise was very cross with me, and how could I tell you after that? We didn't know where you were?'

'Yes, I'm sorry. Thank you for telling me now. And thank you, Dennise, you are a wise woman. You should treasure her, Edmund. One other thing, I need to borrow your shovel.'

'It's in the wood shed, but whatever for?'

'I'll show you. I won't be long.'

When Anthony returned to the dining room, Edmund was refilling the wine goblets. Anthony emptied the diamonds from his purse onto the table and everyone gasped.

'Wherever did you get those, Anthony?' Edmund exclaimed.

'I buried them in the garden after the raid on Cadiz. I had made and lost several fortunes on my adventures, and I decided I should hide this one, until I was ready to use it.'

'Why didn't you put it in a bank?' Edmund asked.

'Have you heard of the collapse of the Medici bank? I knew Francesco Medici well and came not to trust banks.'

'So are you ready to use it?' Dennise asked.

'Yes. I'm afraid I may never see you all again. I'm going to Florence and then Rome. I'm going to marry a beautiful woman. Francesca is her name. It's a long story, but we already have children. I thought I would never see them again, so I have to go. I will leave at dawn tomorrow. But I will write to you and tell you where we are. Perhaps one day you may travel to Italy, and you can visit us. It is so beautiful there, and the weather is warm.'

CHAPTER SEVENTEEN

1605, Rome

It took Anthony and Lightning twenty days to reach Florence and it was early evening on Tuesday, the 23rd of July 1605, when Anthony knocked on Francesca's door once more. The door opened, and a raging storm hit Anthony.

'A couple of months, you said. You've been gone for nine hundred and eighty-six days. I thought at least you might be with me for the birth of at least one of our children. Where the hell have you been all this time? Is there another woman?' Francesca sobbed and Anthony dropped the flowers he had picked. He wrapped his arms around her.

'I'm so sorry. I was betrayed and locked in the Tower of London. I never stopped thinking about you, although I was certain I was going to die. I thought I would never see you again, that I would never see Maria or Antonio again.' From the corner of his eye, he saw Maria carrying a toddler. 'Don't tell me I'm a grandfather now.'

'No, you left Mother with child again when you went away,' said Maria.

'We haven't baptised him yet, we kept waiting for you, waiting and hoping. We thought you might want to name our third child. He's getting a little old to be called baby,' Francesca said, rubbing her eyes.

'Can I hold him?' Anthony asked.

'Yes, of course, you'd better come in,' Francesca said. 'You'll have to tell me again what happened to you, when I've calmed down.' Maria handed Baby to Anthony. Anthony hugged him and kissed him until he began squirming.

'Down, put me down,' Baby said. Anthony put him down and he toddled towards the kitchen, falling and getting up again twice.

'How do you like William, or Walter?' Anthony asked.

'William sounds fine. I'm not sure about Walter.'

'Then tomorrow I will buy a wagon and we will all set off for Rome. We shall be married, and William will be baptised, by Pope Clement. Is there anything we need to do before we go?'

'I will need to tell my sister,' Francesca said. 'She lives in Perugia, with her husband and children. It's on the way. They must come to the wedding.'

'I'll have to tell my boss at the mill,' Maria added. 'Antonio will want to tell his friends, and his boss at the foundry. He should be home soon.'

'I'd better make it a big cart, and maybe buy a second horse,' Anthony said, smiling.

When they arrived at the Quirinal palace, Anthony addressed the senior guard on duty.

'I'm Sir Anthony Standen. We have come to see Pope Clement.'

'Pope Clement died just a few months ago, sir. It's Pope Paul now. Have you got any documentation, sir?'

'I'm afraid not. Is Cardinal Aldobrandini here? He knows me. If you send word to him, I'm sure he will see us.'

'I'll send a messenger to him, sir.' They waited for thirty minutes before the messenger arrived back. 'Very good, sir, carry on through, and the cardinal will meet you by the steps, over there.' Anthony drove through the archway and over to the steps by the main entrance. By the time they had stopped, Cardinal Aldobrandini was walking down the steps.

'Sir Anthony, I am delighted to see you. We heard you were imprisoned in the Tower and were certain to be executed. What happened?'

'Can we go inside?'

'Yes, yes, of course. Come this way. I will have a stable boy look after your horses and cart.' The family got down from the cart and they all followed the cardinal through the corridors of the palace to the pope's reception room.

'Your Holiness, this is Sir Anthony Standen, the man that Pope Clement sent on the mission to Queen Anne.'

'Yes, Pope Clement told me all about it before he passed away. Sir Anthony, we all feared for your life. Whatever happened?'

'May we speak alone?'

'Of course, would you mind, cardinal?'

'Not at all, Your Holiness.' Cardinal Aldobrandini closed the door as he left.

'Do we need to go too, Anthony?' asked Francesca, looking puzzled.

'No, you might as well all stay. Your Holiness, I'm afraid I was betrayed, but I don't know why. When I presented Pope Clement's casket to Queen Anne, I was arrested and shown a letter I had written to Father Persons, concerning our plan. It must have been Father Persons who sent it to London, but I cannot understand why. Why would he jeopardise our plan?'

'Let's find out. I will send for him. Oh, that's an incense burner, the child...' They all looked round and Maria darted over to grab William, who had just started to reach up to the table on which the burner rested. 'I'm sorry, where are my manners. You must all sit down. Is this your wife, Sir Anthony?'

'Not exactly, Your Holiness. Pope Clement heard my confession and said that he would marry us, if I brought Francesca to Rome. When I found Francesca again, on my way to London with the casket, I discovered that we'd had twins in my absence. In the joy of finding each other again, we conceived our youngest, who was born while I was imprisoned in the Tower. We would like to have him baptised William, Your Holiness.'

'It will be my pleasure, but let me call for Father Persons first.'

When Father Persons arrived, he was visibly shocked to see Anthony.

'Robert, join us, take a seat. There. Sir Anthony was imprisoned, as we had heard, but it was a letter that he had written to you which incriminated him. Have you any idea how the English obtained this letter which was in your possession?' Pope Paul asked, raising an eyebrow.

'I think so, Your Holiness. A friend of mine came to see me, but I was out. When I came back, I was told that my friend had been and gone. A few days later, I was looking for Sir Anthony's letter and couldn't find it. I think he must have taken it.'

'Who is this friend of yours?' Pope Paul asked.

'Charles Neville, the Earl of Westmorland, Your Holiness. A good Catholic, and a very old friend.'

'You told me he was dead,' Anthony rasped.

'I wanted to protect him. You'd almost killed him once. I didn't want you going after him again.'

'Where is he now?' Anthony asked, clenching his fists.

'I don't know. I honestly don't know. I haven't seen him since the day he took your letter. I didn't say anything, because by the time I realised the letter was missing it was too late.'

'Your very good friend hates me because I caught him raping a young girl in Mechelin.'

'He said she was only a heretic.'

'Do you seriously consider it permissible to rape a young girl if she isn't Catholic?' Anthony asked. 'What kind of man of God do you think you are?'

'Let us just thank the Lord, our saviour, that Sir Anthony is alive,' Pope Paul said. 'That will be all Robert, please leave us.' Robert left. 'Now, it appears that I have a marriage to perform. Will there be many guests?'

'Your Holiness, my sister and her family will be here in a few days,' Francesca replied.

'Then we shall wait until they arrive. I can hear your confessions first, then when your family arrives you shall be married, and then I will perform the baptism. There is an order for things. Are you expecting any other guests, Anthony?'

'No, Your Holiness. Pope Clement said something about a villa he might be able to sell us.'

'I think I know the one he meant. It's a few miles outside the city, on the outskirts of a village. It has a courtyard, a barn and a stable. There are, I think, about eight bedrooms and several reception rooms. It needs a little attention, as it hasn't been occupied for a few years. There is a vineyard attached, although I suppose the vines will have run away a little.'

'Oh, Your Holiness, that sounds divine,' Francesca said, her eyes wide. 'We will soon have it sparkling. Anthony will get the vineyard in production. You used to work in the wine trade, didn't you, Anthony?'

'Yes, my darling, however did you remember, after all these years.'

'I remember every line on your face and every word

you said to me. I had to save those memories. It was all of you that I had.'

'Do you think eight bedrooms are going to be enough, Francesca?' Pope Paul asked, with a smile creeping across his face.

◇ ◇ ◇

Anthony, Antonio, and Maria were picking grapes when a horseman stopped on the road next to the vineyard.

'Would that be Sir Anthony Standen now?' the horseman asked.

'That is me. Good heavens, is that Hugh O'Neill?'

'The very same. Are you going to invite me in?'

'Have you brought any of that Irish whisky with you?'

'Sadly, I drank it all when I had to leave Ireland. Cardinal Aldobrandini told me you're making your own wine now though. He told me where you were.'

'Come, stay with us for as long as you like. Put your horse in the stable over there. Antonio, would you give our guest a hand with his bags? We can carry the baskets of grapes to the barn, can't we, Maria?'

'Of course, Papa.'

'Heavens, dinner is going to be an event tonight,' Anthony chuckled. Anthony and Maria had just finished with the grapes when Antonio and Hugh came out of the stable. They walked together over to the villa.

'Francesca, we have a guest. Can we feed one more?' Anthony called out as he led them into the kitchen. Francesca turned startled; she was breast feeding their baby — Anna.

'You didn't tell me we had a guest coming,' Francesca said, grabbing a towel to preserve her modesty. 'I'll put Anna to bed after her feed, and it's nearly your bedtime too, William.' Just over an hour later, Anthony,

Francesca, Antonio, Maria and Hugh were tucking into a feast, washed down with Standen wine.

'So why did you have to leave Ireland, Hugh?' Anthony asked.

'Well, after the peace treaty with the English, there was a certain amount of squabbling between the clans. Chichester, who is the governor now, sided with O'Cahan because he thought that if he sided with me, it might spark another war. The dispute continued until I went to London to argue my case with King James. I was warned that I was going to be arrested, so I fled to Spain. Due to bad weather, we landed in France instead. Then we made our way here. I've been trying to gain Pope Paul's support for the return of my lands.'

'How is it going?'

'I think he's trying to help, but it's going to take a long time.'

'You must stay with us while you wait. That would be all right, wouldn't it, Francesca?'

'Of course. We have enough room, for the time being,' she said, smiling.

A few days later, Anthony, Francesca and Hugh were sitting in rocking chairs on the veranda. William was playing in a small sand pit that Anthony had made for him. Anthony was rocking Anna in his arms, and Maria and Antonio were wrestling on the lawns in the courtyard.

'Anthony, I'm very happy you are teaching the children languages, mathematics, alchemy, and all the other things. But I wish you hadn't taught Maria to wrestle. It's very unladylike.' Francesca said.

'Nonsense, Mama!' Maria shouted as she threw Antonio onto his back. 'You know that big lad in the village, Bruno?'

'Yes, six foot three, with shoulders as wide,' answered Francesca.

'Well, I was on my way home from the market last week, and he grabbed me by the hair. He said he wouldn't let me go unless I kissed him. So I threw him on his back and strangled him.'

'I hope you didn't kill him, Maria?' Anthony asked.

'No, I released the pressure after a count of twenty, like you taught us. But he knew I could have done, if I'd wanted to. I haven't had any trouble since. None at all.'

'There, Anthony, you see what I mean. How on earth are we going to find Maria a husband, if they all think she might kill them at any moment?' Francesca asked.

'She looks exactly as you looked when we met. I really don't think she's going to have any trouble finding a host of suitors,' Anthony replied.

'That's for sure,' added Hugh. 'She'll be fighting them off. Begorra, she's started already.' He laughed and they all joined in.

'She may have my looks, but she's already a year older than I was when we met. The clock is ticking. Do you want her to be an old maid?' Francesca asked before being interrupted by a knock on the door. She got up and went to answer it. When she came back, Cardinal Aldobrandini was with her. 'We have another guest, Anthony. I'll go and make some refreshments.' Anthony and Hugh both got up to welcome the cardinal, and Anthony pulled up another rocking chair.

'To what do we owe the pleasure, Your Eminence?' Anthony asked.

'Well, we have a very delicate problem to deal with. It could be a little dangerous, but shouldn't take very long. His holiness and I have discussed what to do, and it occurred to us that we have the perfect team here to see it through. We simply can't think of anyone better qualified to deal with this problem than you two.'

'What's in it for us?' Hugh asked.

'I'm authorised to offer you two thousand ducats, for at most two months' work. How does that sound?'

'Two thousand each?' Anthony asked.

'Very well, two thousand ducats each,' replied the cardinal.

'Well, I could certainly use the money,' Hugh replied, just as Francesca returned with some drinks and pastries.

'What money?' Francesca asked.

'Cardinal Aldobrandini has a job that he thinks Hugh and I can do for him. We have exactly the skills required, that's right, isn't it, cardinal?'

'Yes. It would be very important for the church. There is nobody else who could do it.'

'It isn't dangerous, is it?' Francesca asked, frowning.

'Not very. And it wouldn't take long. A couple of months at most.'

'I've heard that one before,' Francesca said, scowling.

'It's worth a lot of money, darling, two thousand ducats. We are getting through our money quite quickly. It would tide us over until we get the winery into full production. And we will need a dowry for Maria, when she finds a suitable man.'

'We might need an extension on the villa too. I think I'm expecting again, Anthony.'

'Will you be all right if I leave for a month or so? I'm worried, particularly if you're expecting.'

'I think I'm in very safe hands, with Antonio and Maria now, don't you? You must stay for the night, cardinal. Come on Antonio and Maria, you've had your wrestling, now it's time for your next cookery lesson. We shall prepare the feast and then Cardinal Aldobrandini can tell us all what he has in mind.'

ABOUT THE AUTHOR

David West was educated at St. Edmund Hall, Oxford, where he took a B.A. in Engineering Science. During a career in engineering and project management he was commissioned by Gower Publishing to write a book on Project Sponsorship. This led him to study creative writing with the Open University, and a new career as a writer. *The Spy who Sank the Armada* is the first novel in the series *The Sir Anthony Standen Adventures*. He lives in Wiltshire.

AFTERWORD

The Spy who Sank the Armada is my imagined why and how stitched into the known fabric of the incredible life of Sir Anthony Standen, Walsingham's spy who really did sink the Armada. I first met Sir Anthony Standen in George Malcolm Thomson's biography of Sir Francis Drake. "The time had come when Walsingham was no longer satisfied with news that came to him at second-hand, whether from Santa Cruz's kitchen or from the Governor of Guernsey's reports of the gossip on Breton ships or in Rouen taverns. He needed an accurate and detailed stream of information about the number of Philip's ships, their tonnage, the sailors who would man them and the soldiers they would carry. Thanks above all to Standen, he got what he wanted." I hope you have enjoyed my novel. Please leave a review, they are very helpful. The first sequel is Fire and Earth, the second is The Suggested Assassin

Printed in Great Britain
by Amazon

14480034R00173